A CHRISTMAS to REMEMBER

A CHRISTMAS to REMEMBER

JILL SHALVIS, KRISTEN ASHLEY,
Hope Ramsay, Molly Cannon,
& Marilyn Pappano

FOREVER

NEW YORK   BOSTON

Copyright © 2013 by Jill Shalvis, Kristen Ashley, Hope Ramsay, Molly Cannon, and Marilyn Pappano
Excerpt from *He's So Fine* copyright © 2014 by Jill Shalvis
Excerpt from *Own the Wind* copyright © 2013 by Kristen Ashley
Excerpt from *Inn at Last Chance* copyright © 2014 by Hope Ramsay
Excerpt from *Flirting with Forever* copyright © 2013 by Molly Cannon
Excerpt from *A Love to Call Her Own* copyright © 2014 by Marilyn Pappano

Forever
Hachette Book Group
1290 Avenue of the Americas, New York, NY 10104
hachettebookgroup.com
twitter.com/foreverromance

Printed in the United States of America

Originally published as an ebook

First mass market edition: September 2014

10 9 8 7 6 5 4 3 2

OPM

Forever is an imprint of Grand Central Publishing.
The Forever name and logo are trademarks of Hachette Book Group, Inc.

The publisher is not responsible for websites (or their content) that are not owned by the publisher.

The Hachette Speakers Bureau provides a wide range of authors for speaking events. To find out more, go to www.hachettespeakersbureau.com or call (866) 376-6591.

ATTENTION CORPORATIONS AND ORGANIZATIONS:
Most HACHETTE BOOK GROUP books are available
at quantity discounts with bulk purchase for educational,
business, or sales promotional use. For information,
please call or write:

Special Markets Department, Hachette Book Group
1290 Avenue of the Americas, New York, NY 10104
Telephone: 1-800-222-6747 Fax: 1-800-477-5925

Contents

Contents

A CHRISTMAS
to REMEMBER

Dear Readers,

I was so excited to be able to write another Christmas short for the Lucky Harbor world. Sometimes secondary characters make a place for themselves in my heart. They get really comfortable there and refuse to leave until I write their story. That's what Ian and Melissa did, so really, you can thank them for this story. :)

Christmas is one of my favorite holidays. Some of my bestest family memories are attached to Christmas. Like getting bickering teenage girls to wrap presents for charity the year my arm was in a sling. You would have thought I was asking them to head out to the mines and do manual labor. But they did it; they wrapped all the presents, including the ones from me, holed up in their separate bunks so no one saw anyone else's goods.

Then they played Santa for me as well. We didn't get to bed until after 2 a.m. and still we woke up at the crack of dawn, excited, only to find that someone had left the sliding glass door ajar. Raccoons had come in and not only unwrapped everything but trashed it all as well. Complete Devastation. It took hours to clean up, and afterward, I expected bad moods. Didn't get it. Instead we all made breakfast together and, over bacon and eggs, told each other what we loved about each of us. It was the gift of words, and I've never been so proud of the girls or loved them more.

Ian and Melissa have a few things to tiff about in their story as well. But never fear, the spirit of the holiday prevails. After all, this is a Lucky Harbor story...

Love and happy holidays!

Best,

Jill Shalvis

Dream a Little Dream

Jill Shalvis

CHAPTER

1

Ian O'Mallery had been born a firefighter, but there were times when he wished he'd picked a career that didn't interrupt his sleep. Times like right now, when the fire alarm went off in the middle of a really hot dream starring the sexy, love-of-his-life-though-she-didn't-know-it Melissa Mann. She'd been right in the middle of blowing his mind—*and* his favorite body part—when the fire alarm pierced the dream and the vision scattered.

Damn. He listened as dispatch called out the engines required to respond. His, of course. Ian shoved on his gear, trying to push back the dregs of sleep. His dreams kept forgetting that he wasn't seeing Melissa anymore, that after months of being "friends with benefits" and then slowly segueing into a real relationship—at least on his part—she'd dumped the "benefits" part. A crying shame since they'd been the best damn benefits he'd ever had. But Melissa preferred serial dating to getting in too deep. These days they were…friends? Maybe. Sort of. Or not. But whatever they were now wasn't nearly as good as what they'd been.

The fire station was now ablaze with lights, everyone moving at a fast clip toward the rigs. Earlier, volunteers had decorated for Christmas with miles of garland and tinsel, and someone had left a CD of holiday tunes on repeat.

"Christmas is still two weeks off and already my ears are bleeding from that music," Justin, one of the other firefighters, muttered.

"Maybe next year we can tell people we'd rather have a new flat screen." This from Hunter, Justin's partner.

Focused on the task ahead of them, Ian ignored the chatter. As lieutenant of the squad, he had the iPad with the info coming in from dispatch. As they all climbed aboard, he glanced down at the address and froze. From years on the truck, he knew every single nook and cranny of Lucky Harbor, the North Pacific coastal town nestled between the Pacific Ocean and the Olympic Mountains. For that matter, he knew the entire county. Hell, he could find his way through a wormhole all the way to Seattle if he had to.

This particular address was on the outskirts of town, in a neighborhood a few decades past needing a renovation. There were few single family homes. Instead it was mostly apartment buildings, built close together with yards that consisted of dead grass and litter.

This particular three-story building was a known problem. The third floor held a group of party animals who regularly had the police called on them by the other floors.

But that wasn't his biggest issue right now. Nope, that honor went to the fact that Melissa lived on the second floor, and according to dispatch, the building currently had flames shooting out of the top windows and roof.

As they continued to race toward the scene, Ian yanked out his cell phone and called her. His call went straight to voice mail. "Tell me you're out of the building," he said. "Call me. Text me. *Anything.*" He shoved the phone back in his pocket and willed the truck to go faster as he remembered the last time they'd been out together. It'd been six months ago. He'd picked her up from the beauty salon she managed and had taken her to dinner. They'd gone to a seafood place a few towns over, on the water, and she'd hand-fed him lobster, laughing when butter had dribbled down his chin.

"Whoops." Leaning in, she nibbled it off, making sure to kiss one corner of his mouth, and then the other, holding eye contact with him the whole time as her hands traveled south down his chest.

Without taking his gaze off Mel, he handed a passing waiter his credit card.

She laughed as they got the rest of the food to go.

They didn't make it to either of their places. Instead they went to a secluded beach, climbed up the bluffs by starlight until they found a private little plateau that overlooked the water, and had a picnic that had nothing to do with food.

When he finally brought her home, a police squad car was in her lot. One of the idiots on the top floor had let a party get out of control.

Again.

Ian held on to Melissa when she went to get out of his truck. "You need to move," he said. Not a new conversation for them. "Closer to town, to a better neighborhood. I can help you find a place."

"I'm working my way out of debt," she reminded him.

"You know I can't put down a new security deposit and first and last months' rent."

There was a solution to that. *"Move in with me."*

She sucked in a breath. Her bright green eyes went even brighter, but she shook her head. "Don't be silly. I'd drive you nuts in a week, tops."

"You drive me nuts now," he teased.

She put a finger over his lips, stared at his mouth for a long time, and then looked into his eyes. "You, Ian O'Mallery," she whispered, "terrify me."

"Me? I'm a pussy cat."

She laughed her wonderful laugh and kissed him. "Yeah. If a wild mountain lion counts as a pussy cat."

Knowing she'd had it rough, that letting someone in was hard for her, his smile faded. "You have nothing to be afraid of with me, Mel."

She held his gaze but didn't respond.

"You're still not ready," he guessed softly.

"I'm working on it," she said, just as softly.

Glancing at her building, he felt his jaw tighten, but nodded. What else could he do? "Work faster."

Instead, she'd broken things off the next day.

The radio crackled to life, jarring him back.

"Victims trapped on the top floor," reported the dispatcher.

It was midnight, ensuring that the building was filled with its tenants.

"Shit," Justin muttered at his side.

They pulled into the lot. The police had beat them to the call and were out of their vehicles, holding back traffic.

The building was engulfed, and Ian's heart stopped

when he saw several terrified faces peeking out of the second- and third-story windows.

One of the cops jogged over. "Apparently the building isn't up to code," he said tersely. "A tenant told us the landlord had forbidden Christmas lights because of it, but that the idiots on the top floor had used them anyway. Someone up there had a party tonight, and their Christmas tree went up in smoke and caught the curtains. That was all it took."

A few lucky people had somehow gotten out and were sitting on the curb in their pj's, in shock.

Melissa wasn't one of them, but her car was in the lot, which meant one thing—she was still in the building.

Ian leaped into the fray, barking out directions to the men in his charge, one word bouncing in his head on repeat.

Melissa.

CHAPTER

2

Melissa clutched her ears, grimacing at the pounding in her head, which was pulsing in tune to the fire alarm still going off somewhere nearby. She'd awoken to it, and smoke so thick she couldn't breathe. She'd immediately grabbed the blanket from her bed, wrapped herself up, and crawled to the door.

Hot. Everything was so hot she felt like she was melting.

Panic had taken over for a moment but she reminded herself she hadn't survived the things she'd already been through to go out like this. She pulled her T-shirt up over her nose and mouth and crawled to the window.

Stuck. Again. The damn landlord hadn't gotten to it yet. Not that it mattered; it was too far to jump. Ian was right about moving. Ian...God. She'd made a mess of her dating life, always flitting from one man to the next without getting in too far. Without giving anyone a piece of herself.

But with Ian, she'd been incapable of holding back, of

keeping her walls up. She missed his hard, chiseled body and the way he used it to take hers. She missed his sweet baby blues that were deceptively playful, and how they heated after he kissed her. She missed how he never let her hide, how he kept at her until he knew her secrets, all of them.

She missed *him*.

She coughed until her ribs hurt, and she looked around, wondering what the hell to do. The air was so thick and so hot that she couldn't suck a breath into her lungs. There was too much smoke, and no viable exit. A second wave of panic consumed her, and desperate to make a smart move, she crawled into her bathroom and to the coolest spot she could find—her tub.

Smoke snaked under the bathroom door. She stuffed towels beneath it and waited for her life to flash before her eyes. She wouldn't mind revisiting some of the good stuff about now. But instead, she thought about all her regrets, and there were many. Having grown up under the strict thumb of her parents, she'd rebelled early. They'd simply turned their backs on her. One strike and she'd been out. Fine. She'd gone on without them, living in the moment for years, never letting herself plan for the future. She'd been friends with the wrong girls, gone out with the wrong men, and made some wrong choices. Burned to the point that she'd changed her tactics to avoiding any real attachments—even when the man of her dreams had come along, never really believing he could be hers.

Anyone who knew her thought of her as wildly independent and brave. But the brave part was a lie. A big, fat lie. She was a chicken, too afraid to get hurt.

Above her, the ceiling started to collapse, and she

thought how dumb she'd been because here she was, about to get really hurt. She was going to die here, and that pissed her off. She had a full bag of chocolate chips she'd not eaten so she'd be bikini-ready this summer. She'd spent her paycheck paying off the last of her credit card debt instead of going to Seattle for a shopping trip. She hadn't had a chance to try out the new hair care products that had arrived at her salon yesterday.

And worst of all, six months ago she'd looked into Ian's eyes and felt her entire heart melt, and she'd walked away instead of risking her heart.

And now she was going to die.

Over her own coughing, she heard someone yelling her name.

Ian?

She clutched the side of the tub and strained to hear over the roar of the blood in her ears. Had she conjured him up, or had he really arrived? "I'm here!" she tried to yell, but her smoke-ravaged voice didn't carry far, and yet another coughing spasm overtook her.

No one came. Not Ian, not anyone, and she hugged her legs in close and dropped her head to her knees with a little sob.

Then, from above her came a terrible creaking and groaning, as if the entire building was about to cave in. She screamed as a heavy piece of burning ceiling broke free. She dodged that one but the next hit her hard, and she screamed again.

The bathroom door burst open to a firefighter in full gear, looking like a vision with flames behind him.

"Ian?" she tried to ask past her ravaged throat, having to hold her aching head up with her hands.

He said something into his radio, which she couldn't catch. She couldn't hear a thing over the loud roaring around her. He dropped to his knees before her, and she nearly cried in relief. It *was* Ian. She could see his intent, urgent expression behind his face mask. He was saying something to her; she just couldn't grasp it. Then he was scooping her out of the tub and into his arms, cradling her close, taking them both clear just as more of the ceiling crashed into the tub.

Oh my God...She clutched at him, even as her head spun and ached so badly she thought she was going to be sick. "You came for me," she managed past her raw throat. Marveled. He'd literally walked through fire for her. For *her.* "No one's ever done that..."

Tightening his grip on her, he turned to the door to get her out of there. She wanted to tell him she could walk, but she couldn't. She couldn't do anything but float in her own thoughts. When he'd asked her to give them a real shot at having a relationship, she'd dug in her heels and let her need for independence push him away.

That's what she did. She pushed people away until she was alone. Her stubbornness and determination to make it on her own had always been stronger than her good sense.

But he'd never gone far.

Around them, the whole place was crashing in, and she cringed, clutching at Ian's fire gear.

"You're okay, you're safe now," he said, and she stared at his mouth, reading the words.

She was safe. Because he'd made her so. Usually she relied only on herself. Always, she relied only on herself.

But not this time.

"Mel, look at me."

She was trying, honest to God she was trying to keep her eyes open and on him, but her head hurt like a bitch, and worse, everything was going dark. Her eyes were closing. Logically she knew this, and she attempted to open them again but her lids were too heavy...

"No, don't you dare leave me," Ian said firmly, voice low and gruff, muted by his gear. "Open your eyes, babe."

Damn, she loved that tough, obey-me voice of his. When he spoke like that, she wanted to give him the moon.

But she'd never been able to give him what he needed, never, and she let the dark take her...

CHAPTER
3

Ian raced down the stairs with Melissa in his arms, his gaze on her ashen face.

You came for me, she'd murmured, the surprise in her voice slicing through him. She had no idea what he'd do for her—and that was their biggest problem.

He'd grown up in a big, boisterous, loving family, but not Melissa. She'd never had someone at her back like he had. She'd never experienced unconditional love, and as a result, she didn't trust it. "I've got you," he told her as he ran out of the burning building. "Always will."

He was met just outside the burning building by Cindy, pushing a gurney toward them. The paramedic took over, but Ian kept a firm hold of Melissa's hand. She was out cold, bleeding from various cuts, including a deep one on her temple. "She was conscious," he said.

"How long has she been out?"

"Two minutes."

Cindy, a longtime friend, put her hand over his and squeezed gently. "We'll take good care of her."

He knew that, but damn it was hard to let go. Leaning over Melissa, he whispered, "*Always*."

Cindy flashed him a sympathetic smile as she and her partner pushed the gurney toward the ambulance, and Ian was forced to put thoughts of Melissa aside and turn back to the scene. They pulled ten more people from the building with various degrees of injuries, ranging from first- and second-degree burns to broken bones to smoke inhalation. Not good, but it could have been much worse.

He'd heard nothing about Melissa's condition, and it was two interminably long hours before he could get to the hospital to check for himself. "Melissa Mann," he said at the front desk, "brought in from—"

"Tonight's fire." The woman nodded. "She's here."

"Where?"

"Last I heard she was in x-ray but—"

He strode down the hall and rounded the corner to the x-ray department.

It was empty.

His heart stopped, and he whirled around, nearly plowing over the receptionist, who'd followed him. "But," the unflappable woman went on, as if he hadn't walked away from her in the middle of a sentence, "if she's done there, she's been brought upstairs. Room two-ten."

He took the stairs instead of waiting for an elevator and stopped at the nurse's desk. He knew Dottie. They'd gone to school together and had dated in their freshman year. And their junior year. And then about three years back for a few months, until they remembered that they didn't like each other for more than a week at a time.

Dottie smiled at him. "Hey, Hot Stuff. You look like you fought the good fight tonight. You were on that apartment building fire?"

"Yeah. You've got Melissa Mann in room two-ten. How is she?"

She grimaced sympathetically. "Honey, you know I can't divulge information except to next of kin."

Yeah, he knew. And if he'd been successful at convincing Melissa to move in with him, he might've convinced her to marry him next, and then they would be next of kin. "We're seeing each other."

Dottie expressed surprise with a lifted brow. "I didn't know that."

Few had. They'd kept it quiet—Ian because he liked having something to himself in a town that loved gossip more than just about anything, and Mel because... well, because what they'd had scared her. "How about her parents? Have they been notified?" To say that Melissa wasn't close to her judgmental parents was an understatement, but they should be told.

"We're here."

Ian whipped around to face them. That they'd already made it from Seattle told him they'd sped here, which wasn't helping his impending heart attack any.

"How is she?" her father asked.

Dottie stood up. "Dr. Josh Scott's in with her now. I'll get him for you."

Five minutes later, Ian stood next to her parents as Dr. Scott gave the news. Minor concussion accompanied by some swelling. The plan—watch and wait—was something he should be good at by now but had never mastered.

• • •

Three hours later it was nearly dawn, and Ian was alone in Melissa's hospital room. Her parents had gone to the B&B for the night to get some rest. The lights were still dimmed, and the monitors beeped and hissed softly.

Melissa was still out.

The doctor had assured both him and her parents that this was okay, that her brain was taking the rest it needed, and that her last scan looked clear. She was young and strong and vital. They'd know more by morning.

But Ian knew better than most that a clear scan didn't always mean jack-shit. A little over a year ago, he'd lost his sister Ella to a head trauma after a skiing accident. The doctors had stood at her bedside, where Ella lay in a coma, and said the prognosis was tentatively "looking good."

Confident in their word, Ian had gone back to work for the rest of his shift, leaving Ella with the rest of the family to stand vigil.

Ella had died before dawn. She hadn't died alone, but she'd died without Ian.

He wasn't going back to work this time. Nope, he was sitting right here, his hand gripping Melissa's, and he was going to keep holding it for as long as it took.

A nurse came in to check her vitals. "Talk to her," she suggested. "I think it helps them find their way back to us."

When the nurse was gone, Ian looked into Melissa's still face. So unlike her. Awake, Melissa was the life of the party, more alive than anyone he knew. "Mel." He stroked the hair from her face, carefully avoiding the large bandage on her temple where she'd been stitched up.

"I was about sixty seconds too late getting to you. Bad timing." He blew out a breath. Just like their relationship. He lifted her hand to his mouth and kissed her palm. "I miss you, babe."

Her fingers tightened on his, just a reflexive gesture he knew, but his gaze flew to her face. "Mel? Can you hear me?"

Nothing, but he took heart anyway. "I'm right here," he promised, leaning closer. "And I'm not going anywhere."

The beeps and hisses of the machine were his only answer. *Talk to her*, the nurse had said. Ian wasn't, and never had been, a big talker. That was one of Melissa's biggest complaints, actually. "I dreamed about us last night," he said, and let out a breath. What the hell. No one was listening. "I dreamed we'd worked things out. We were doing up Christmas like I haven't since..." He broke off.

Melissa had known he hadn't celebrated Christmas last year, that he hadn't celebrated anything since Ella had died. Hell, he hadn't even managed to go back to his parents' house, only a two-hour drive away. He'd tried a few times but found he couldn't do it, forcing his family to come to Lucky Harbor when they wanted to see him. "There's more," he said softly. "You brought a tree for my place. *Our* place," he corrected. "You got me over the hump on that, Mel." He had to smile at the memory. "And you were dressed up as an elf." A sexy-as-hell elf whose little green outfit—emphasis on little—had shown off her gorgeous curves to perfection. "You'd made cookies to leave out for Santa," he went on, "and the house was lit up like...well, like Christmas." He smiled again because generally he was the only one who cooked. "We had..." He broke off to drop his forehead to their linked hands and let out a low laugh because he couldn't believe he was saying this. "We had a kid. A little girl who had your beautiful eyes and smile. You named her Molly." His throat tightened. "We were married, which means that I must have eventually worn you down, right?"

Melissa still didn't answer, didn't move, and he let out a long, shaky exhale. "Just wake up, Mel. I know we're not together, and that none of what I dreamed matters anymore, but just wake up. I can handle you not in my life if I have to, but I can't handle you not *having* a life."

CHAPTER

4

Melissa shuddered out a sigh as her dream began. It was Christmas, and she was dressed in a . . . sexy elf costume? Huh. Interesting since she'd given up the crazy partying a few years back. But it got more interesting. The dream was being narrated by Ian. She could hear his voice, and God how she loved the timbre of it, low and slightly husky, talking about how she'd made cookies for Santa and decorated the house.

Okay, so she wasn't at a party. Or at least if she was, it was a party for two. Then the vision panned out like a wide-angle camera, and she realized she was in Ian's house, standing by a huge Christmas tree, and she was holding the sweetest little baby she'd ever seen. Theirs. Ian was looking at them, "his women" as he called them, "Mel and Molly." Wanting to memorize this, wanting to memorize everything, she took a wild look around. Ian's mouth was still moving but suddenly she couldn't hear him. All she could hear was an annoying *beep, beep, beep* . . .

• • •

Melissa opened her eyes to an antiseptic smell and the beeping of monitors. Oh, crap. A hospital. Her first thought was *don't make me wake up, I love this dream!* Her second thought was that she had a huge insurance deductible, and—

"How do you feel?"

Turning her head, she found Ian sitting in the chair next to her bed. Six months, and her heart still clutched every single time she saw him. She kept waiting for that to go away, wondering when her pulse would stop leaping from just being near him. Hell, she didn't even have to be near him to feel it. She could simply *think* of him and it would happen.

She'd been so certain that would fade after she'd slept with him. Their first night had been a crazy, wild, sex-on-the-beach thing that still revved her engines when she thought about it. Not a thing had faded. Instead, it'd gotten better and better.

She hadn't been the same since she'd broken things off, and that baffled her to the core. She'd never been the type of woman to need a man. Enjoy, yes. Need? She knew how to get the most out of life without one. But with Ian, everything had been different. He'd never tried to control her, tell her what to do, or who to be. He'd accepted her as she was, flaws and all.

And she'd still pushed him away. She'd regretted it instantly, but hadn't had any idea how to fix it.

But that had been before her dream.

Now, she still didn't know how to get him back, but she knew she had to try because she wanted the life she'd envisioned. *Desperately.* "I saw you," she whispered. Or tried to. Barely recognizing her own raw, scratchy voice, she tried to sit up and gasped as her head swam.

Ian was there in a blink, hands on her, lowering her back to the bed. "Easy," he said. "You don't have your sea legs yet."

"What happened?"

His eyes met hers. "You don't remember?"

"I remember the fire," she said. And the horror. The bone-numbing fear. The unbearable heat. She made a sound of duress, and he wrapped her hand in his much bigger, work-roughened one. "I couldn't get out the door," she told him softly. "And the window was jammed, or I'd have probably tried to jump even though it was too far."

Speaking of jumping, a muscle in Ian's jaw was doing just that. "It *was* too far down," he said. "What else?"

She thought about it. "I remember crawling into the tub. And just as my life started flashing before my eyes, you showed up."

He gently stroked his thumb over her IV line. "Not soon enough, though."

Something in his voice had her meeting his gaze. His hair looked finger-combed at best. He was in his cargos and long-sleeved firefighter polo that both looked as if maybe he'd slept in them.

But it was his eyes that caught and held her attention. In her dream, they'd softened when they'd landed on her, broadcasting his emotions in a way that he'd been extremely careful not to do since they'd stopped seeing each other.

His eyes were hard to read now, but there was no mistaking the strain in them. Usually he was the epitome of cool, calm, and collected, but not today. "I'm okay," she said softly, and then paused. "Right?"

An almost-smile tugged at his mouth, and he brushed

his lips against her temple. "Yes," he said in that voice that always meant business.

She relaxed. If he said she was okay, well then, she was okay, but she knew there was a reason he looked so tense.

"You had some brain swelling," he said, "but your body repaired itself before surgery was required. You were out for a while."

Ah. The reason. "A while? How long is a while?"

"Eighteen hours."

"*What*?" She sat up again, more slowly this time and with his help. "But I just got here."

He gave a slow shake of his head and gently stroked the hair back from her face. "It's been almost two days, Mel."

Two days... "I dreamed..."

"Of?"

She didn't answer.

"I talked to you," he said. "Did you hear me?"

"No," she said with real regret. She'd have loved to hear what he'd said to her. Her eyes drifted shut, and she turned her cheek into his big, warm, callused palm. She remembered him whispering to her, *I've got you*. Dream? Or real? "Thank you," she whispered. "For saving my life."

"You scared the hell out of me."

She opened her eyes and met his. "I scared me, too," she admitted. "I thought I was cashing in."

"No." He shook his head. "Not on my watch."

Unbearably touched, she leaned on him, setting her head on his broad shoulder. Maybe before the fire she'd been too afraid to go for what she wanted, but now she knew how ridiculous that was. She'd huddled in that tub, sure she was going to die alone with her regrets, but she'd been given a second chance. She wouldn't blow it. Life was short, *too* short. "Ian..." She paused. "I need to talk to you."

He looked down at her. "Talking's never been our strong suit."

She knew that but she had to try.

Unfortunately, it seemed like the whole world suddenly realized she was awake. A nurse bustled in, and then another. They nudged Ian aside to check her vitals, and then her doctor was there, too, asking her all sorts of annoying questions.

Melissa never got to tell Ian a thing. It was okay, she decided. She'd just show him. But it was another two long days before she was released: two long days of doctors, nurses, friends, and...this had been the hard part...her parents.

It was awkward since they'd not had much of a relationship in the past years, but they were mature enough not to bring up her past, and she was mature enough not to poke the bears.

When she finally left the hospital, she joined her parents, who'd gotten two rooms at the local B&B. They all stayed there a few days, made a few trips to Target to replace some essentials, had a few meals. The subject of Melissa's immediate future was broached, and her parents hadn't quite hidden their relief that she wouldn't be going home with them.

Her building hadn't been cleared for her to return to, but she knew she wasn't going back there, either. She was on a mission to fix her life. To get a life.

To get Ian back.

He just didn't know it yet.

CHAPTER

5

Two days later, Melissa had set her plan in motion. She was temporarily staying at the hair salon, on the futon in her office. It was in town, relatively safe, and best of all, free. She'd made calls and arrangements and was ready for action.

Ian had no idea what was about to hit him.

First, she headed to the fire station with a box of cupcakes from the bakery run by her friend Leah. This meant they were the best cupcakes ever, perfect bribery material. As a whole, the fire station was a close-knit, closed-mouthed group, but Melissa knew for a fact that free desserts turned the first responders into social butterflies. She handed them out and learned that Ian was "pissy" and in his office.

She left the guys and headed down the hall. Ian's door was open. He stood in front of his desk on his cell phone, a hand in his hair.

A little breathless at the sight of him, she gave him a little wave as she kicked the door shut behind her and set a cupcake on a corner of his desk.

Eyes on her, Ian finished his phone conversation. Then, looking amused, he tossed his phone aside and sat on the corner of his desk. He didn't say a word as she stepped between his long, spread legs and put her hands on his broad-as-a-mountain shoulders. Shoulders strong enough to carry a lot of weight, a lot of burdens, most of which weren't his. "Hi," she said softly.

"Hi." He stroked a finger lightly over the bandage still on her temple. "You okay?"

"Yes, thanks to you."

His hands went to her hips, but he didn't pull her in as she'd hoped. Leaning in, she put her mouth to his ear. A hot spot for him, she knew. She let out a soft breath and licked his lobe and was rewarded when he groaned. She took his lobe between her teeth and held it.

His fingers tightened on her, as if maybe he was going to push her away, but he didn't. His eyes drifted shut. And almost as if he couldn't help it, he very slightly tilted his head to the side to give her better access. "Mel."

His voice held a warning tone, but she didn't stop. Instead she tugged just a little.

"Feeling all better, I'm guessing," he muttered, but he didn't fool her. His eyes were his sexy, half-mast bedroom eyes. She loved his sexy, half-mast bedroom eyes.

"Can I see you tonight?" she asked.

"We're not bed buddies anymore, remember?"

His voice remained even but she knew she'd caused him pain in the past. She was going to make it all better. And then never hurt him again. "I have something I want to show you."

"I think I know this game," he said dryly. "And it's a great game. But we already played it out, Mel."

"It's not that," she said softly. "It's something else."

Their gazes locked and held. He studied her for a long beat and then slowly shook his head. "I can't."

"Can't, or won't?"

"Won't," he said.

Unexpected roadblock. She absorbed the pain and forged through it. She'd never been easy; she couldn't expect him to be. "Please?" she murmured, cupping his face, loving the feel of his two-day scruff against her fingers. "Just this one last time?"

She knew it was the *please* that did it. He'd never been able to resist *please* from her. And she should be ashamed of herself for using it against him, but she wasn't above doing whatever she had to do to prove herself. "Ian?" she whispered, holding her breath for his response, and after a heart-stopping beat, he gave it, a single almost imperceptible nod. He'd see her tonight.

Now all she had to do was get it right.

She enlisted the help of Ian's older sister Kaley.

"Remember the deal," Kaley said, letting Melissa into Ian's house with her key. "I do this for you, and you—"

"I'll hold up my end of the bargain," Melissa promised.

Kaley looked at Melissa. "You know I didn't want you for him," she said.

Melissa nodded and ignored the pang of hurt. "I know."

"I wanted someone to love him."

"I do," Melissa said.

"I wanted someone to keep him."

"I intend to," Melissa said.

Again Kaley looked at her. "For whatever reason, I

actually believe you," she finally said. "Don't stop loving him, even when he's pissed at you for this. And he *will* be pissed."

Melissa knew it. But Ian had risked all for her, including his own life. She had to risk back, and if it meant making him mad in order to reach him, she'd do it. She'd do anything. "I know what I'm doing," she said, and hoped to God that was true.

The sun was just coming over the horizon when she heard Ian's truck pull into his driveway. Melissa jumped up, carefully put his present in the pantry, and was skidding back into the living room when Ian walked in the front door.

Melissa smoothed her outfit and stood there, her heart pounding so loudly that she was shocked she could still hear the front door swing open.

Ian took one look at her and blinked in surprise. "What the hell?"

"I'm an elf."

He opened his mouth and then closed it again. "Since when do elves wear tutus and wings?" he finally asked.

"Since all the elf costumes were taken, and the only thing left that was green was this fairy costume." She thought she saw his lips twitch and took heart in that. "I would've gone for Mrs. Claus," she said, "but there were none of those left, either."

There was a funny look on his face, but then he distracted her by sniffing the air dramatically. "Cookies?" he asked, heavy on the disbelief.

She understood the sentiment. She was a terrible cook, and he knew it. She could burn water without trying. He'd never appeared bothered by that in the least; instead he'd cooked. He was good at it, having learned out of necessity at the firehouse. He'd always said he didn't mind.

But *she'd* minded. She wanted to be able to give him a fraction of what he gave her. "Chocolate chip cookies," she said proudly.

He paused again. "You made me chocolate chip cookies?"

Okay, so she'd bought the dough from Leah, but hey, it was close enough. The first batch was in the oven, giving off a delicious scent. "Yep."

Ian eyed his living room. Every corner now dripped with the holiday decorations she'd spent all night putting up. Garland, lights, trim...She'd brought in a tree, too. A huge one that she'd had to bribe the high school kid at the tree lot to help her drag into the house. He'd left before she could coax him into helping her put the tree in a stand, but Melissa had sort of leaned it back into a corner and called it good. She had used her own decorations. She hadn't had very many, but thankfully her small holiday box had been in her shop's storage closet and not in her apartment.

Ian's gaze came back to her, veiled as he looked over her "elf" costume. "I thought you said you didn't hear anything I said to you when you were unconscious," he said.

"I didn't."

He kept looking at her. She had no idea what he was thinking because he was good at hiding his thoughts when he wanted to. He walked to the tree and fingered a tiny set of shears hanging from a gold ribbon. "I don't decorate for Christmas."

She moved in close. "You used to."

"You know why I don't now."

She ran a hand down his back, feeling the easy strength of him. And the tension that was barely leashed. "I know you love Christmas," she said quietly. "And Ella wouldn't want you to keep ignoring it."

Closing his eyes, he turned away. "Why are you here, Mel?"

To win your heart. She'd been careless with it once, but she'd never be again. "Everyone needs a little holiday spirit," she said.

"*Everyone* has plenty. Downtown is practically glowing from all the lights and decorations. It's enough."

"I was hoping to bring *you* some cheer. Your family's hoping you—"

"Melissa." He scrubbed a hand over his face. "Don't."

But she had to. She'd promised Kaley. "It's just one meal, Ian. Brunch, tomorrow, at your parents' place. They—"

He moved to the front door and opened it. A not-so-subtle invitation for her to get the hell out.

Instead, she turned back to the tree and added a few last ornaments.

The door slammed, and she went still, afraid to look and see if he'd left.

"I wish you hadn't done this," he said from right behind her, making her jump. The man moved like smoke. "Or spent your own money—"

"I didn't spend much money," she said. "I used my own decorations." She kept herself busy fussing with the tree. She could feel him strong and warm at her back. She let her eyes drift closed, having to fight the urge to lean back into him.

Reaching around her, he lightly tapped on a plastic

firefighter hat swinging from a red ribbon. She'd written his number on it in black Sharpie. "I just got that one," she said. "I tell myself it will keep you safe."

"And what about you? What will keep you safe?"

She moved to the couch, to her purse. Pulling out her phone, she brought up a craigslist ad. "I've been looking for places to move," she said, showing him.

He looked at the duplex on the screen, silent.

"It's only a few blocks from here," she said. "A better address, yes?"

He looked into her eyes. "Yes," he finally said, but she got the feeling he'd nearly said something else.

Once upon a time he'd have said *live here, with me*. But she'd thrown that away. Her heart ached as she dropped her phone to the couch and then climbed onto a stepstool to place the star on the top of the tree. "There," she said. "All done."

Ian didn't say anything as she backed down the ladder, moved it across the room, and once again climbed it to tie a sprig of mistletoe to a ceiling beam.

She worked her way down the ladder to the bottom rung and realized that there were two strong forearms surrounding her, securing the ladder. Already breathless, she stepped to the floor, turned, and found herself practically in Ian's arms.

He glanced up at the mistletoe she'd placed overhead and then into her eyes. "You looking for a kiss, Mel?"

He was teasing her, which she took as a good sign. Better than showing her the door again. As she knew all too well, Ian had come from a large family, including four sisters. He'd probably known how to distract and redirect a female by age two.

But *Melissa* wasn't teasing. She was serious, and a day ago she'd nearly been *dead* serious. "Yes," she said. "I want a kiss." Among other things...

Ian looked into her eyes for a long beat, then gave one shake of his head. He started to move away but then he stopped. Staring down into her face, he slowly pulled her in. He still wasn't showing much, but that was okay. She had a lot of catching up to do. Feeling her throat tighten, hoping she was going to be able to reach him, she slid her hands up his chest. "I missed this," she murmured. "Missed you."

"Melissa," he said on a ragged groan as her arms wound around his neck. "What are you up to?"

"If you don't know, I'm doing it wrong."

His hands were still at her hips, his fingers digging in as if he was getting ready to push her away from him. She held on and met his gaze. "I'm trying to show you something."

"What is that, exactly?"

"That I want you," she said.

"Wanting was never our problem," he said, and nudged. He was hard.

This gave her a surge of anticipation that made her entire body tremble. She wanted to kiss him more than she wanted her next breath, but this wasn't going to be their usual "friends with benefits" situation. This time, she wanted it all. "I want to give us a *real* shot, Ian."

"Because of what happened the other night," he said, not sounding impressed.

"Because of what *almost* happened the other night," she corrected. "A near death experience makes people rethink things." She paused. "Like mistakes they've made."

"Yeah, it does." He never took his eyes from hers. "I've seen hundreds of people go through it. It wears off," he said flatly.

"This won't."

He didn't move. So she did. She pulled his head to hers, then looked at his mouth.

And then that mouth was touching hers, lightly at first, then not lightly at all.

"You believe me," she whispered in relief against him.

"I don't know what I believe," he said, voice rough. "But I know I want you back." Gently fisting his hand in her hair, he tilted her head to suit him before kissing her like he meant it, parting her lips with his and slowly stroking her tongue with his own. When they were both breathless, he pulled back to look at her, let out a low, innately male sound that made her quiver, and then took her mouth again. And again. And again, until a huge crash sounded.

They both jerked and whipped around in time to see the tree still vibrating from its fall. Broken glass and ornaments littered the living room, a virtual graveyard of Christmas, and as Melissa stared at it in horror, the fire alarm went off.

Oh no...

"My cookies!" She ran to the kitchen—the smoke-filled kitchen—and hurriedly turned off the oven. Then she pulled out the cookies. Burned to a crisp.

Ian strode to the window and shoved it open to let in the twenty-degree, icy winter air before turning with an intense look in the direction of his pantry.

"Melissa," he said with shocking calm in the middle of such chaos, "why is my pantry barking?"

Tossing aside the oven mitts, Melissa opened the pantry and scooped up the eight-week-old black lab puppy with the red bow around her neck. "I didn't plan for it to go like this," she said. "But..." She tried for a smile as she thrust out the puppy. "Merry Christmas?"

Ian stared at her, and then at the wriggling, panting, happy creature in her arms. "You got me a puppy?"

Melissa set her in his arms.

The puppy went ape-shit ecstatic at having a new person to lick to death. Trying to get at Ian, she was running a marathon in place, desperate to get closer. The second he pulled her in she made happy little puppy sounds, then sighed a big puppy sigh as she relaxed into a boneless state and...peed on him.

CHAPTER

6

Ian tucked the puppy under one arm, opened a second window, and turned on the oven fan, then strode into the living room. He'd already unplugged the tree lights, but now he made sure everything else was turned off. "Don't come in here," he said over his shoulder to the silent woman in the doorway. "You're not wearing shoes."

Melissa hugged herself. "I'm so sorry. This isn't how I thought things would go."

Ian wondered how she thought things *would* go, but he said nothing as he went into his bedroom next. There he set the puppy on the floor. "Stay," he told her, and changed his shirt.

Less than ten seconds later, the puppy was already chewing on a shoe. Ian scooped her back up and got licked across his chin for the effort. "You're as big a troublemaker as she is, aren't you?" he asked.

The puppy panted happily, blowing warm puppy breath into his face.

Ian carried her into the living room. Melissa had found

a broom and a trash can. Still dressed as a fairy-slash-elf, she was cleaning up the mess. She'd shoved her feet into a pair of his winter boots. They were huge on her but she didn't appear to notice as she struggled to right the tree. Coming up behind her, he took over. "Melissa."

She didn't look at him so he turned her around. Her eyes were wet, her face blotchy. "I'm so sorry, Ian—"

He put a finger to her lips. The puppy leaned in and tried to lick her, but Ian tightened his grip on Miss Wild Thing. "You did all this for me," he said.

Melissa nodded her head miserably. "Yes. I burned your pan, nearly destroyed your kitchen, *did* destroy your living room, and got you peed on by Molly. All for you." She sniffed noisily.

"Molly?" Ian asked, still as stone.

Melissa let out a long, shaky breath. "Okay, here's the thing," she said, sounding heartbreakingly unsure. Even a little scared. "When I was in the hospital, I had this dream. We were living here, in this house. We were..."

"Together," he said.

"Yes. Like maybe as if I'd never screwed things up. And—I realize this is going to sound crazy—but we were married. It was Christmastime, and I'd decorated your house, and made Santa cookies, and..." She nibbled on her bottom lip and blushed. "We had a baby named Molly." Her voice lowered, even as the pulse at the base of her neck beat like a hummingbird's wings. "We were happy. So happy. And you looked at me like..."

"Like what?"

"Like I was your entire world."

Ian was staggered. She'd *dreamed* all the things he'd told her when she'd been unconscious. She'd loved those things so much she'd woken up and tried to make them a reality.

"I just wanted to give you Christmas back," she said softly.

"By dressing up as a sexy elf, decorating my house, and making cookies?" He laughed softly. "Were you going to give me a baby, too?"

She grimaced. "I didn't actually make the cookies. I bought the dough."

He stared at her and then laughed again. Christ, she was priceless. Precious. *Worth waiting for...*

"I forgot how much I love your laugh," she said softly. "But as for the baby, I didn't want to get ahead of myself, not to mention we aren't together that way. So..."

"You went with a puppy."

"Yes," she said.

"Named Molly."

She nodded, looking worried. "Too much, right? Of course it is. It's—"

"Perfect," he said thickly. Her mascara had run a little bit, there were a few unidentifiable smudges on her costume, and her hair was crazy. She'd never looked more beautiful to him. "Do you have any more surprises for me?"

She nibbled on her lower lip. "Will I scare you into running off screaming if I admit that I do?" she asked. "That in fact, there are two?"

"Should I call the station, put them on standby?"

She choked out a laugh. "Not necessary." She paused. "I hope."

God help him. God help the both of them. The puppy had fallen asleep on his shoulder. He set her back in the pantry, in the box and blanket that he assumed was her bed, and held his breath. She made a few soft puppy noises, snuffled, and then fell back asleep.

He turned to Melissa. "Bring it on," he said. "Surprise number one?"

Staring at him, she pointed to the very thin, silky red bow around her neck.

CHAPTER

7

You're my present," Ian said with his bad boy smile.

Melissa's heart knocked into her ribs as she nodded.

"Say it," he ordered.

She wanted to say she was his *forever* but she didn't want to rush this. Didn't want to rush *him*. "I'm yours."

"Love the sound of that," he murmured, and yanked her in close. He tugged on the bow around her neck until it came loose. Then he scooped her up in his arms and carried her down the hallway and to his bed, where he followed her down. "When does this present expire?" he asked, working on removing her "elf" costume.

"When you're over it."

At this, his focus came back to her face. He looked at her for a long beat, and then his expression softened and he bent to kiss her. "Scared, Mel?"

"Terrified," she whispered.

"Trust me," he murmured, his mouth so close that his lips brushed hers as he spoke.

She nodded before she could even think about it. She

did trust him. She trusted him with her life, her heart and soul . . .

He turned his attention back to getting her naked, his gaze heating every inch of skin he exposed. He further warmed her by following each hot gaze with a touch. And then a kiss. She'd long ago learned that his patience and endless attention to detail carried over to the bedroom. He liked to touch and kiss, everything. A *lot*. He could spend hours loving her body, driving her to the point of madness and beyond.

His mouth on hers, he trailed his fingers across her breasts. She clenched her stomach and arched her back for more.

But he changed direction and headed south. South worked. Except she was already gasping for more and he still had his clothes on. As if reading her mind, he slid off the bed and stripped, quickly and efficiently, which didn't mean her tongue wasn't on the ground at the sight of him, hard. Perfect.

Seeing her expression, he smiled a just-for-you smile as he crawled up her body. He knew exactly what he did to her, and he liked it. "Kiss me," she demanded, wrapping her arms around his neck.

His mouth immediately covered hers, warm and sure. His hands were just as warm and sure, moving over her body, alternately making her sigh in pleasure and cry out for more. She got lost in the sensations, unable to think or worry, or even remember the reasons she'd held back from him. Why had she resisted this, resisted him, knowing that this was what had been waiting for her?

His arm slid beneath her, yanking her even closer to him. Eager for just that, she wrapped her legs around his waist, her need for him stronger than anything she'd ever experienced, stronger than anything she'd ever believed could exist. And that's when she remembered why she'd tried to hold back. *Because she loved him.* Irrevocably. Ripping her mouth from his, she gasped in air, the emotions battering her, searing through her chest.

"Trust me," he whispered again, and then those lips dragged down her throat, over a collarbone to her breast. His tongue laved her nipple before his teeth gently closed around it, biting, creating a shock of desire that took over the space where all the panic was sitting in her chest. "Ian—"

His mouth was busy, working his way to her other breast, and then down her belly. Nibbling at a hip, he then nudged his way between her thighs. "Mmm," he said, and stroked her with his tongue.

It was all she could do not to scream. At that moment, he could have done anything, asked anything of her. But he didn't. He never did. He only gave.

She flipped him. Or she tried. She knew he only rolled over because she wanted him to, allowing her to press him to the mattress. Then she took a tour of his body in the same way he had of hers, using her tongue, her teeth, her entire being to love him.

He threaded his hands in her hair, tightening them into fists as he quivered beneath her, and then, when he was panting for air, her name on his breath in a half curse, half prayer, he rolled them again and slid into her.

They both gasped then, and he dropped his forehead to hers. "This isn't just for now," he said, his voice thick with need and desire. His eyes bore into hers, fierce, intent. Her heart swelled, even as she promised herself she wouldn't hold him to it, to the words he gave her in the heat of the moment. But then he said three more, which were going to be damn hard to let go of.

"You *are* mine."

She shifted against him, desperate for the feel of him moving within her. "And you?" she managed.

His gaze locked onto hers. "Babe, I've always been yours."

Her eyes filled, and all the air left her body as she arched up to meet him thrust for thrust, trying to get closer, and then closer still. But she was as close as she could get, and still she struggled, needing something, needing—

"I love you, Mel," he said, his mouth at her ear. "Always have."

It was what she needed. Her heart soared, and she tightened around him. With him filling her body, her very spirit, she completely shattered. Clinging to him, she pressed her face into the crook of his neck and let go, whispering against his damp skin, "I love you, Ian."

He forced her head back, his eyes burning into hers. "Again."

"I love you," she repeated. A promise, a vow.

Groaning, he held her head for a kiss, deep and demanding. She wrapped her arms around him—her legs, all of her, pulling him in as close as she could. It was the same between them, and yet different. *Better.* In the past, this level of passion had frightened her, but now . . . now she couldn't imagine being without it.

Without him.

CHAPTER

8

Melissa woke up alone in Ian's bed and blinked. Pinpricks of soft light were just edging into the room around the shades. She glanced at the clock. Seven fifty.

Seven fifty?

Crap! Her last present to Ian was going to start without her. Heart in her throat, she jumped out of bed, shoved herself back into the fairy costume—all she had—and ran through the house, skidding to a stop in the kitchen.

Man and pup were at the stovetop, and the scent of sizzling bacon filled the air. Ian flipped a pancake with one hand, cradling the puppy to his chest with the other.

The sexy adorable sight sucked the air right out of her lungs.

Ian took one look at her in that fairy costume and grinned, making her heart skip a beat. "Hey," he said, and came toward her. Leaning in, he gave her a long, hard, hot kiss. "Merry Christmas."

"You're really okay with all this?"

He set the puppy down and cupped Melissa's face,

holding her gaze prisoner. "Mel, I'm so far beyond okay that I can't even tell you."

Molly began to run circles around their feet, but then got distracted by Ian's shoelaces.

"I have one more present," Melissa whispered against Ian's lips.

"A repeat of last night?"

She paused, getting a hot flash just thinking about last night. "Maybe later," she said. Definitely later. *If he forgave her for what was coming next...*"But I have to drive you to this present."

He looked at her for a long moment. "I have to be at the station in ten minutes."

"I got your shift traded. Doug's going to take it for you."

"Doug has family."

"They're coming to the station to be with him," she said. She picked up Molly, who began to wriggle in sheer excitement, short little legs cycling the air, her tongue attempting to reach Melissa's face. "No peeing in my car," she told the puppy.

Molly grinned at her like *Who, me?*

They all piled into Melissa's car. She made a quick stop at the salon and changed out of her fairy costume. When she got back in the car and pulled onto the freeway, Ian fell silent. He remained silent when she exited the highway nearly two hours later. And by the time she pulled into the driveway of a large ranch-style home in the suburbs north of Seattle, he'd stopped breathing.

His parents' house.

She turned off the engine and looked at him. He was staring at the house as if it were a spitting Cobra. "You okay?" she asked quietly.

"Why." Just the one word, gutturally uttered.

Melissa took in his tension as her own. "Because I'm not the only one who's retreated instead of dealing with emotion."

"Jesus, Melissa. This is hardly the same thing."

"It's not your fault Ella died," she said softly.

"I wasn't there." His voice was strained, tight.

"You couldn't have changed what happened by being with her at the hospital. Ian..." She squeezed his hand and waited until he looked at her from hollow eyes. "She's gone, and I'm so sorry. But your family doesn't deserve to lose both of you."

He kept his hand in hers but he closed his eyes. "It hurts to be here, where she's not, where I'd always seen her so full of life."

"I know."

"And now so much time has gone by, it's not right. I deserted them last year."

"They still want you to come. They miss you being here."

Ian opened his eyes and looked at the house. As they both watched, the curtains were pulled aside and one, two, three, and then four faces peeked out. His mom, his dad, and his two older sisters. He made a sound that was a mixture of grief and laughter. Behind them, the puppy barked once from her traveling crate.

Ian let out a shaky breath and shoved the car door open.

Melissa waited until he was out and then put her car in reverse.

"Hell no, you don't." Ian leaned back into the vehicle and snagged her keys. "You brought me here. You're coming, too."

"Oh, no, I—"

Not interested in what she had to say, he pulled her out through the passenger side.

Melissa tried not to panic as they strode up the walk, the puppy now in Ian's arms. Either Molly was still sleepy or she was sensing the tension coming off Ian in waves, but she behaved like a little angel.

They didn't have to knock. Before they got to the top step, the door flew open wide and Ian's mother Nancy stared at her son, eyes shimmering with unshed tears.

Ian managed a weak smile. "Hi, Mom. I—"

She yanked him into her arms and hugged him so tightly that Melissa would've been surprised if he could breathe. "You came home! Oh thank God, my baby finally came home."

Ian froze, then dropped his head to his mom's shoulder, his free hand fisting in the back of her sweater. "I'm sorry," he whispered hoarsely. "I'm so sorry I haven't been here—"

"Shh," she said, and cupped his head. "You're here now. That's all that matters."

His sisters got in on the hug. And then his dad gathered them all in, giving Ian the male slap on the back. "You're just in time," he said. "She was about to shove us all in the car to come get you. Something about how you'd been a stubborn lout for long enough and it was time, past time, to have you back here, with us."

Melissa blinked back tears and couldn't swallow the ache in her chest no matter how she tried. This was a family, a *real* family. She was so very happy for Ian and so very...sad for herself.

Ian pulled free and reached for Melissa, his eyes holding a suspicious sheen as he tugged her in.

"Um," she said, gesturing vaguely to her car. "I need to—"

Nancy grabbed onto her as well, and then the next thing Melissa knew, she was being pulled into a bear hug, too. And she'd been right. Nancy hugged so tight that air was optional.

It was the best hug she'd ever had.

"You brought my baby home," Nancy said, then pulled back and held Melissa's face. "I can never thank you enough."

Melissa wanted to tell her that it was her pleasure but knew if she opened her mouth she'd embarrass herself by crying.

"Mom," Ian said quietly, "can you give us a minute?"

"You're not leaving," she said fiercely.

"I won't," he promised.

With reluctance, the front door shut, leaving Ian and Melissa alone on the porch. He took her hand and brought it up to his mouth. "Thank you."

Melissa, still not trusting her voice, nodded.

"You're amazing," he said. "You know that, right?"

She managed a smile because the way he was looking at her was everything she'd ever been too afraid to hope for. "Call me when you want a ride back, okay?"

He tightened his grip on her. "No."

She soaked up the sight of him, wanting to remember this, always. "I just want you to know," she said, "last night was the best night of my life." She paused. "Well, minus the part where I almost burned your house down and the puppy peed on you." She searched his gaze. "And yes, I'm leaving. I don't want to rush you."

"Rush me through what?"

"Us."

He let out a low laugh. "Babe, I've been here waiting all along. Waiting for you to be ready." He tugged her into his arms. "*Please* rush me."

"Do you think they're looking at us?"

"Oh yeah. And you know they've got front row seats, so you're going to have to try to keep your hands off my—"

"Ian!"

He smiled, and at the sight, her heart caught and swelled against her rib cage. "I'm sorry I was so slow," she whispered.

Still looking amused, he ran a finger along her healing temple. "You about ready to be over that now?" he asked.

She turned her face into his palm and kissed the center. "Yes."

"Then stay," he said.

"For brunch?"

"For brunch. For dinner. For the night. And then for the rest of my life." He touched his forehead to hers. "*That* can be my Christmas present."

She wrapped her arms around his neck. "And what will be mine?"

"Me."

Sometimes the most important life decisions come down to a blink of an eye. "Best present ever," she said, and to the tune of cheers from inside, she pulled him in for a kiss.

Dear Reader,

Growing up, it's impossible to write about one Christmas that was a Christmas to remember.

See, when I was a kid, we didn't have a lot. My mom worked hard and made sure we had everything we needed, but she was rarely able to give us what we wanted.

Except at Christmas.

My sister and brother and I would have to take turns, every third Christmas, getting the "big gift" (like a tape recorder, a record player, or a small black and white TV). But we didn't mind, seeing as Mom saved all year to spoil us on that special day in a myriad of ways that maybe weren't so big but were always precious.

And she did. We lived with my aunt and grandparents on a small farm in Indiana and Mom and my Auntie Bec took the stockings down, placed them where we were to sit on Christmas, and stuffed them so full they were overflowing. As the days led up to Christmas, they held tons of gifts back, pulling them all out and spreading all the presents across the floor of our mudroom so when we woke up on Christmas Day, the entire room was taken up with Christmas.

It didn't even matter what was wrapped in those boxes.

What mattered was that, even at a young age, it was not lost on us that it wasn't just a day, but an entire year Mom had worked hard and saved precious money to light up that family holiday and make it special for the kids she loved.

And it wasn't just that day we knew how much she loved us. It was just that she knocked herself out so that on Christmas we would be in no doubt.

We never were.

Not back then. Not until the day she died. And beyond.

We still do up Christmas like nobody's business. Last year, moving home from England after a decade, I finally got to have another Christmas with my family.

We had it at my sister's house.

And my sissy took the stockings down and filled them to overflowing. She set them where each of her loved ones would sit during the festivities. And she spread the presents across the floor so when the big day dawned, the room was filled with Christmas . . .

And love.

Kristen Ashley

To Emily Sylvan Kim and Amy Pierpont,

*both of whom talked me into writing this story
when I was certain I didn't have the time,
and I wasn't certain I could do "short."*

*I loved spending Christmas with the Allens
and the Cages.*

*And I'm glad Emily and Amy didn't give
up on me so I got that chance.*

Every Year

Kristen Ashley

D o you think this is a good idea?" I asked.

"No," Tyra answered, but she had a smile in her voice.

We were standing outside on the deck next to Tyra and Dad's house in the foothills of Colorado outside Denver. It was two a.m. In other words, the early morning hours of Christmas Day.

And it had just started snowing.

The darkness before us was cut with a floodlight. Therefore, Ty-Ty and I could clearly see what was happening around the huge, tall tree at the other side of the drive.

"If Shy falls off that ladder and breaks his neck, I'm blaming Dad," I joked, and it was a joke because this wouldn't happen. My man could do anything, including what he was right then doing up on a ladder out in the snow.

"Where Tack's standing, if Shy falls off, he'll fall right on your father," Tyra replied.

I grinned because this was true.

Out in the dark, my dad and Tyra's husband, Kane "Tack" Allen, my man, Parker "Shy" Cage, my brother,

Cole "Rush" Allen, and Shy's brother, Landon, were all working by the bright light of the floodlight at the tree.

In truth, they weren't all working at the tree. There were two ladders on either side of a stout branch. Shy was up one, Rush was up the other, and those two were currently working at tying a rope to the branch. At the bottom of the rope a tire was tied. So it was only Shy and Rush who were working.

The reason for the tire swing?

It was a Christmas present for my baby brothers (Dad's kids with Ty-Ty), Rider and Cutter. This present came about because six-year-old Ride had seen some kid on a TV show on a tire swing and he'd gone ga-ga over it. It had been all he'd talked about for the last four months. And by talking about it I mean begging Dad for one.

Since Ride'd been talking about it (or begging), four-year-old Cut got in on the action. And Cut hadn't even seen the show with the swing. But it sounded like all kinds of fun to him and Cutter was all about fun, the wilder the better.

In other words, neither he, nor his big brother, fell far from the tree.

So Dad, being just that kind of dad (always), was giving it to them.

Except he wasn't. He was standing at the base of the tree barking orders up to my man and my big brother, and although Dad supplied the tire and the rope, he wasn't the one up the tree.

For Landon's part, he wasn't bothering to hide the fact that he thought the whole thing was hilarious—primarily how long it was taking—and he was doing this by shouting jokes.

That said, since he showed, I was getting a weird feeling from Landon. Shy's brother was usually a teasing, laid-back, fun-loving guy. That wasn't to say he couldn't be intense, especially when it came to his brother. They were tight and looked out for each other. Life taught them to be that way. Mostly, though, he was funny and mellow.

But now, something about Lan was just...off.

This tire swing situation had been going on for an hour. The lateness of that hour was due to the fact that Ride and Cut were so excited Santa was coming they wouldn't go to sleep, and it hadn't been safe for "Santa" to go out and give them their swing.

The fact that it had started snowing made the hilarious event of three Chaos Motorcycle club bikers and a soldier tying a rope to a tree *seriously* hilarious.

"Give it a yank!" Shy called down to Dad.

Dad moved forward and wrapped his hands around the rope, giving it a hefty tug.

For once (and that would be once in about twenty tries), the knot didn't slip.

"You want me to climb in?" Landon offered. "Test it out? Give it a whirl?"

"You climb on that fuckin' tire while this ladder is resting against this branch and I'm on it, I'll rip your head off," Shy returned.

I stifled a giggle even though it appeared my man was losing his Christmas spirit.

Dad gave the rope another tug.

It held.

"I hope this is done," Tyra whispered to me. "I need the whole three hours' sleep I'm going to get before the boys wake us up."

"And Rush needs the next three hours to wrap his Christmas presents," I whispered back.

This was the truth. Every year my brother delayed shopping until the very last moment. Then he brought his Christmas stash over on Christmas Eve and spent hours wrapping. And bitching. Though I didn't know why it took hours or why he was bitching. He wrapped his presents in newspaper and didn't put bows or tags on them or anything. He just wrote in a Sharpie pen on the paper in big letters who they were for. So it wasn't that strenuous of an endeavor.

"Come down," Dad called. "We'll test it when you got your feet on the ground."

Shy and Rush descended.

Tyra and I watched.

They moved the ladders and Shy went to the tire. He cautiously put a foot into it and gave it his weight. Then he started to swing.

God.

My man was hot even swinging on a tire in a snowstorm in the middle of the night.

Seriously.

Though, I was thinking this mostly had to do with the fact that I had his back, which means I had a line of sight to his ass in his jeans and his shoulders in his thermal.

Nice.

"Finally, we're done," Tyra murmured. "Let's get out of this snow."

We're done?

I grinned again at Tyra's words but this time to myself, since Ty-Ty and I *really* had no part in Operation Tire Swing except to provide moral support from afar.

I left the men to the cleanup and started to follow her inside. But I gave a last look at the men and saw Shy approach his brother. Since the Christmas preparations were winding down, I had a feeling Shy had also felt the weird vibe from Lan and was having a word.

I left him to it and went inside.

Tyra was at the stove.

I closed the door behind me and looked left at the brightly lit Christmas tree where, earlier, Tyra and I had spent an hour on our hands and knees spreading all the presents out in a single layer across the living room carpet, adding Santa's addition. This meant there was very little carpet left. The room looked like a Christmas explosion.

It was *awesome*.

"Cocoa for the men," Tyra called, but softly because there was no doubt my little brothers were sleeping lightly. I looked to her as she finished, "Warm them up."

Three bikers and a GI drinking cocoa?

Was she Christmas crazy?

"Uh...not sure Shy's into cocoa," I informed her as I made my way to the kitchen.

She opened a cupboard and pulled out a bottle. Turning to me, she held it up.

Peppermint Schnapps.

"That'll work," I mumbled on a smile.

The milk was warming in the saucepan and the mugs with powdered cocoa were at the ready when the men came in.

They didn't bother to dust off the snow in their hair and on their shoulders. They also hadn't bothered to put on coats or even jackets although it was below freezing. We were up in the Colorado foothills and everyone knew (and was excited) that after a very dry winter, we were forecast to have a white Christmas.

This meant every last one of the guys was in nothing but a thermal, jeans, and biker boots, except Landon, who had on construction boots.

This wasn't a surprise. As reigning Chaos princess (Dad was president of Chaos) and also as an old lady, I'd known my whole life alpha badass bikers were impervious to cold. And it wasn't a stretch to learn that military men were just as badass.

"Congratulations on doing that without anyone sticking anyone with a knife," I said as the men moved into the kitchen.

My man grinned at me.

When he did, my belly got warm and my lips tipped up.

My eyes moved to Landon and I saw he was gazing at the Christmas tree, an expression on his face that made my belly stop being warm and my lips droop down. Before I could get a lock on it, Dad spoke.

"Brothers can work together," Dad noted. "It's bitches who get bitchy."

I decided not to argue this, though, truth be told, there wasn't anything to argue with. For the most part, Dad wasn't wrong.

Shy slid an arm around my shoulders. I shivered as the cold still clinging to him transferred to me. So I turned into him, pressed my front into his side and wrapped my arms tight around his middle in an effort to warm him up. This had the effect of his arm around me tightening.

"Spiked cocoa, fuckin' great," Landon muttered, eyes now on the mugs. He moved his gaze to Shy. "You in a tree in the snow and loaded hot chocolate. Think I'm gonna like Christmas with the Allens."

My belly got warm again and I looked to Tyra. When I did, I saw her green eyes were on me. They were soft but lit with a happy light that corresponded with the feel I had around my heart.

This was because Shy and Landon Cage had not had a true family Christmas since Shy was twelve and Landon was ten. That year, on New Year's Eve, their parents had been murdered. They'd been raised from then on by a shrew of an aunt who'd detested them and the added responsibility and drain on finances they represented, and she didn't mind showing it.

This was going to be my first Christmas with my man; we'd just hooked up this past summer. And I was totally excited about that—Christmas *and* hooking up with my man.

But I was more excited about giving him, and his brother, a real, honest-to-God family Christmas.

And the look on Ty-Ty's face said she was looking forward to the same.

I studied Lan from under my lashes and I hoped, instead of bringing up unhappy memories of all he'd lost, that he looked forward to it, too.

"I coulda done without the me-in-the-tree part," Shy murmured as I gave him a squeeze before I let him go in order to help Tyra, who was now pouring the milk in the mugs.

"That was the best part," Landon told him.

Shy gave Landon a look and I saved Landon from his retort by pushing a mug of cocoa in Shy's chest.

Shy looked away from his brother to look at me. But

he didn't take the mug until he bent his neck to touch his mouth to mine.

And there it was again. My belly getting even warmer.

"Tyra, where's your newspaper?" Rush asked, and again I sent a smile Tyra's way.

Tyra handed Dad a mug and answered, "Out in the garage, honey."

"Right," Rush muttered, and moved that way, taking his mug with him.

I moved back to Shy, got close and up on my toes to whisper in his ear. "That's our cue to get the heck outta here. Rush is gonna start wrapping, not his favorite chore, so it also means he's gonna start gettin' pissy."

Without delay, Shy announced to everyone in the kitchen, "Tabby and me are goin' to bed."

Dad gave Shy a chin lift. I made my way to my father and gave him a hug. He gave me one back and a kiss on the cheek.

"See you in the mornin', darlin'," he said softly in my ear.

"Yeah, Dad. Merry Christmas."

He gave me a squeeze. "Merry Christmas, honey."

I handed out more hugs to Ty-Ty and Landon, the one I gave Lan included me looking into his eyes and giving him a cautious Christmas smile.

He smiled back but I could tell he wasn't entirely committed to it.

Hmm.

I avoided my brother, who was coming back from the garage, his arms loaded with newspapers, a Sharpie between his teeth, calling out my good night to him as Shy and I headed to the basement.

Sleeping arrangements were that Shy and I got Rush's old bedroom in the basement, Landon was on the air mattress in the office, and Rush, since he'd be up for several more hours, would hit the couch in the living room.

This meant privacy for my man and me.

Which meant this worked perfectly for me.

As Shy sucked back some of his cocoa, I approached the subject of his brother.

"Is Lan cool?" I asked quietly, and my man leveled his gaze on me.

"He'll get there."

That wasn't a good answer.

"I didn't think this would be hard on him. Or you. I thought—"

Shy moved from where he was standing at the dresser to me, standing in front of the bathroom. He lifted a hand, curled it around my neck, and dipped his face close to mine.

Then he proceeded to break my heart.

"Me and Lan, we aren't used to happy."

Oh God.

"Maybe we shouldn't have gone whole hog this year. Maybe we should have just had a little Christmas thing, you and me and him," I suggested way too late.

That's when he mended my heart.

"And maybe me and him should learn to get used to happy."

I pressed my lips together to hold in the swell of warm his words caused and leaned forward, touching my forehead against his, knowing my man was getting used to happy and hoping his brother learned the same.

I watched his beautiful green eyes smile before I felt

his lips touch mine. They tasted of cocoa, peppermint, and Shy, which was a brilliant combination. Then he broke away, downed the last of his cocoa. We each did the brushing our teeth, changing clothes business and ended up on opposite sides of the bed.

Shy pulled back the covers.

I studied my long, lanky, loose-limbed man with his messy dark hair and his beautiful green eyes and that got another smile out of me that had nothing to do with Christmas.

"Hey," I called, and he looked up from the bed.

When his eyes caught mine, they were questioning. But when he got a load of my smile, they turned soft.

And, just saying, when Shy saw me smile, that always happened.

Loved my man.

"What, baby?" he asked gently.

Oh yeah.

Loved my man.

"Merry Christmas," I whispered.

That got me another look but this new look was not soft.

It was dark and hot.

"Come here," he growled.

With his look and that tone, I didn't delay.

I went there. In my tight red camisole and cream pajama shorts with big black and red snowflakes on them and a wide, red satin drawstring, I hit the bed on my knee. I added the other knee and moved across the bed to him.

The instant I got close, he snaked an arm around my waist and pulled me closer. In fact, he plastered me against him, hauling me up at the same time and I had no choice (not that I'd pick another one) but to wind my arms around his neck.

He drove a hand into my hair, fisted it, tilted my head, slanted his the other way, and slammed his mouth down on mine.

Then he thrust his tongue in my mouth.

I held on, pressed close, and enjoyed my first Christmas kiss from Shy Cage.

And I enjoyed it a whole lot.

When he broke the kiss and lifted his head half an inch, he whispered, "Merry Christmas, Tabby."

Oh yeah.

Loved my man.

Not a second later, his hand left my hair so he could sweep his arm over my ass, down the backs of my thighs to my knees. He curled it in, yanked my legs to the side, and then I was on my back in the bed with Shy on top of me.

Now we were talking.

His mouth found mine again, his tongue slid inside, his hand drifted up and in to curl around my breast, and I wrapped all four limbs tight around him, thinking this first family Christmas with Shy was starting out *great*.

"Sanna! Sanna! Sanna, Sanna, *Sanna!*" I heard Cut's excited voice as well as his little feet pounding on the stairs, making it clear he was heading our way.

I (sadly) blinked away sleep as I felt Shy's arm give me a reflexive squeeze.

Once I opened my eyes, I noted the basement bedroom was pitch-black. I felt like I'd had two minutes of sleep. I was, not unusually, pressed down Shy's side with an arm thrown over his stomach and a cheek to his shoulder.

It was good I got back into my Christmas pj's after our late-night Christmas activities, but Shy was totally nude. This made it also good that the covers were up to my shoulders.

"Jesus," Shy muttered when the chant of "Sanna, Sanna, Sanna!" hit the room.

I saw a blurry shadow move like lightning and my eyes adjusted enough to the dark so I could see Cut climb up on the bed. He got up on his feet, still chanting, and walk-wobbled down our bodies, stepping on one or the other of us every other footfall until he threw himself down, arms out, landing flat out on the both of us.

"*Sanna came!*" he screeched, and after imparting this crucial information, he rolled off Shy's way. We heard his little feet hit the floor, then thud across it as he kept shouting, "Sanna, Sanna. Sanna! Sanna came!"

Then he was up the stairs and gone.

"I think that means it's time to get our asses outta bed," Shy noted sleepily, and I let out a soft laugh.

"Yeah," I agreed. "I think that's what it means."

I bent in, aimed a kiss at his shadowed throat, and hit my mark. But as I was moving away in order to roll away, I had two arms around me and I was rolled the opposite way. Shy rolled with me and I was again back to bed with my man on me.

After getting me in position, he laid another Christmas kiss on me. It was warm. It was soft. It was lazy. It was a little sleepy. And it was *long*.

In other words, it was *the bomb*.

When he lifted away to kiss my forehead, I remarked breathlessly, "You know, if that's the only thing you give me today, I'm good." And this was no lie.

Yes. The kiss was *that* good.

Then again, they always were.

I felt his eyes on mine in the dark before I heard his gruff voice say, "Christ. Fuckin' love you, Tabitha."

I pressed into him and gave him a squeeze. "Love you, too, honey."

He dropped his head to kiss my jaw before he dipped down to kiss my throat. Then he rolled again, taking me with him until we were off the bed and on our feet beside it.

We retraced our steps of a few hours before to do the teeth-brushing, hair-brushing thing again (me with the hair brushing, that is; Shy didn't bother). Shy added pulling on a pair of seen-better-days dark blue sweatpants and a white thermal that was skintight and gave more than a vague indication of the muscled lusciousness that lay beneath it.

I gave myself a moment to appreciate the view before I pulled on a thin black cardigan and a pair of thick socks and headed upstairs, hand in hand with my man.

The minute we made an appearance through the door to the upper level, Rider cut us off at the pass.

He did this by rushing to us, skidding to a halt on his own socked feet two feet in front of us, and tipping his head back to announce, "Santa was here! He left presents and filled stockings and even took the carrots for the reindeer!"

There was a reason Santa, having shown, was a surprise at which to rejoice. This was because my two baby brothers were Hellions with a capital Hell. They were normally unruly but October through December afforded Tyra the opportunity to threaten them with Santa bringing coal rather than presents, and she did this often. They ignored it often. So, until this morning, the jolly one making an appearance was a crapshoot and both the boys knew it.

"Right on," Shy replied, and I looked up at him to see him smiling down at my little brother.

His eyes were soft again, as was his entire face.

After knowing Shy for years, the road to us more than a little bumpy, having Shy in my life, my home, my bed (or, I should say, our home and bed since we lived together)—there was a lot I loved about all of that.

And one of those things high at the top of the list (a long list, seriously) was how he was with my brothers and the fact that he didn't hide how deeply he cared about them.

Ride was a big fan of Shy's, too, and this was proved when he jumped forward, grabbed Shy's hand, and started tugging (I'll note, totally ignoring me), declaring, "Come on! Dad said we can open our stockings!"

"Your old man said you can open your stockings when everyone was up and had coffee," Dad contradicted as I followed Shy and Ride into the living area that was really one huge room including kitchen and living room, with a fabulous view of the mountains from every window.

When I got there I saw, not surprisingly with Cutter's earlier excitement, that both Landon and Rush were also up and sitting in the living room. Their eyes glazed with sleep, hair a mess, and at the sight, I couldn't stop my lips from twitching.

Rush, like Shy (and, incidentally, Dad), was wearing a thermal and seen-better-days sweatpants. Landon had on a tight white long-sleeved tee and a pair of navy blue workout pants with a wide white stripe down the side.

Tyra, in the kitchen at the coffeepot, was dressed like me but her Christmas pj's included pants, not shorts. They had a sky-blue background and white snowflakes all over, with the addition of miniature snowmen and penguins wearing scarves.

"Coffee!" Cut half-shouted in disgust, half-whined in despair.

"Coffee, boy," Dad agreed, and I saw his eyes on his youngest. "It's brewin'. You got about two minutes to wait. The presents'll still be there when it's done."

"Coffee's stupid!" Cut informed Dad.

"Don't tell your mother that," Dad warned Cut, and this was the God's honest truth. Tyra liked her coffee.

I hit the kitchen and a second later I hit Dad for a kiss on the cheek and a hug.

Then I moved to Tyra, gave a hug, got one in return, and exchanged heartfelt, whispered Merry Christmases.

"Do we gotta wait until Tabby hugs everyone, too?" Cut asked as I shifted to the cupboards that held the mugs.

"That would be an affirmative," I heard Dad mutter.

"Affirma-what?" Cut demanded to know.

I pulled down mugs, looked at Ty-Ty, and we both giggled.

But Dad didn't think this was amusing and he was also done.

I knew this when he ordered, "Son, sit your ass in the living room, shut your trap, and *wait two minutes.*"

Tyra, not a big fan of Dad cursing in front of the boys (something she let him know often, something he didn't care about and continued to do when the spirit moved him, which was all the time) whirled and snapped, "Tack!"

"Thank fuck Christmas comes only once a year," Dad,

unrepentant at his language (obviously), ignored Ty-Ty's snap to say under his breath.

Tyra gave her husband a glare, which deflected off him completely (as usual) and turned back to the coffee.

She poured.

I moved around the space and passed out the mugs, giving another cheek kiss and "Merry Christmas" to Landon and Rush. Again, with Lan, I checked the pulse of his mood by looking in his eyes.

They were, as I'd noted earlier, sleepy. They were also something else, and that something else had to do with the fact that the minute I moved away, his gaze moved direct to my two little brothers, who were barely containing their excitement. He looked contemplative, not joyful, and my Christmas spirit took a hit.

I gave Shy a look. Shy gave me a head shake that I interpreted as him saying *let him work through it*.

It was tough but Shy knew his brother better than me so I did as I was non-verbally told.

Finally hitting the living room with my own cup, I noticed that Ride and Cut were firmly in position, both fidgeting on their booties, obviously impatient.

Tyra had a Christmas tradition where stockings were stuffed and placed where you were supposed to sit during the unwrapping festivities. This was mostly because they couldn't stay hung since she stuffed them so full of presents and candy, they overflowed. It was also to give some order to the proceedings.

This meant that Rider and Cutter's stockings were on the floor by the presents. Rush's was, too, seeing as he played Santa every year and had since we were kids, way before Tyra entered the picture and (finally) made my dad happy. Even after Tyra arrived, Rush was still the one who passed out the presents. Now, since Ride and Cut could coordinate their limbs on command, Rush just sat there and told them which presents to take to people.

Rounding out the crew, Dad and Tyra were on one couch. Shy and I were on another. And Landon had the armchair.

The minute Tyra's ass settled on the couch next to Dad, Dad gave the go ahead.

"Tear it up, boys."

Rider and Cutter did not delay.

I didn't, either.

Neither did Rush.

It was arguable, but I thought stockings were the best part of Christmas. I didn't know why. I always got stuff like deodorant, magazines, gift cards, things to put in my hair, lip gloss, shit like that, all of this wrapped in Christmas tissue paper (another Tyra tradition). So it wasn't like I was unearthing diamonds and pearls, but instead stuff I usually bought myself at the drugstore on a regular basis.

Still, I loved it.

I was halfway through tearing through my stash when something hit me. A warm buzz that vibrated in the air—indistinct, almost elusive—but I felt it coming at me from my left side. I lifted my head from unwrapping a plastic spatula shaped like a Christmas bell and looked that way.

And at what I saw, I went still.

This was because both the brothers Cage were not unwrapping their stockings. They were watching Rider and Cutter as if they were mesmerized. But their mesmerization left warm looks on their faces, the kind of warmth mixed with nostalgia that made me catch my breath.

My eyes drifted to my brothers, all three of them, the big and the little.

All of Kane Allen's children looked like him, including Rush and me. Ride and Cut were no different. A mess of dark, thick hair, and even as little boys you could see they were going to have Dad's tall frame.

Both my baby brothers got their mother's green eyes, however.

Rush got our mother's eyes. Luckily, I got Dad's, which meant I got nothing from my mother. I was down with that, seeing as we didn't get along since she didn't much like me from approximately the day I was born and I returned the favor.

Landon, being dark like Shy, made Tyra, a redhead, the only odd man out in the assemblage.

We looked like family, though. All of us.

But I knew Shy and Landon didn't see how cute those two little boys were, tearing into their underwear and socks with abandon. Or how awesome it was that Rush, a badass himself, got off on sitting on the floor with his little bro buds and passing out Christmas presents. Shy and Landon also weren't thinking how beautiful Ride and Cut were with their father's coloring, features, and frame, and their mother's extraordinary eyes.

No.

They were seeing themselves in happier times.

And, for once, in fact, for the first time in sixteen years, that nostalgia didn't hit them like a knife in the gut.

Instead, it was hitting him with a feeling that was sweet.

I knew Shy was going with that flow; he had been since he became a part of my life.

It was Landon who now was letting the sweet feeling of love, joy, and family seep into his pores.

And liking it.

And I liked that.

Feeling my own not-so-vague hint of sweet, I came unstuck, moved the part of my stash that I'd tucked in the seat between Shy and me, and shifted closer to him.

I put my hand on his thigh and when I got his eyes, I encouraged quietly, "Baby, open up your stocking."

"It'll get opened, Tab," was his quiet reply.

I held his eyes, saw the sweet burning in them, felt it burn into my soul, and nodded.

Then I went back to my stash.

"Now presents!" Cut shouted, clearly done with his stocking and ready to move on.

"Lan and Shy aren't done with their stockings, honey," Tyra told him, and Cutter sliced his narrowed, impatient gaze to Shy and Landon.

"Hurry up!" he snapped.

"We're good," Landon told him, and looked Tyra and Dad's way. "You can keep goin'. We'll catch up."

Dad gave him a look, assessed what was going on (Dad was far from dumb; he knew all about Shy and Lan). Then he gave a chin lift and his gaze moved to Rush, "Start it, Rush. Think this year it's youngest to oldest."

"*Yee ha!*" Cutter, the youngest, screeched, his arms going straight up in the air right before his body fell on a big package. He slapped his hand on it and said to Rush, "I wanna start with this one."

"That'll be hard, buddy, since that's for Ride," Rush told Cut.

Cutter's face fell.

"Though, this one's for you," Rush said as he reached and slid an even bigger package out from behind the tree.

Cutter's eyes got huge.

Jeez, my brother was cute.

I gave up on finishing up my own stocking in order to drop sideways so I could lean into my man and watch Christmas unfold.

Shy readily accepted my weight and slid an arm around my shoulders to tuck me closer, settling in himself by stretching his long legs in front of him and crossing his ankles.

And, sitting tucked close to Shy, we watched Cutter rip into that package like nobody's business.

When Mom was around, Christmas at the Allen house could mean anything, including Mom throwing a hissy fit and breaking all the stoneware in the kitchen (no joke, this happened—*twice*). Therefore, we spent the day on eggshells, all of us, including Dad, wondering if it would be good or very, very bad.

But not now.

No, not now.

Not with Tyra. Not with Ride and Cut. Not with Shy and Landon.

Now, it was still not good.

No, now it was *amazing*.

"That's it," Ride decreed when the last package was opened (but the tire swing had yet to be unveiled). "Can we play now, Momma?" he asked Tyra.

"Got two more," Dad said, and Rider's brows snapped together as Cutter looked around the sea of decimated paper, lonely present-less bows and ribbons, and stacks of loot, likely hoping one of those two was for him (or more likely hoping both of them were).

But it was Shy that set me aside and straightened out of the couch.

I watched him go, wondering if he was heading for more coffee or, since it took hours to unwrap presents—the sun was now up, its blinding brightness glinting off the blanket of snow and tufted bunches on the pine boughs—going for a beer.

Instead, he went for the Christmas tree.

In order not to step on any Christmas treasure littering the floor, he had to stretch his long arm out to reach into the branches. But this he did, coming out with a little box beautifully wrapped in gold paper with a silver bow.

He then came back to me.

Oh God.

My eyes went from the box to him.

He folded back into the couch beside me and since I didn't move, he grabbed my wrist, lifted my hand palm up, and put the almost weightless—definitely holding jewelry—box in my hand.

Then his eyes came to mine and locked there.

"Every year," he murmured, and I knew.

I knew.

Oh God. I knew.

I knew that every year they were together, Shy's dad gave his mom a beautiful pair of earrings. I knew this because I had seven of those pairs.

After they died, his aunt had confiscated those earrings as her "due" for taking care of family.

When Shy had finally, years later, processed the loss

of his folks, he'd gone to his bitch of an aunt's place and confiscated them back.

He had seven pairs, which meant I had seven pairs. Landon had the other seven pairs to give to the woman he (eventually) took as his own.

And this was a searing memory for both men. This show of generosity and love on a day that was about joy and family. The memory had become a symbol of all the beauty they lost when their parents were ripped away. Not only two parents who loved them, gave them a home, nurturing, affection, and pride. But also losing being able to witness the deep and precious love their parents had for each other.

It was important.

It was treasured.

Now, a nuance of that lay in my hand.

But more, Shy's love for me lay there.

Deep and precious.

My eyes stung with tears.

"Open it, baby," he whispered.

I nodded, pressed my lips together, and looked down at the box.

I tore away the wrapping and let it fall unheeded to the floor. Using my thumb, I flipped open the blue jeweler's box with its gold scrollwork.

And then the tears came.

Inside were two emerald-cut sapphire earrings. So deep blue the color seemed to go on forever.

The color of my eyes (and Dad's).

And they were not small.

So, obviously, when I said the tears came, what I meant was, I burst into them, loud and sobbing.

Shy pulled me into his arms.

I wrapped mine around him, shoved my face in his neck, and held tight. I'd thought I'd done a bang-up job, getting Shy that awesome, custom-made, huge-ass silver skull ring with shining black onyx for eyes as his Christmas present that, when he opened it, he obviously loved. I knew that when he put it on immediately and hadn't take it off.

But his present beat mine by a mile.

"Th...th...thank you, honey," I stammered, but I couldn't quit crying.

I wanted to. But it was all just too beautiful. The earrings. The love behind them. The memory he'd created that I'd never forget.

So I burrowed deeper and let loose.

Seconds later, I felt something burrowing into me and I tipped my head down to see Cutter crawling into my lap, pushing in, looking up, his little boy face anxious.

"Why're you sad, Tabby?" he whispered.

"I'm not, honey," I whispered back.

He pushed closer to both Shy and me, his face now confused.

"But you're cryin'," he told me.

I curved an arm around my baby bro and explained, "Sometimes, something so beautiful happens, you can't process it and it builds up inside so big, you can't do anything but cry."

"I hope that never happens to me," he replied.

"And I hope it happens to you all the time," I returned.

His face scrunched up, not liking that idea. It was cute but I wasn't going to explain. Not then. I was just going to hope to God he felt what I was feeling right then one day. Or felt for a woman what Shy felt for me in giving me those earrings.

I felt more love enveloping me, and this was my dad getting close and leaning in to touch his lips to my hair.

I pulled my forehead out of Shy's neck, looked up at my dad, and gave him a shaky grin through my tears.

Dad grinned back. Then he moved his eyes to Shy and the grin faded. But the look he gave my man had my hiccoughing back another wave of tears.

He liked Shy for me.

Like, a lot.

And I liked that.

Shy accepted Dad's look, then pulled Cutter and me deeper into his arms.

It was then, I peeked through my man and my brother and saw Landon sitting there. I held my breath at the look on his face, his eyes aimed at my hand, holding the jeweler's box.

Then those eyes lifted to mine and my breath came out in a whoosh at the shine I saw in them.

He liked me for Shy.

Like, a lot.

And I liked that, too.

Like, a lot.

Better, this wasn't nostalgia we were creating.

Just happy memories we got to look forward to making more of.

Every year.

Cut took my attention by lifting a hand to swipe clumsily at the wet at my face, which I took as indication to get my shit together. Through deep breathing, I did.

"Right, boys. Jackets," Dad ordered.

Cut peeked out from under the people huddle Shy had affected on the couch and looked up to Dad. Then my little brother (not always a hellion) gave me one last assessing look to ascertain I was all right. He waited for my non-trembling smile before he climbed off my lap and dashed after Rider, who was going for his coat.

Tyra and I went for our coats as well.

Shy, Dad, and Rush, being badasses, even now just in sweatpants and tees, did not. Though Landon took off, to where I didn't know and didn't look, because I didn't want to miss anything.

"Boots," Dad demanded when the boys had their jackets on, and both scrambled for their boots.

"Hats!" Tyra cried, dashing for their hats.

"Momma!" Rider shouted his impatience.

"No hat!" Cutter agreed, swiping at his hair while Tyra tried to pull a knit cap over it.

"They'll be all right, baby," Dad murmured to Ty-Ty, getting close to her, sliding an arm around her shoulders, and she gave up.

I stood in my jacket, socks, and Christmas pj's, watching Rider roll excitedly up and down on his toes while Cut swayed excitedly side to side and Dad moved to the door.

Hand on the handle, he turned back. "Santa left one more thing," he told his youngest sons and opened the door.

They raced out.

Landon, coming back from wherever he'd gone, got close and murmured to Shy, "Next year, you up a tree in a Santa suit."

I giggled.

Shy grunted, "Bite me."

Landon chuckled.

"*Holy smokes!*" Rider screamed.

"*Yee ha!*" Cutter screeched.

The adults moved out to the deck that someone (probably Dad, Rush had a severe allergy to anything that even remotely resembled housework) had cleared. And we watched the boys race in their jackets, boots, and pajamas toward the swing.

"Hope to Christ that doesn't fall down," Shy muttered.

I turned into him and wrapped my arms around him.

"It won't, baby," I assured him as he shifted and wrapped his arms around me.

Rider climbed on the top of the tire. Cutter climbed in the middle.

Lan walked through the snow and I saw he'd disappeared to put on his boots (though he eschewed the jacket, of course). He made it to the boys and gave them a shove.

The minute he did, their shrieked glee rang in the air.

And I was right.

It held.

"Push us harder, Lan!" Cut ordered, and when the boys swung his way, Lan pushed them harder. They went higher and their happy screeches again filled the air.

I watched as Lan's gaze moved to his brother.

I saw his huge smile.

And I knew Landon Cage was getting used to happy.

"Cut, Ride, hang on, babies," Tyra said to her sons.

We were sitting at the dining room table, an addition to the house Tyra made after she moved in with Dad. An addition she utilized daily, seeing as even if Dad was off on Chaos business, she had a family dinner every night with her two boys, Dad when he was around, and the same with Rush and me (and now Shy) when we were at their house.

Rider and Cutter weren't the only ones dying to tuck in to Christmas dinner. Dad had put his special rub on two beef tenderloins, then roasted them to perfection and I couldn't wait to eat.

My father could cook anything and it was always spectacular. But he only cooked his special rub beef tenderloins for Christmas and birthdays. We were all itching to dig in because we knew the delights that awaited us.

As for me, I also couldn't wait for Shy and Landon to be introduced to the mouthwatering meal.

Tyra looked at Dad, then lifted her wineglass.

Her intentions were clear so the men went for their beers. I grabbed my wineglass and Ride and Cut, looking at each other kind of confused, finally joined in, grabbing their sodas.

"Nothing," Ty-Ty started, and I looked to her to see her gaze on my side of the table where I was sitting between Shy and Landon. "Is more important than family."

Uh-oh.

I had a feeling I was going to cry again.

I reached a hand under the table and wrapped my fingers around Shy's hard thigh. When I did, Shy's hand moved to mine, his fingers curling around, forcing mine from his thigh to curve around his. And then he held tight.

I reciprocated the gesture as Tyra kept talking.

"So it's a blessing when that family grows." She looked at her husband, then her boys, to Rush, then back to my side of the table. When she spoke again, her voice was soft. "Shy, Lan, welcome to our family." She lifted her glass higher and finished, "Merry Christmas."

I forced a "Merry Christmas" through my tight throat and heard my dad's rough "Merry Christmas, baby."

I looked to Dad to see his gaze soft and sweet on his wife, and I felt that familiar thrill I got whenever I was with them, knowing the love and happiness Tyra had finally brought to my dad's life and how very much he appreciated it. Through this, I heard Shy, Rush, and Landon muttering their Merry Christmases.

We drank to Ty-Ty's toast.

Then we tucked in.

Or, that was to say, everyone else did.

I stared at Tyra until she felt my eyes and looked at me.

"Thank you," I mouthed to her.

"You're welcome, honey," she mouthed to me.

I sucked in a deep breath.

Then I put down my glass, picked up my fork and knife, and dove in to the delights awaiting me.

I followed Shy into our little apartment. He stayed at the door and held it open for me. Once I cleared it, I heard it close and the lock go. I turned on the lamp and dropped the three shopping bags full of Christmas stash right where I stood. Then I tore off my hat, shrugged off my coat, and threw them on the chair. After that was accomplished, I moved to the couch and fell on it on my back, my hands going to my belly.

"I'm not eating for a week," I announced.

About an hour after dinner, we'd come down the mountain (and yes, I was *still* stuffed), Rush and Lan leaving at the same time as Shy and me. It was time to let Dad and Tyra have their time with their boys. It was time for Rush to get to whatever girl was on his hook these days (I couldn't keep up). And it was time for Landon to carouse (yes, on Christmas. Then again, Lan didn't take many breaks from carousing, especially when he was on leave).

More, it was time for me to have Shy all to myself.

Some of the apartment was packed up. This was because Shy and I were moving to our new house in a few weeks and I was so excited to start that part of our lives together, I couldn't wait to box up the old in preparation for the new.

My mind on this happy thought, I got another happy thought when Shy entered my line of sight and I saw him grinning down at me.

"That's too bad, baby, seein' as you have a mountain of Christmas candy to get through."

His words tugged at my heartstrings so hard, I had to draw in breath.

This was because, back in the beginning, and that was the beginning of what would become Shy and me, he'd come over because he thought I was sick and he'd found me under a mountain of discarded Christmas candy wrappers that I'd consumed the night before while watching scary movies.

I remembered it like it was yesterday, watching his long, lanky, loose-limbed body stride through my apartment, then bend to clean up the wrapper mess.

That day, he'd set about building a friendship with me, taking care of me during the single-most toughest time in my life, and bringing me back to the me I'd lost somewhere along the way.

And, in the end, giving me him, the best gift I'd ever

received, even better than the sapphire earrings right then in my ears. Since those were the absolute bomb that was saying something.

This must have shown on my face because Shy suddenly folded his body to rest a hip on the couch beside me. He leaned in and his hand came to my jaw.

"What's on your mind, Tabby?"

"You," I whispered, "and Christmas candy wrappers."

I knew it hit him when his eyes flashed and he moved. Getting off the couch, he bent and shoved one arm under me at my waist, one at the back of my knees, and he lifted me into his arms.

He didn't go in for the kiss when he had me up and pivoted toward the hall that led to the bedroom.

I did.

So my mouth was on his, my tongue in his mouth, when my back hit our bed and Shy landed on me.

The minute he did, I put a foot to the bed, bucked my hips, and rolled him, going with him, not breaking the kiss. But once I had him where I wanted him, I lifted up and yanked off my sweater.

The room was dark and it was clear Shy didn't like it that way. That was why I felt his hands span my ribs as he sat up, twisting us. He took one hand away to reach to the lamp and he turned it on. Then both his arms curled around me tight and I was again back to the bed with my man on me.

He didn't delay in burying his face in my neck, working there, then working his way down to drift his lips across the edge of my lacy red bra.

When his lips hit the valley between my breasts and started gliding up the other side, I liked it so much I slid my fingers in his hair to hold him to me. He went up my other breast, then he went back down and my belly flipped when he kept going down my midriff, down my stomach, to stop and roll his tongue around my navel. Then down he went where he brushed his lips along the waistband of my jeans.

Oh yes.

I felt a surge of heat between my legs as his lips disappeared.

Oh no.

I lifted up on my elbows to watch as he tugged off my boots and my socks.

Then he gained his feet at the side of the bed and pulled off his thermal.

I felt a nag of disappointment because I wanted to do that, but it was only a nag seeing as he exposed the planes and hollows of his chest and abs.

My mouth watered and my hands went to the buttons on my jeans.

Shy's green eyes watched my hands work even as his fingers did the same on his jeans.

My eyes dropped there and I hurried up.

I got my jeans over my ankles and Shy was back. Better yet, when he came back he was naked.

I loved his hair, how thick it was, how long, how soft, but when his mouth was again on mine, I didn't go for his hair. Squirming under him, I fed on him through touch, running my fingers everywhere I could reach, wanting to go slow but liking what I felt too much to pull that off.

So I gave up and took all I could get as fast as I could get it.

Shy returned this favor, but he was able to go slow.

Agonizingly slow.

Which made me even more fevered to get *more*.

Finally, I felt Shy's hands on the sides of my hips, his pinkie and ring fingers pressing into my panties and tugging them down.

I didn't care what his intentions were, mostly because I knew they were going to be good. So I moaned against his tongue a second before I lost it and his lips again trailed down my body as his fingers dragged my panties down my legs.

He had them over my ankles, then he wrapped his hands around those ankles and pulled them apart.

That was when I knew what I was going to get.

And I couldn't wait.

"Baby," I breathed.

That was all I could get out before my legs were over his shoulders and his mouth was on me.

My back arced from the bed, my heels dug into his lats, and I drove my hips up into his mouth as he worked me there.

God, so beautiful.

Every time, so damned beautiful.

With nowhere else for them to go where I might want them to be, I slid my fingers back into his hair to hold him to me as the whimpers and soft cries glided up my throat and he built it. Slow at first, then making it roar higher and higher until I was panting and whimpering and my fingers were fisted in his hair.

It was coming. Another Christmas present. Not as good as the earrings but *far* from shabby.

Suddenly, his mouth was gone from between my legs and his lips were kissing my belly.

I lifted my head and whispered my plea. "Don't stop."

His head came up, his eyes locking on mine even as he slid farther up my body. I watched him drop to kiss the skin over my ribs and I liked that. It was sweet.

But I wanted his mouth back between my legs.

Or something else a whole lot better.

"Baby," I begged.

He lifted his head and his eyes caught mine again.

"Wanna watch," he murmured, and his words and what they meant slithered through me, leaving me trembling.

Then his fingers were between my legs, toying, playing, again creating beauty.

My lips parted and my hips moved as Shy rested his chin against my midriff, his eyes still locked to my face, and he built it again for me. Higher, God, so high, it was searing through me.

"Shy," I breathed, one of my knees cocking reflexively, closing over to trap his hand there as my back arched off the bed and it burned through me.

In the throes of my orgasm, I felt him push my legs apart roughly and then he was there, driving inside me, hard, fast, deep, God, so, *so deep.*

He pulled my legs around him but it was me who wound my arms around him, holding him tight with one arm at his shoulders, clasping his hips with my legs, gliding one hand down his spine to curl my fingers and hold fast to his ass.

"Mouth, Tabby," Shy ordered and I tipped my chin down, my first orgasm drifting away, Shy's cock driving in, his mouth claiming mine. His tongue thrusting inside started the next one building.

One of his forearms was planted in the bed; he shoved his other hand under me and cupped his hand on my ass like mine was on his. But mine was grasping him, encouraging him to take me harder, rougher, faster. His was yanking me up so he could take me harder, faster, rougher.

Oh God.

Beautiful.

Amazing.

It was going to happen again.

I tore my mouth from his and shoved my face in his neck.

Shy's thrusts increased in pace and velvet brutality as his arm in the bed moved to become fingers in my hair and he tugged back.

"Show me," he demanded.

"Baby," I whimpered, trying to focus on his face.

"Hold it," he ordered.

Oh God.

He liked us to come together.

But I wasn't sure I could give him that this time (then again, I never was and it was hit and miss if I did).

"Shy, honey, I—"

He kept pounding as he growled, "Hold it, Tabby."

"God," I panted, my limbs tightening around him. I slid my arm from around his shoulders to cup his jaw as our eyes locked and he drove deep.

I wasn't going to be able to hold it.

"Shy—"

"Hold it, baby."

"I—"

His mouth came to mine and his rumbled, "*Hold it,*" drove down my throat.

I slid my thumb over his lips, his tongue came out and touched the pad and I liked that so damned much, my back left the bed, arching into him.

The movement of his hips went out of control.

"Now, honey. Give that to me," he groaned.

Thank God.

I let go and gave it to him.

He sucked my thumb in his mouth and when he did, what was scorching within me ratcheted up about five levels and *blistered* through me.

His neck bent and I slid my thumb out of his mouth and my fingers into his hair as he thrust deep through his climax and buried his face in my neck.

I held on and took it.

Gladly.

Finally he stilled, buried deep, connected to me.

As my breath left me and Shy's started to come more easily, I turned my head, closed my eyes, and took him in. All of him. Everything. All of it mine. His weight. His solidness. His smell. The feel of his hair curling around his neck and tickling my nose. The exquisite tenderness between my legs. The even more exquisite feeling of Shy connected to me.

I memorized it even though I knew this was my life. This man and me. My bed being our bed. My home being wherever he might be. His love represented in the posts through my ears, precious stones on the lobe, a symbol of everything he felt for me.

It was a good life.

The best.

And I didn't have to memorize it because in a myriad of ways, it was every day for me.

But I still did. I'd learned to burn the precious memories into my brain.

So I burned that deep into me.

"Clean you up," he murmured against my skin. "Then I gotta crash, honey." He lifted his head and caught my eyes. "I'm wiped."

"I'll go clean up," I offered, something I didn't do often seeing as Shy liked washing himself from me.

"No."

That was it. *No.*

See? Shy liked doing it.

He gently pulled out, kissed the underside of my jaw, my chest, then rolled off the bed. But I knew he didn't lie when he said he was wiped because usually he took his time, but this time, although he was his usual tender and sweet, he didn't linger.

As he moved back to the bathroom to get rid of the washcloth, I moved under the covers and threw his side back, waiting for him.

He slid in and reached out to turn off the light before he turned to me. He gathered me in his arms and pulled my front to his. I tangled my legs with his and pressed both hands into his chest, feeling his warmth, his strength, as he shifted to snuggle us even closer.

Oh...so...*totally* loved my man.

I felt his body ease and my body eased into his.

I knew he was drifting into sleep so I lifted my chin and kissed the base of his throat, about to say my last Merry Christmas and my good night.

But Shy beat me to it.

"Thank you for a great Christmas, Tabby."

His voice was thick and I closed my eyes at the emotion sitting deep in every syllable.

It said everything, and with Shy, everything was always *everything*.

I didn't know how to tell him that. I didn't know how to explain what having his everything meant to me. I didn't know how to tell him how much I treasured giving him his first great Christmas in years. I didn't know how to tell him what a gift it was that it was me who got to give him everything.

I just knew one thing.

So I said that.

"Every year, baby."

Dear Reader,

Nothing gets me into the holiday spirit faster than listening to Christmas music.

And I have a little secret: my favorite Christmas music is the traditional stuff. Every Christmas you'll find me with the stereo cranked up, singing along to all four hours of Handel's *Messiah* while I bake cookies.

So, when I was asked to contribute a story to this collection, of course I went looking for inspiration from music. I put together a playlist of favorite carols and songs, most of them traditional. I plugged in the earbuds, found a comfy spot on the couch, and waited for the Christmas muse to find me.

She did—right at the moment "Silent Night" came up on the iPod. I suddenly realized that I'd picked a playlist composed entirely of carols and songs with images of a stable and a star and a bunch of wise men searching for a miracle—all traditional Christmas themes based on the story of the first Christmas.

And that's how my story, "Silent Night," was born. It features a single mom, a baby, a stable, and a man looking for a miracle.

I wish you all a wonderful holiday season, filled with laughter, love, light, and peace.

Merry Christmas,

Hope Ramsay

Silent Night

Hope Ramsay

The engine sputtered a couple of times and died. Maryanne swallowed back a curse and guided her ancient Honda Civic to the side of the road.

She stared at the fuel gauge. She'd run out of gas, which was hardly surprising because she'd also run out of luck. And money.

Her last few dollars had gone into the gas tank, and now here she was two miles short of her destination.

She turned in the driver's seat to check Joshua, her three-month-old son. He was fast asleep like an angel.

She was going to have to walk to the farm. And if Cousin Jennifer didn't open the door for her, she'd be officially homeless. And spending Christmas here.

In her car.

The thing was, Maryanne had no guarantee that Cousin Jennifer would even remember her. They had only met that one time. So, all in all, coming here had been a crazy idea. But then crazy ideas usually came from being desperate. And desperation had set in yesterday when

Maryanne's landlady had thrown all her possessions out onto the street.

She unfolded the wrinkled Google Maps printout that she'd made at the library early this morning. She couldn't be entirely sure, but it looked like she was just a mile short of the turn-off onto Ridge Road. From there it was only a mile or so to her final destination: the Carpenter family farm, where her father had been raised and where her grandfather had grown peaches.

Maryanne had visited the farm one Christmas when she was six years old. She remembered Cousin Jennifer as a sweet teenager who had played dolls with her. Maryanne was banking her future on that memory.

And what the heck—if Maryanne had nowhere to go, going to Nowhere, South Carolina, kind of fit the bill. Not that this itty-bitty town was really called Nowhere. No, it was called Last Chance. And that was what Maryanne needed more than anything else.

She looked up at the sky. It was lumpy with dark clouds that hung low over the brown fields on either side of the road. The weather had turned cold.

And rain was coming. Maybe even snow. Maryanne had never really seen any appreciable snow, having grown up in Montgomery, Alabama. But those clouds looked menacing.

She had to find shelter. So it looked like Cousin Jennifer was about to have unexpected Christmas guests.

She pulled together a change of clothes, and some diapers and other baby stuff, and threw it all into a tattered backpack along with her last two Clif Bars. She bundled Joshua into the BabyBjörn front carrier she'd found at the Salvation Army, zippered her two-sizes-too-big North Face jacket around the both of them, and started walking.

What was a couple of miles? She could probably walk it in less than an hour. And if she was lucky, she might get there before the skies opened up.

But this wasn't her lucky day. She was maybe a mile down Ridge Road when the first cold drops of rain spattered her parka. Good thing it was GORE-TEX.

She saw the big red barn and the white farmhouse just as the rain changed from a drizzle to a downpour. She ran up the drive and onto the porch.

The house was weathered, and the porch seemed way smaller than the one she remembered. In fact, the house of her long-ago Christmas memory had been grander in every respect. She remembered the lights—all different colors strung along the eaves—and a gigantic tree in the front windows. She remembered a bay window.

This house didn't have one of those.

But that didn't mean much. Over the years, she had certainly embellished her memories. That's what abandoned kids did. In fact, as a lonely girl living in a succession of foster homes, she'd gone so far as to imagine a pretend life for herself, right here on Ridge Road in Grandpa's farmhouse, with a boy next door named Joe, who was her best friend in all the world.

Maryanne had never really had a best friend. Except in those pretend moments. So she couldn't be absolutely sure about anything here in South Carolina, except that being here was better than being in a women's shelter in Montgomery.

Still, the house of her memory, or her fantasy, had never seemed dark and abandoned like this one.

She knocked on the door and got only an echo for her trouble.

Her feet were wet, and her toes were starting to go numb. She looked toward the barn. She'd only been inside a barn once in her life, that same Christmas Eve, when Mom had left her with her grandparents. Grandpa had told her that on Christmas Eve, if you sneaked quietly into the barn, you could hear the animals talk.

And of course she'd gotten up in the middle of the night and tried to find out if it was true.

It hadn't been.

Joshua started to wiggle and fuss. He was making his hungry noise. It was sort of amazing how she could tell what he needed just by listening to him. That noise triggered her let-down reflex. She needed to feed him.

She pulled her soggy hood back over her head and dashed to the barn. Thank God it was open.

And empty.

It didn't look like there had been animals here for a long time. The stalls were barren earth, and the only hay she found was old and up in the loft. She headed up that way and found a musty horse blanket. She settled into the hay, took off her wet socks, and found a pair of dry ones in her sack.

And there, nestled in some straw, covered by an old blanket, she nursed her baby.

Daniel Jessup pushed the grocery cart up the aisle at the Last Chance BI-LO. He was headed for the freezer section when the big spiral-cut hams caught his eye.

He stared down at them, lost in happier memories. Momma had always cooked a huge ham on Christmas Eve. And a couple of pies. And mashed potatoes.

His stomach rumbled.

"Can I help you with one of the hams?" the guy behind the meat counter asked.

Daniel shook his head. "No, I just wish they weren't so big. It's just me this year."

The guy smiled. "You could get a canned ham. They're on aisle five. They're already cooked. You can just slice and eat. Or you can warm it up in the oven."

"Really?"

The guy nodded and gave him one of those looks—like Daniel had been living under a rock somewhere. And in a way he had been. Ever since Julia had walked out on him.

For five years, he'd been barely managing to feed himself, living on frozen dinners and takeout. Daniel headed toward aisle five, where he found the canned hams. The directions on the back seemed easy enough. He found himself putting the ham in his basket.

But how was he going to manage mashed potatoes? What about pie? And why was he doing this?

He continued up and down the aisles. He found a box of instant mashed potatoes that required nothing more than a little water and milk. He could nuke some frozen butter beans. And the bakery still had one apple pie left. A bottle of inexpensive merlot would make the icy night go faster.

He wheeled his cart down the seasonal aisle on his way to the checkout line. The offerings were picked over on this Christmas Eve afternoon, but there were still a few bright and shiny new toys that hadn't found homes. It was kind of sad. They'd all be marked down the day after tomorrow.

And that's when it all caught up to him.

He didn't have anyone to share a dinner with. He didn't have anyone to buy a gift for.

He wasn't expecting any gifts, either. But that didn't bother him in the least. He had everything he needed, except his family.

He picked up a stuffed reindeer with a red nose and bells inside. It was the sort of toy you hung over a baby's crib. It had an elastic loop on the top. A baby was supposed to pull on it to make it bounce and jingle.

"Daniel Jessup, this is a surprise."

Daniel looked up to find Miz Miriam Randall wheeling a shopping cart in his direction. Miriam had to be pushing eighty-five. But the old gal was pretty spry. She sure was a character, with her Princess Leia hairdo and those 1950s rhinestone trifocals. Today she was wearing a sweatshirt with a big Rudolph on the front. She looked festive.

"Hey, Miz Miriam. How are you doing?" Daniel said.

"Oh, same old, same old. Just picking up a few last-minute items before the sleet starts falling. So, what brings you home to Last Chance? I'm sort of surprised." She gave him this enigmatic smile. She was onto him. Like every church woman in Allenberg County, she read him like the daily paper.

He managed a smile, although the guilt gnawed at him. He'd often been absent these last few months as Daddy's health and mind had faded. But it had been so hard to visit. It hurt so bad to have his own father look him in the face as if he were a stranger.

"I know I was a terrible son," he muttered.

"Oh, Daniel, I didn't mean it that way. I can hardly blame you for staying away. Ruben didn't know who anyone was toward the end. I'm sure that was hard on you. I was just saying that it's surprising to see you here over Christmas when your kin are all gone. Atlanta must be a much livelier place to spend the holidays."

"I'm putting the farm up for sale. Christmas seemed like a good time to go through the last of Momma's and Daddy's things and get the house ready. It's a slow time for me at work." He didn't know why he added the last bit, because it wasn't true. Maybe it was a cry for help. Maybe he was truly burned out. Or maybe he was just hiding out.

Christmas was hard. He wanted to be left alone.

The old woman studied him from behind her thick glasses, her brown eyes sharp.

"Son, there's something I need to remind you of." She pushed her cart up next to his and reached out to touch his arm. It was strange to be touched. It had been a long time since anyone had touched him like that—person to person, with friendship and caring.

"I'm sure you know the story of the three wise men. How they each looked up at the sky and saw that star. How just the sight of that light was all they needed to get going. They just saddled up their camels and went off to find a miracle. But have you ever stopped to think about the fact that the star was there for everyone to see? Why didn't everyone go to Bethlehem?"

Daniel stood there. He had no answer for Miriam. He'd never given this much thought at all. And besides, Miriam had a reputation for talking in parables, when she wasn't working hard to match up all the unsuspecting single people in town.

She nodded as if she understood his confusion. "I'll

tell you why. Because everyone else decided to go back to sleep. The point is, Daniel, most folks didn't really see that light—not with their hearts, anyway. So they just stayed home and waited for the miracle to come find them, instead of going out looking for one. I'm a firm believer in folks working for their miracles."

She smiled and patted his arm again, and then she gestured toward the toy. "You know, you might think about buying that toy and putting it in the charity box at church. You have a merry Christmas, now, you hear?" she said. She turned and wheeled her cart down the aisle.

Daniel looked down at the toy. Miriam was right. He ought to get on with his life. And he'd been trying to do that.

But mostly failing. He'd just heard that Julia and her new husband were expecting a child. And the news had eaten into him like acid.

He stared at the little reindeer. And then he put it in his shopping cart.

Maryanne rigged up a temporary place in the hay for Joshua to sleep, swaddled in her big, warm, North Face jacket. Without her jacket it was cold in the barn, so she draped the old horse blanket around her shoulders. It stank, but it kept her from freezing.

If no one came home, it was going to get dark in the barn tonight. She needed to find a lantern or something. So she left the baby asleep and climbed down from the loft.

Twenty minutes of searching netted nothing like a lantern. Weren't barns supposed to be cluttered with junk? This one was practically pristine.

The rain beat on the tin roof, and from the little ticking sound, she could tell that it had ice in it.

She cracked the big barn door and gazed out. The trees were taking a beating. Ice formed on the long, thick leaves of the big magnolia in the front yard. The tree stood at least thirty feet tall, but its branches were beginning to sag under the frozen weight.

The farmhouse remained dark. It brooded there in the fading light, making a mockery of her long-ago Christmas memories and the fantasy life she'd created out of them.

Maryanne squeezed her eyes closed and berated herself for the decision to leave the car. She would have been better off there. It was easier to warm a car's interior with body heat than a big, wide-open barn. And besides, someone was sure to have found her out on Route 78 sooner or later.

But, then again, a single mother in a car with all her worldly possessions and a three-month-old baby was the sort of thing that brought out the do-gooders. She needed to avoid them at all costs. You could never trust a do-gooder. They always had ulterior motives.

Just then, a car pulled into the drive, its LED headlights looking ghostly blue in the rain. She ducked back into the shadows and watched the silver car's back wheels spin as it struggled up the drive.

Wow, Cousin Jennifer was doing all right if she could afford a BMW 535i. In all the scenarios she'd spun about this moment, she'd never seen Jennifer driving a luxury car. She'd never thought of her cousin as being a rich person. Rich people were mostly mean, in Maryanne's experience. They looked down on her. Or they self-righteously tried to "help" her.

In the end, all those well-meaning people tended to see her as a stereotype—a product of the foster care system. And lately, since Joshua, as a "single unwed mother" or a "welfare queen." Half of them tried to get her to give Joshua up so she could finish college and make a better life, and the other half called her names for keeping her baby, like they thought being on public assistance was her goal in life.

Rich people had no idea what it was like to be a waitress, making less than minimum wage and hoping for tips. Rich people didn't have to work that hard. Rich people didn't have thankless jobs that provided no health care or child care. Rich people didn't know what it was like to work your way through college one course at a time because that's all you could afford. They didn't know what it was like to fall through the safety net.

It was her own damn fault that she'd fallen, though. They certainly had *that* right. She'd allowed herself to love someone. And, of course, he'd left her. Everyone she'd ever loved had left her.

The BMW's door swung open, and a tall dude with sandy hair and a little cowlick got out. He wore a black, double-breasted overcoat—probably cashmere. It accentuated his shoulders. He looked like he was coming home from his job as a stockbroker or something.

That's when Maryanne noticed the license plate on his car. It lacked South Carolina's palmetto and half-moon. But it sure did have a Georgia peach.

Where the heck was Jennifer? Was this her husband?

Maryanne hid in the shadows as he unloaded groceries and unlocked the farmhouse. The lights came on, and the spill of yellow light from the windows set up a longing inside her.

She ought to go introduce herself, but she'd planned on talking to Jennifer, not some stranger in a cashmere coat. She couldn't just stride up to his door and use the line she'd rehearsed. Obviously he hadn't been there that long-ago Christmas.

So she stood there, looking at the light, weighing her options, and trying to make up her mind.

Daniel unloaded his ham and fixings onto the kitchen counter.

Damn, he'd forgotten to stop by the church on the way home to drop off the little reindeer toy. It lay there in the bottom of the grocery sack mocking him.

He left it there, out of sight, as he reached for the corkscrew he'd bought to go with the wine. Then he went searching for a juice glass. Momma and Daddy had never been drinkers so there wasn't a wineglass to be found in this kitchen.

He was just pouring the wine when he heard a noise coming from the barn. It sounded...

He stilled, all his senses going to full alert. His ears were playing tricks on him. It was probably just the wind, or maybe a stray cat howling at the rain.

The noise came again.

He put down his juice glass and went digging into the drawer in search of a flashlight. And lo, it was right where it was supposed to be. Daddy had always been just a little OCD, and the dementia only made it worse.

The flashlight worked.

He threw on his overcoat and minced his way over the ice to the barn. An iron band formed around his chest. He could hardly take in a breath.

The door was open a crack, and that was odd because he'd closed the door before he'd left the place last weekend. An open barn door was an invitation to stray cats and other critters.

But the noise coming from inside the barn wasn't a stray cat.

He shoved open the door and hit the ladder to the loft at a run. When he was halfway up, he shined his light into the corner.

Oh holy God.

The girl flinched when the light hit her eyes, and if anything the baby in her arms howled even harder.

"Turn that damn thing off." She shaded her eyes, and he aimed his light up toward the rafters. It bounced back, giving the loft a dim, shadowy glow.

He'd gotten only a fleeting look at the woman, but her glossy brown hair and deep, dark eyes made an impression. The baby in her arms was maybe three or four months old. The child wasn't happy in the least.

"Who the hell are you?" he shouted above the baby's cries. The words came out like bullets, harsher than he'd intended. It was freezing cold in the barn. No wonder the baby was screaming.

"Are you Cousin Jennifer's husband?" she said, bypassing his question.

"Cousin Jennifer? Who's that?"

"Jennifer Carpenter."

If the situation hadn't been so strange he might have laughed. "Jenny Carpenter? You think I'm her husband? Lady, Jenny Carpenter is a professional spinster. She's never going to have a husband."

"How can anyone be a professional spinster?" she

asked. There was something in her voice. He couldn't decide if she was sassing him or teasing him. Either way, he didn't like it. She was the one with a baby in his barn on an icy cold night.

"What the hell are you doing here?" he barked.

"Looking for Jennifer...uh, I mean Jenny. And I take it you're not her husband."

"What gave you the idea I was her husband?"

"Uh, well, you're here at her farm."

The light dawned. "This is the *Jessup* farm. Old man Carpenter's orchard is down Ridge Road another mile, maybe. Lady, you've holed up in the wrong barn."

"Oh." It was too dark to see the expression on her face. But he heard both apology and embarrassment in her voice.

"I guess I'll be going, then," she said. "Just let me get Joshua in his carrier and then—"

"You can't go anywhere tonight. They're calling for three inches of ice on the roads. And besides, I didn't see a car."

"Oh, well, my car broke down on Highway Seventy-Eight, about a mile short of Ridge Road."

"You walked here? With a baby? In the rain?" He went on alert. This had serious child endangerment written all over it.

"Well, don't get up on your high horse. I wasn't going to stay in the car when I could walk. Besides, it wasn't raining when I started out. I've got a good North Face coat. I'll be fine."

"You'll be fine doing what?"

"Just walking down to the right farmhouse."

"The Carpenter farmhouse burned down ten years

ago. The barn is all that's left. I think Jenny leases the land to Mr. Nelson. But Jenny lives in town at the moment, although I heard that she's planning on moving into The Jonquil House and turning it into a bed-and-breakfast."

"Oh." There was a depth of emotion and desperation in that single word. It hit him in the chest. Maybe she wasn't a goofball of a mother. Maybe she just needed some help.

He softened his voice. "I gather it's been a while since you've seen Cousin Jenny. And something tells me she's not exactly expecting you for the holidays."

Busted. She was so busted. The rich BMW guy had managed to see right through her, even in the dark.

Although he did have the advantage since he'd halfway blinded her with his flashlight right at the start. Now she had this big purple glowy splotch right in the middle of her vision. It was going to be hard to get Joshua in his carrier and get the heck out of here.

Before he called the cops.

She definitely didn't want cops involved. Cops were going to get in touch with the do-gooders, and then she and Joshua would end up "in the system." And the system would grind them up and spit them out.

But then again, if Grandpa's farmhouse had burned, she was stuck here. Last Chance was a good five, maybe six, miles down Route 78. So all told it might be seven miles to Cousin Jennifer's house. She couldn't walk there with Joshua. Not in the rain and ice.

She positioned the baby up on her shoulder and swayed while she rubbed his back. His distress ate into her. This sudden bout of crying was so unlike him. He was usually a content, practically serene baby.

Maybe he was sensing the fact that Maryanne had come to the end of her rope, and she didn't know what to do.

The baby raised his head for a moment and then he put it back down on her shoulder and kind of snuggled down against her. He gave one or two last little hiccups and relaxed. She gave him a little squeeze. She had never loved anyone or anything more than Joshua.

The man on the ladder let go of a long sigh. She could see a plume of steam. It was freezing cold in this barn.

"C'mon. You can't stay in here," he said. "And I won't have you walking to town in an ice storm. I've got food inside." He paused for a moment. "You wouldn't happen to know how to heat up a ham, would you?"

He was kidding, right? "Uh, that's not actually very hard."

"Yeah, well, it is if you've never done it before. And I have some instant potatoes. Who knew they even had anything like that? I certainly didn't know you could get potatoes from out of a box."

"I'm an expert at instant potatoes." She didn't tell him that she also knew how to make real mashed potatoes.

"My name's Daniel. Daniel Jessup. And you are?"

"Maryanne Carpenter. And this is Joshua."

The farmhouse wasn't at all like the one Maryanne had visited when she was six. This one was smaller than her memories.

Her grandfather's house sprawled in every direction. This house had a prim, center-hall design. The house of her memory had been stuffed with furniture and a gigantic Christmas tree. This place was empty, except for a bunch of boxes stacked up in the dining room and a lonely, threadbare couch in the living room. There were no holiday decorations here—not one shred of tinsel that would give away the season.

But both of these houses had big kitchens. Daniel's groceries, such as they were, were sitting on the butcher block counter along with an open bottle of wine.

"So, you were planning on drinking alone, huh?" she asked, suddenly curious about this man and his almost-empty farmhouse.

He bypassed her question with one of his own. "I'm going upstairs to see what I can find to make a bed for the baby. Are you good here?"

She turned to look at him. He was standing in the kitchen doorway, studying her as if he were trying to decide if she was good or evil.

So she studied him right back. He was tall, with sandy blond hair and deep-set blue eyes. His gray business suit couldn't hide the farm boy inside. That cowlick, his big hands, and those broad shoulders gave him away. She could just imagine him in jeans and a plaid shirt tossing around hay bales or something.

In fact, he looked exactly like one of her deepest fantasies. The one that went along with the make-believe life she had imagined for herself at her grandfather's farm. He looked like the farm boy next door.

"I'm good for now," she said. "Did you grow up here?" She suddenly wanted to know. Because if he had grown up there, then he *was* the farm boy next door.

He nodded but didn't elaborate. He turned away, and a moment later, the sound of his footsteps going up the stairs echoed through the empty house.

She had never imagined the boy next door growing up to become a stockbroker with a BMW and a cashmere coat. Which just proved how dangerous fantasies could be.

She pushed her disappointment aside and assessed the contents of Daniel's refrigerator and pantry. She was hungry and not ashamed to admit it. Joshua seemed to be taking all her extra calories these days.

Unfortunately, the cupboard was almost bare except for the ham, a box of potatoes, some frozen veggies, and several boxes of cereal. At least he had fresh milk.

She had just started up the oven when Daniel's footsteps thumped down the stairs. Boy, he sure was heavy on his feet. She braced herself for another confrontation. But he didn't come into the kitchen right away.

He stayed out there in the living room, moving stuff around.

She opened the canned ham and put it in the oven to heat, and was just rummaging through the cabinets looking for a second juice glass, when he spoke again. She almost jumped out of her skin.

"I fixed up something for the baby."

She turned. Oh boy, he had reverted to type. He'd lost his suit and come back wearing a pair of faded jeans and a red flannel shirt that was surprisingly festive. He wasn't wearing farm boy boots, though. The tasseled loafers were like a flashing danger sign.

"What did you fix up? I can't imagine that you have a crib or a cradle," she said.

"Well, no. But I had an idea for a bed, kind of. I'm sure you're tired of lugging him around."

"Not really," she lied. She *was* ready to put Joshua

down, but she didn't want Daniel thinking she didn't care about the baby. He already had the wrong idea about her.

Or maybe it wasn't the wrong idea. She'd made some truly boneheaded decisions today. She shouldn't have taken Joshua out into the rain. She shouldn't have thought about spending the night in an unheated barn. She probably shouldn't have even left Montgomery.

"What kind of bed?" she asked, breaking the sudden silence.

"Come and see." Was that a twinkle in his eye? No, certainly not. Any guy who had been planning to drink a bottle of wine all by himself on Christmas Eve was incapable of having twinkles.

Anywhere.

She followed him to the living room. "It's my mother's bureau drawer," he said, explaining the obvious.

A couple of baby blue velour towels had been folded into the bottom of the drawer to make a little bed that would fit Joshua perfectly.

Some of Maryanne's defensiveness crumbled. "Thank you," she muttered, her throat suddenly closing off the air. It had been a long time since someone had done something kind for her. The whole world wanted to reform her. But very few people were actually kind.

Cousin Jenny had been kind. Grandma and Grandpa had been kind. In fact it was their kindness she remembered the best. It was their kindness that had drawn her to this place when she'd come to the end of her rope.

And Daniel was kind, too. It was a rare thing in the real world.

So she decided not to lie to him. She decided to kind

of trust him. "It would be nice to put the baby down for a bit," she admitted. "My shoulders are tired."

He smiled and nodded. "I thought that might be the case."

She wrapped her arms around the sleeping child and slipped the carrier off. Joshua fit very nicely in the bureau drawer. She dug into her backpack and found a receiving blanket and swaddled him tight. Joshua liked being wrapped up tight when he slept.

"I don't think he's going anywhere for a while," Daniel said. "Why don't we pour some wine and figure out how to make instant potatoes?"

The woman—Maryanne—was exhausted. The weariness showed in the dark circles under her deep brown eyes. The baby probably kept her up all hours of the night. And she was obviously down on her luck. She looked like she'd dressed herself in Salvation Army castoffs. Her sweater was unraveling at the neckline. Her jeans were frayed. And she didn't have a wedding ring on her left hand.

But she wasn't some runaway teen mom. He'd guess she was in her mid to late twenties and fairly well-educated by the way she spoke. She was pretty in the way of the girls he'd grown up with here in Last Chance. She wasn't all made up or dressed to the nines like the women of Atlanta tended to be. Like Julia had been.

He found her lack of pretension refreshing.

And despite his first impressions, he now knew she loved her baby. He'd watched her wrap him up in that faded receiving blanket and kiss his downy head before leaving him in the living room. The tender look in her eyes had lanced through him.

He pulled himself away from thoughts that were likely to turn maudlin. Instead he made himself useful, pulling another juice glass from the cabinet. "Can I interest you in some inexpensive merlot?"

She had found a saucepan and was putting some water on to boil. She looked like she actually knew what she was doing.

"I thought you'd never ask," she said with a little tilt to her mouth.

Wow. The smile transformed her. She had dimples, and the corners of her eyes turned up. She was more than pretty when she smiled.

He handed her the juice glass. "Merry Christmas," he said.

They touched glasses and sipped their wine. "Not bad for the BI-LO in Last Chance," he said. He took a seat at the kitchen table, a beautiful oak antique that the auctioneer said would fetch a very nice sum. He wished he had a place for it in his Atlanta apartment. In fact, the idea of selling the house, which had been in the family for more than a hundred years, still made him queasy.

"So, you're a wine connoisseur?" she asked.

He let go of a nervous laugh. "Not really. I never touched a drop until I was in my twenties. My wife liked wine, and I got in the habit."

She turned to look over her shoulder. "She *liked* wine. Past tense?"

"We're divorced."

"Ah." She moved to the refrigerator and took out some milk. The room grew silent except for the sound of sleet hitting the windows on the windward side of the house.

He'd come up here to be alone—to push all the holiday noise aside—and now, suddenly, the quiet seemed unbearable. He knew Maryanne didn't want to talk about herself. And God knew he didn't want to unburden himself to a stranger. But they couldn't sit here in silence, could they?

"So," he said, "how old is Joshua?"

"Almost four months. He's just about learned how to roll over. I'm going to have to watch him in that drawer. That's why I swaddled him so tight."

"He's got a healthy set of lungs."

She poured the box of potato flakes into the boiling water, followed by some milk. "You know, it's strange. He doesn't cry much. I mean, he cries when he's hungry and when he needs a diaper change. But he doesn't fuss without a reason. So his crying jag tonight was kind of unusual." She placed the saucepan of instant potatoes on the stove top and turned around to face Daniel.

She folded her arms across her chest, the gesture defensive. "I know you think he was crying because he was cold. But he wasn't. I had him all wrapped up in my down jacket. I was kind of cold, but he was toasty warm. I didn't set out with the intention of spending the night in a barn, you know. I mean, what mother would do that?"

He gave her a smile in the hope that she would relax and maybe trust him a little bit. He wanted her trust. He'd only just met her, but he was coming to admire her grit and determination.

"Don't be so hard on yourself," he said. "I'm sorry I yelled at you before. I was just surprised, is all. And when you think about it, Jesus spent his first night in a barn."

She blinked at him and then turned around. "Please don't tell me you're one of those churchy people."

"Churchy?"

"You know, a holy…" Her voice trailed off, and she picked up the sack of frozen butter beans and began poking holes in it with a fork.

"A holy what?" he asked.

She didn't say a word, but there was a savagery in her movements as she put the frozen veggies in the microwave and punched in the cooking time. The microwave whirred into action, momentarily drowning out the sound of the rain and sleet hitting the windows.

She turned around. "A holy roller." She said the words with utter contempt.

"I'm not a holy roller, Maryanne. I was raised as an Episcopalian, and we kind of frown on holy-rolling, to tell you the truth. We're pretty tame as a congregation. Although I will admit that the Ladies' Auxiliary is a bunch of busybodies. The knitters among them go into overdrive whenever a new baby is born. And when someone passes they all show up with casseroles. They do a lot of praying for the sick. And they are unrelenting matchmakers."

He knew all of this firsthand. The ladies had shown up in droves each time death had darkened his door. They'd prayed for Daddy this last year, and they'd visited him on a regular basis at the nursing home. And ever since Daniel's divorce, the ladies had been pushing one single woman after another in his direction, including Jenny Carpenter, who was actually a Methodist.

But today was the first time Miriam Randall had ever given him any kind of advice, and Miriam was reputed to have special abilities when it came to helping single people identify their soul mates.

Of course, it was hard to see how her little sermon about the wise men could be interpreted as marital advice. Maybe she was just trying to tell him to quit being a sourpuss.

"I don't much like churchy people," Maryanne said. "They always have ulterior motives. And I don't need people like that telling me what to do or where to go or how to be." The microwave chimed. She turned around, opened the door, and rotated the bag of veggies.

"Okay," Daniel said. "I get it. But the truth is, you aren't the first mother who ever took shelter in a barn. Better to do that than to walk on in the rain and discover that a blackened and crumbling chimney is all that's left of the Carpenter place. Of course there's a barn there, too. But it's almost falling down. I don't think it would keep the rain out."

She leaned on the counter, her back to him. "I remember that barn," she said in a little voice.

"You do?"

"I was six. My grandfather told me some BS story about the animals talking on Christmas Eve. I decided to check it out."

He chuckled.

She turned. "You think it's funny?"

He shook his head. "No, I think it's par for the course. Every farm kid in Allenberg County has gotten up in the wee hours of Christmas Day to visit the animals. The thing is, though, if you just walk into the barn all brazen and sure of yourself the animals are going to clam up. You have to sneak up on them. And that's practically impossible to do. They can smell you coming before you even get there."

She stood there blinking at him. The expression on her face was kind of cute. Clearly she was a woman who had stopped believing in miracles. And right then it occurred to Daniel that maybe he'd stopped believing in them, too.

Objectively the ham and instant potatoes weren't much of a Christmas Eve dinner, but to Maryanne they might have been manna from heaven. It had been several days since she'd had a good, hot meal. A nursing mother couldn't survive on Clif Bars for very long before deep hunger set in. And, of course, she'd done a stupid thing spending her grocery money on gas to get here.

What would happen if Cousin Jenny wasn't the same kind person she remembered? Obviously her memories were suspect.

Although Daniel Jessup was clearly a kind person, even if he did prove to be a master at prying out Maryanne's secrets. By the time they were sipping after-dinner coffee, he'd learned that she'd come all the way from Montgomery. That her mother had been married to Ezra and Maggie Carpenter's only son, John. That John had died in a barroom fight when Maryanne was no bigger than Joshua. And that she'd met her grandparents only once, twenty years ago. At Christmastime.

"I may have heard Momma and Daddy mention your father once or twice," Daniel said. "And I might even have heard that Ezra and Maggie had a long, lost grandchild. I reckon that was you. I guess John Carpenter had a chip on his shoulder even as a young man."

She put down her coffee cup. "My father was a drunk. And Mom never let me forget it." She looked toward the dark window over the sink. The storm was blowing the rain against the house. She shivered. She was grateful to be inside.

And so angry at herself for falling for Gary Duggan, Joshua's father. He was probably a carbon copy of her own, no-account father. What a fool she'd been for following in her mother's footsteps. If she ever saw Gary Duggan again, she'd spit in his eye.

But then he hadn't been the first person to abandon her.

She looked back at Daniel. He didn't have that come-hither look in his eyes that had so attracted Maryanne to Gary. But he was very handsome. And he was like some walking and talking dream. In her secret fantasy life, she and the imaginary Joe had grown up together, doing all kinds of things, like fishing, and climbing trees, and going to the eighth grade dance together. She imagined whispering secrets to him. She imagined him as a true friend—the kind who would never leave her.

"Why are you here?" she asked, and immediately regretted her words.

"It's my house," he said. Of course he hadn't understood the true meaning of her question. And now she had to backtrack or he'd think she was crazy.

"No, that's not what I meant," she said. "I'm just trying to figure out why you're here all alone without any decorations and nothing but boxes everywhere."

He studied the remnants of the pie he'd just consumed. "Daddy died about two months ago, and I'm putting the farm on the market. I don't live here anymore. I live in Atlanta."

"Well, that explains the Georgia license plate and the BMW. What are you, a stockbroker or something?"

He looked up, met her gaze, and shook his head. "No, I'm a lawyer."

And just like that her bubble burst. She hated lawyers more than do-gooders. She had to ignore the flannel shirt and the jeans and remember the tasseled loafers and cashmere coat. He might have grown up right next door to Grandpa's farm, but he was not Joe. Joe was not a real person, even if he sometimes seemed as real as Cousin Jennifer.

Just then, Joshua started to fuss. Thank goodness. She could escape Daniel's blue-eyed stare for a few minutes. She pushed up from the table and hurried into the living room.

The baby had managed to unwrap his blanket and was on his way to rolling right out of the bureau drawer. She greeted this development with mixed emotions. He needed a crib to keep him safe. And she didn't have the money for a crib.

She didn't even have a place to *put* a crib.

She picked Joshua up, and he gave her a big, wide, toothless grin that made her heart fill up. She loved him so much. And each day she got the feeling that he loved her back. She sat down on the couch, draped the blanket over her shoulder, and nursed him.

There were times, like right this minute, when she wondered if allowing Joshua to love her was the right thing. She couldn't give him anything. Even on Christmas.

She had no gift for him. And now she didn't even have a home or know where her next meal was coming from.

Even in foster care, she'd gotten something every Christmas. Of course it was never something she'd wanted. In fact, there had been only one year when she'd gotten the gift of her dreams—that year at Grandpa's farm. There had been a baby doll under the tree for her.

She had cherished that baby for about three hours until Mom came back.

Mom was not supposed to come back on Christmas Day. She was supposed to come back after she married Derek, her boyfriend. Mom had told Maryanne that she would be staying with Grandma and Grandpa for a while.

A while had turned out to be two days. Mom had come back all tearful and announced that she and Derek were taking Maryanne back to Houston, where Derek was from. Grandma had been unhappy about this news, and there had been a screaming fight. And then Mom had dragged Maryanne out of the house before she could even get her baby doll and take it with her.

Maryanne had howled all the way from Last Chance to the Georgia border over her lost doll. And at the first gas station, Derek had spanked her for it. Hard. And Mom had told her that she had to obey Derek from now on because, if she didn't obey him, she might have to go live with her grandma and grandpa, forever. And even though Maryanne had kind of liked her grandparents, the idea of not ever seeing Mom again was very scary.

So she promised to obey Derek, even though he was kind of mean. But having to obey him didn't last all that long. The night they reached Montgomery, Derek wanted to go out partying. Mom didn't really want to go, but she had to obey Derek, too. So Maryanne got dropped off with a friend of Derek's for the night, a really scary lady who smoked a lot of cigarettes.

That night, Mom and Derek got themselves into a fatal car wreck. Many years later, Maryanne had discovered that alcohol was involved. It sure looked like Mom had a weakness for drunks and jerks.

Of course, Derek's friend took Maryanne right to social services, and at the age of six, she'd entered foster care. For years she had assumed that Grandma and Grandpa hadn't wanted her.

Then, about two years ago, she'd finally screwed up the courage to look into her own files—only to discover that no one in Montgomery had ever tried to contact her grandparents. Probably because Maryanne didn't know their names or even the place where they lived, except to say South Carolina.

So maybe Grandpa and Grandma would have given her a home if someone had given them a chance. And if that had happened, then she would have grown up next door to Daniel Jessup.

That thought set her heart to racing, just as Daniel walked into the room. And there was this look on his face. Like he kind of understood where she was coming from. Or like maybe he felt the same strange connection or something.

But that connection couldn't be real, could it? It was just her desperation and her loneliness.

She couldn't just sit there staring at Daniel, so she looked down at Joshua, who had fallen asleep. Feeling suddenly embarrassed and awkward, she buttoned up her blouse and pulled down her sweater.

Daniel stood on the threshold between the dining and living rooms, unable to move. The light from the table lamp haloed Maryanne's hair, making her look almost like a Madonna. The tender look on her face as she gazed down at the baby opened up Daniel's heart in a palpable way.

He thought about the things Miriam Randall had said to him that afternoon. Maryanne's appearance here, tonight, when he'd been prepared to drink himself into a stupor, was nothing more than a miracle. A real, everyday miracle.

Maryanne had changed everything by her presence here tonight. It was as if she'd thawed something frozen inside of him. And listening to her talk about that one Christmas she'd spent here with her grandparents made him realize how blessed he'd been in his life. He was the lucky one. He'd had his mother and father for a long while. He'd grown up here, safe and sound and loved.

Maryanne hadn't had any of those blessings. But she would have them now that she'd come home. And the moment he realized that this *was* a kind of homecoming for Maryanne, it made him wonder why the heck he was selling the farm. Why he'd been so anxious as a younger man to move away to the big city.

Maybe he could come home, too.

He turned and headed back into the dining room, where he'd stacked a bunch of boxes that had been designated for the Salvation Army. Now he knew he was a fool to have even thought about giving Momma's Christmas stuff away. Sure, the boxes were loaded with memories. But maybe it was time to go looking for the good ones instead of dwelling on the bad ones.

He carried the box with the tree into the living room.

"What's that?" Maryanne asked as he set the box down in the middle of the room and started pulling out green branches.

"It's a Christmas tree. Wanna help me decorate?"

She cocked her head. "It's a little late for that, isn't it?"

"It's not Christmas yet. And it's never too late for a little holiday spirit."

This won him a big smile. "Yeah, I guess."

She put the sleeping baby back in his makeshift bed, and the two of them put up the old tree in the front window, just the way Momma used to do it. The tree was a little worse for wear. It looked as if some mice had gotten to some of the branches. But when the lights were on, and the old ornaments came out of the box, it didn't look half bad.

"Oh, it's so pretty," Maryanne said as she stood back to admire the angel he'd put on the top. Her eyes danced in the lights like a kid's. And that look of exhaustion had faded away. She turned and headed out to the porch. "I want to see what it looks like from the outside."

And out into the icy night she ran, slipping and sliding down the steps. He wanted to shout out to be careful, but somehow her enthusiasm caught him, and he found himself following after her to stand in the freezing rain looking at the lights.

"Gosh, it's like the way I remember it," she said.

"Huh?"

"Oh!" her voice sounded strained, and her joy faded. "I mean it looks like something in a greeting card."

He chuckled. "Not really. You should have seen the house when Momma was alive. She had pine roping draped on everything."

Maryanne nodded, as if she really remembered.

Oh boy, she was losing her mind. But the sight of those colored lights through the lace curtains was like something from a deep memory. Never mind that it wasn't a real memory. She'd imagined living in a place like this for so long that sometimes it seemed more real than the awful reality she'd experienced.

She needed to back off and get a grip. It would be so easy to let herself trust Daniel. Or trust this situation. Or believe that maybe she'd found what she had been wishing for.

She turned and made her way over the ice back to the warmth of the farmhouse. Joshua was awake and making cooing sounds. He was also working hard to get himself unwrapped.

Maryanne felt another pang as the reality of her situation settled back on her shoulders. It was all well to sit here and pretend that she lived in a pretty little farmhouse with Joe, her best friend who would take care of Joshua no matter what, when in reality she was homeless. And Joshua was getting older, and taking care of him while trying to finish school or find a decent job was going to be impossible.

Her life was impossible.

"Can I play with him?" Daniel asked. He had snuck up behind her, his body warm against the chill from outside. His voice was deep and masculine.

Of all the things Daniel could have said to her in this moment, this one thing surprised her. She turned to look at him and came right up against his endearing aw-shucks, open-faced look. "We have a Christmas tree, and I even have a Christmas present to put under it for him. But you wouldn't mind if I gave it to him early, would you?"

"You have a Christmas gift for him? How can that be?"

He shrugged. "It's a miracle." Then he turned and headed into the kitchen. A moment later, he came back with a little stuffed reindeer in his big hands. "It's not much. Just a little jingle toy." He shook it. And the sound of bells filled the room. Joshua started looking around.

From his last comment about miracles, she knew better than to ask why he was in the possession of a toy that looked brand new. She certainly didn't believe it was a miracle. There had to be a rational explanation for it.

He crossed the room and sat down on the floor, Indian style. He really had to fold up his long legs to sit like that.

He finished unwrapping the baby and then he dangled the little reindeer toy just within Joshua's reach. The baby had been learning how to reach for things, and the bright, red-and-brown Rudolf immediately captured his attention.

His little legs kicked, and he got a fierce look on his face as he slowly reached out and grabbed the reindeer's leg. Then he let the toy go. It bounced on the elastic that Daniel was holding crooked in his finger. When the toy bounced, it jingled.

Joshua smiled and made a little sound that might have been a laugh.

Daniel held the toy back within reaching distance. The baby caught the reindeer and let it go again. This time there was no mistaking the noise that issued from his little body. It was the deepest, most infectious belly laugh Maryanne had ever heard. It was Joshua's first laugh, and it made a joyful sound.

Daniel found it impossible not to laugh along with the baby, or to let Maryanne's enjoyment of the Christmas tree creep into his heart. It had been so long since he'd felt anything like this.

He'd come here to hide from Christmas and to be alone with his grief. But here he was, miraculously, given the one thing he thought utterly impossible. He wished he had toys and gifts to put in the old stockings he'd found in the Christmas box. He wished he'd come here a few days ago and put up the lights out front on the porch the way Daddy used to.

He was tired of living in the dark. He wanted to light up the world, if for no other reason than to see those holiday lights shining in Maryanne's eyes.

He couldn't put up the lights now. It was too icy outside. He might not have anything for the stockings, but he *could* start a fire. What was Christmas without a fire burning in the hearth?

He had to haul in some firewood from the stack out back. But he didn't mind, especially after the fire was crackling in the hearth, giving the old living room a real Christmas glow.

Maryanne let Daniel hold the baby for a while. He played with the boy until Joshua got a little fussy. And then he walked the floor with him until the baby settled into a blissful, innocent sleep.

When the child was finally snoozing, Daniel didn't have the heart to put him back into his improvised bed. Instead he sat beside Maryanne on the couch.

"So, by the way you manage Joshua, I guess you and your ex have kids, huh?" Maryanne asked.

And just like that, Daniel's warm, fuzzy feelings evaporated.

"No, we never did," he said, and swallowed back an overwhelming surge of guilt and sorrow.

Maryanne must have sensed something because she didn't press the point. Instead she moved a little closer to him and rested her head on his shoulder, and together they watched Joshua sleep for a long, quiet while. And, oddly, the silence made him want to tell her everything that was in his heart. How had she managed to open him up like that? He'd been keeping all of it so close for so long.

"I lied a minute ago," he finally said. "Julia and I had a child." His voice was surprisingly firm.

"Had?" Her head remained on his shoulder.

He drew in a deep breath. "He was born with a congenital heart defect. The doctors couldn't fix him. He lived for about a month. He never came home from the hospital." The tell-tale tremble in his voice was like a warning. "We discovered that the problem was genetic. Julia and I each carry a recessive gene for something called Zellweger syndrome. So if we tried again, we had a twenty-five percent chance of having another sick baby. Julia couldn't deal with that. So she left."

He braced himself for Maryanne's pity. But it didn't come.

"What was your son's name?" she asked. The question struck him as odd. No one ever asked that question. They always wanted the details of the disease. They always wanted to dive into the facts and figures and all that. As if the facts and figures and details could obfuscate the fact that his son had been, for a brief time, a living human being.

"We called him Christopher," Daniel said. It had been a long time since he'd spoken that name aloud. "He died on Christmas Eve, five years ago. That's why I was planning on drinking alone. So I'm glad I found you in the barn."

He said these words and the moment they left his mouth he knew he was deeply grateful. Not just because she'd given him a moment to play with a baby. But because, somehow, even though she had nothing, she'd walked into this house and brought light into it. And just being here with him, sharing a meal, putting up a tree, resting her head on his shoulder, had brought him back into the land of the living.

Daniel's story broke Maryanne's heart and made her realize that there were worse things than being homeless on Christmas Eve.

Daniel had a home, but his parents were gone. His wife was gone. Even his child was gone.

Maryanne had spent a lifetime being alone. She knew what it was like. And her life had changed, for the better, when Joshua had come into it. She was the lucky one.

Maybe that's why she had been hanging on so tight to the baby, even though having and keeping him meant giving up her job and school, and now, ultimately, her home. Of course, it was crazy to even think about raising a child without a home. She knew that.

But here was a man who had a home with no one to fill it up. And somehow that seemed to be way worse. What good was a home without anyone living in it?

They put Joshua down in his makeshift bed and sat in front of the fire and talked for hours.

He told her boyhood stories about living on a farm, and it was almost as if she already knew them. As if, somehow, that secret other life she had pretended was true. As if there really was a boy next door who climbed trees, and made hay, and milked cows, and went fishing in the river. A boy who had a mother who baked him pies and put up pine roping above every window during the holidays.

Maybe that's why she'd come up Ridge Road this afternoon and mistaken this farmhouse for the one she'd visited so many years ago. Maybe in her mind she'd been visiting this place for years.

So in that instant, hours later, when he leaned in and kissed her, it felt like the most natural thing in the world.

His mouth awakened a dangerous desire inside her. For just one moment, a whole range of new possibilities opened before her. And then reality clicked in her head. She hardly knew this guy. He was a high-priced lawyer from Atlanta, not the fantasy she'd created for herself as a child.

More important, she didn't want to make the same mistakes her mother had made. She wasn't going to go from man to man. She was going to learn how to be independent and stand on her own two feet.

Maryanne gently disengaged. And he let her go, as if he, too, remembered that this was impossible.

They sat there staring at one another. "I—" he started, but she interrupted.

"That's not going to happen again, okay?" she said. "I mean, you don't need me. And I don't need your pity. And besides, you're some rich lawyer dude and I'm a homeless, welfare mother. So maybe I should go back to the barn and get some sleep."

"Don't be ridiculous." He stood up and checked his watch. "You know, it's only one thirty. Jenny is probably just getting back from midnight services." He dug into his jeans and came out with one of those big-screened, expensive smartphones. Exactly the kind of phone a rich Atlanta lawyer would be carrying around.

"Here," he said, handing her the phone. "I'm sure Jenny's number is listed. Why don't you give her a call?"

The phone ended up in Maryanne's hands.

Oh boy. The very last thing she wanted to do was call Cousin Jennifer in the middle of the night. What the hell was she supposed to say?

She looked up at Daniel, unable to read the expression on his face. He looked a little like the man who had come charging up the ladder a few hours ago, wanting to know how she could be so stupid as to think about sleeping with a baby in a barn.

"I have no idea how to look up her number. I don't have a smartphone like this. I can't afford one." She handed the phone back to him.

He ran his long fingers over the device in a dance that was both mysterious and sexy. He handed the phone back to her. "All you have to do is press the little green button and the phone will make the call for you."

She stared down at Jennifer's name and number. "I can't call her at one thirty at night."

"She'll be awake. Trust me. Almost everyone in Last Chance goes to church at midnight on Christmas."

She looked up. "They do? Really?"

"It's a pretty churchy place, Maryanne."

She stared at the number, increasingly disturbed by her own reluctance. "She might not remember me. And if I call her at this hour of the morning, she'll think I'm desperate or something."

"Aren't you?" he asked. His voice wasn't hard. It was

as soft as it had been all night, but somehow having him point out the truth hurt.

"You're right. I *am* desperate. And I'm a coward. But I'm not the only coward in this room." She raised her head. She wanted to take the words back almost from the moment she said them. Daniel was the last person in the world she wanted to lash out at.

"Coward? How do you figure?"

"You have to be brave to go on with your life," she said. "When people abandon you, you just have to suck it up and go on."

He pressed his lips together. "Yeah."

And they stared at one another for the longest moment. She wanted to run to him and tell him she didn't mean it. She wanted him to say the same thing back.

But neither happened. Instead he said, "All right, we'll call Jenny tomorrow morning, and I'll take you and the baby into town." He cocked his head. "Listen, it's stopped raining. According to the forecast, the temperature tomorrow is going to be in the forties with sunshine. The ice will be gone by mid-morning."

"Thank you." She handed the phone back to him, knowing that the time for saying the right things had come and gone. The moment had passed them both by.

He nodded, then glanced at the baby. "I'll sleep upstairs, You're welcome to the couch. Merry Christmas."

Idiot. He was a stupid, dumb idiot. He should never have kissed Maryanne. He shouldn't have moved that fast. But for an instant, that kiss had been a freaking miracle.

But maybe Maryanne wasn't looking for miracles—at least not that kind. Because he sure as hell had frightened her. And when she'd pushed him away, it had brushed up against those old wounds. So he'd done what he always did whenever Julia pushed him away. He lashed out and said the most hurtful thing he could have said. He'd made her face her own homelessness. He'd made her face her own desperation.

As if he wasn't desperate himself.

As if he didn't want to give her a safe place to stay.

He'd done all that damage when he'd just wanted to let her know how her appearance had changed everything.

If not for Maryanne and Joshua, he'd have spent the night alone, trying to numb his pain with a bottle of wine. If not for them, he would never have figured out the ham and potatoes. If not for them, he would have put the toy in the charity box this morning and some kid would have gotten a reindeer for Valentine's Day. If not for them, he'd have been so caught up in his own misery he wouldn't have seen the truth.

She called him a coward. And she was right. He had been afraid of sucking it up and moving on with his life. Afraid that somehow by moving on, Christopher would be forgotten.

But he'd been wrong.

Maryanne didn't go to sleep. She sat watching the coals in the fireplace burn down to ashes. Joshua slept on like an angel.

Her heart was full of so many conflicting emotions right at the moment. Daniel had called her bluff, hadn't he?

He'd handed her that fancy phone and made her look right into herself and realize how stupid her actions had been. Why on earth would Cousin Jennifer want anything to do with her? They were kin, but that didn't mean a thing.

And she wasn't going to mistake a kiss for something permanent or even real. She'd kissed him because he was exactly like the guy she'd been dreaming of all her life. And he'd kissed her out of charity. Or maybe because he was lonely and missed his wife and child.

He didn't care for her. They were practically strangers, no matter how much she might feel connected to him. He may have grown up on a farm and had a wonderful childhood, but he was still a complete unknown. He was a lawyer, for heaven's sake, a man from an entirely different world.

She thought about that for a long time. She thought about his big silver car and his tasseled loafers. He had a home. He had a steady job. He had a big heart. And he was good with Joshua.

Maybe he wasn't a complete unknown. Maryanne already knew that he was a good person. A steady person. A pillar of society.

He'd made Joshua laugh.

He'd also made her see the truth. She was never going to escape the sad facts of her life. She'd screwed up. She'd been working hard and making progress and then she'd gotten pregnant.

She knew what the do-gooders said about her. She was bad. Her mistakes were a sign of her wickedness. She didn't even get approval for deciding to have Joshua instead of throwing him away. Instead, the do-gooders started in on their harangue about how she could never give Joshua what he needed. About how, for the good of the child, she should give him away. And she'd stubbornly insisted that she could give him love the way no one else on earth could.

And yet, tonight, she'd learned otherwise.

Daniel Jessup had looked down at her child with such a tender expression on his face. He could give Joshua the childhood that Maryanne had wanted so badly that she'd made it up in her fantasies.

Maybe the do-gooders were right. She wasn't ready to be anyone's mother. She could play Santa tonight. She could give a truly amazing gift. And maybe by letting go, she could get her life back in the right place. Maybe she'd come full circle and had to leave her baby behind to truly find herself.

She sat there for hours, mulling these things over until they became utterly clear in her head. And then she went into the kitchen and found some paper and wrote a long letter.

And later, she bundled up in her hand-me-down jacket and walked out into the crystal night. She realized right then that she didn't exactly know where she was going or how she would get there.

It was icy on the driveway. But she discovered she could walk in the grass along the roadside. The ice crunched beneath her feet. She got to Ridge Road where she had intended to turn left and head back toward Route 78 and her abandoned car.

But something stopped her.

She stood at that crossroads, her heart breaking. She wondered for a moment if Mom had felt like this on the day she'd left Maryanne with Grandma and Grandpa. The day she said she'd be gone for a while.

Had Mom wanted to give her the gift of a better childhood? Or had Mom just been selfish? And why had Mom come back? Why had Grandma been so angry? Maryanne would never really know. She'd only been six, and all she had cared about on that Christmas, so long ago, was her baby doll.

Maryanne's throat closed up, and tears stung her eyes. She felt like howling out her pain the same way she had on the day she'd left her doll at Grandma's house.

There was no way to understand why or how things had turned out the way they had. She just needed to be brave and move on. And stand on her own two feet. Because that was the only way she would ever make any progress.

But where to now?

She should have turned left, toward the state road, but instead she turned right and headed up a long rise.

She walked along the icy road for about fifteen minutes before she saw the barn and the crumbling chimney where once a farmhouse had stood. There was no point in trying to be stealthy as she walked up the drive to the barn. There weren't any cows here anymore to miraculously talk on Christmas Eve. Besides, it wasn't Christmas Eve anymore. It was Christmas Day.

She remembered this barn, even though it was falling down now. Its doors stood open like a warm invitation.

She walked inside and found the stalls still piled up with hay. A black cat emerged from the darkness and meowed a welcome. For a barn cat, she was surprisingly friendly. She sidled up to Maryanne and rubbed her head against her ankles and then walked back into the darkness.

Maryanne followed the cat into a stall, where she sat down, drew her knees up, and cried like the day she'd left this place, twenty years before.

Daniel startled awake from out of a dream. Something wasn't right. He lay there a moment trying to get his bearings, and then he realized Joshua was crying.

Hard.

He slid from the bed, stepped into his jeans, and hurried downstairs. It was not quite dawn. The house was dark.

He turned on the lamp beside the couch and discovered Joshua howling in his bureau drawer. His little face was red with fury, and his hands were balled up.

"Maryanne?" Daniel called, and got no answer.

He picked up the baby, who continued to cry as Daniel put him up on his shoulder. "Maryanne?" Daniel called a little louder as he walked into the kitchen and switched on the light.

He saw the note on the table. He picked it up. His chest constricted, and his heart started racing. He'd driven her away just like he'd driven Julia away.

He knew his words had cut deeply last night, but he never thought she would leave. He'd made the same damn mistake.

How could she have abandoned both of them?

He felt like howling in harmony with the baby.

Instead, he rocked the baby a little bit back and forth and then looked that little face right in the eye. "We aren't going to let her go," he said. "So don't cry. I won't let her leave either one of us, you hear?"

The baby stopped crying. He didn't smile or anything, but he gave a couple of hiccups and looked at Daniel like he understood. He was a most remarkable baby, wasn't he?

"Okay, kid, you and I are going to have to go look for her. She couldn't have gotten too far." He went back into the living room and put the baby back in the drawer for a moment.

He stepped out onto the porch to take a look. Maybe she left tracks in the ice.

He found them, along the side of the driveway. If only he could use his car, he'd catch up with her fast. But the ice was thick on the road. And it would be madness to drive with an unsecured baby in the front seat. He was going to have to follow her tracks on foot.

He turned back toward the house. The eastern sky was turning from black to midnight blue, and there, hanging on the horizon, was the morning star.

It wasn't any kind of amazing or miraculous celestial display, just Venus rising in the east. But it shone so brightly that it pulled him out of his panic.

He stood there staring while it flickered in the early morning dark. He'd never stopped to think about how beautiful Venus looked on clear, crisp winter mornings like this.

The world was a beautiful place.

Miracles happened here every day.

And just like that, he knew where he'd find Maryanne. All he had to do was follow a bright light in the sky.

He hurried inside, bundled up the baby, and managed to figure out the baby carrier Maryanne had left for him. And then he made his way in her icy footsteps down the hill to Ridge Road.

When he turned right and walked on, the morning star was in front of him.

And when he got to the Carpenters' place, it almost

seemed that the star was right above the barn. And the door was open. A black cat wandered out into the yard and practically smiled at him. And even though she only said "meow," it was almost as if he heard the words, "What took you so long," inside his head.

The cat had abandoned her, too. For a long while, it had curled up beside Maryanne where she had collapsed after sobbing her heart out. Its defection put a punctuation mark on the state of her life.

She would never get over giving up Joshua. She wasn't entirely sure she was ever going to get over leaving Daniel. And that surprised the crap out of her.

She told herself that Daniel was a stranger, but the more she insisted on that, the more she knew it wasn't true. Somehow, she had connected with him through the miles that separated this place and Montgomery. She had been there in spirit as he'd grown up. He was the boy she'd invented. Only he was real.

And her heart insisted that this was true, even though her mind knew it couldn't be possible.

"I'm sorry."

Was she imagining his voice now? She pushed up from the hay.

No, Daniel was standing right there, wearing his cashmere coat and a baby carrier. He'd lost his loafers, though. Those boots on his feet looked like authentic farm boy attire. And the baby carrier didn't look out of place, either. A rush of relief spread through her, warming up her chilly hands and face and feet.

"You're sorry for what?" she said, brushing away the last few tears of her crying jag.

"For making you feel bad last night. I only did that because you pushed me away, and I'm so tired of being pushed away. Julia abandoned me when I needed her most. And I don't exactly understand why, but now I need *you*."

"You need me?"

"I want you, too. I mean, I want you in my life, Maryanne. I can't explain it but I know it's something that's meant to be. I almost feel like maybe I've been waiting for you. Only this morning I knew I couldn't wait anymore. I had to come find you."

"But I'm a screw-up," she said. "I don't have a college degree. I got myself pregnant. And now I'm homeless and broke. So you're a fool to want me in your life. And if you think I'm just going to take charity from some guy, you're crazy. My mother did that all the time, and it never made her happy. I want to make it on my own."

"I understand. I'm not giving charity. And I realize that you're going to need time to get back on your feet and figure things out. And I'm happy to wait. But I'm not letting you give Joshua away. And I'm not letting you run away from me, either."

She stood up. "You don't want Joshua?"

He blew out a breath. It formed a big cloud of steam. "I know we just met, but certainly you've figured out that I want a family. I've always wanted one. But I'm not about to take your baby. I want so much more than a baby. It's a package deal, Maryanne."

"But I'm not ready. And—"

"Look, first of all, encouraging women to give up their kids is not what I do. So my behavior last night was truly reprehensible. When I kissed you, it felt like something

I'd been waiting for all of my life. You, not the baby. I want to get to know *you*. I want to help *you*. And not just because it's what I do."

"What you do?"

"I told you I was an attorney. That's true. I used to be a corporate attorney back when I was married to Julia. But ever since Christopher, I...well, I just decided that I needed to do something more important. Julia didn't understand. She used to call me a do-gooder."

Maryanne's stomach double-clutched. He didn't seem to be the judgmental type. How could he be a do-gooder?

"So, what, you just go around doing good deeds or something?"

He laughed at her sarcasm. "No, not exactly. I gave up a very lucrative law practice to become a children's advocate. I work hard to keep families together. And I want to help you. All you need is some day care and a job to get back on your feet. There are loads of people right here in Last Chance who can help with that. Jenny is one of them. She's a good church woman, and she's starting a business. I'll bet she needs help at the new B&B.

"But the thing is, I don't want to be your advocate. I want to be your friend."

"Friend?" Maryanne whispered the word out loud. A friend was precisely what she wanted most of all. She wanted a friend like the boy next door. The one she had made up in her head.

Daniel took several steps toward her so that Maryanne had to look up to see his face. Dawn was breaking out, and his blue eyes looked so bright and earnest. His face was so kind, and he had this red-cheeked jolly kind of expression. It was definitely a Christmas kind of look.

"I didn't tell you this before," she whispered, allowing herself to give voice to the ridiculous notion that they *were* connected by something, maybe fate. "When my momma died in Montgomery, I told the authorities I had a grandma and grandpa in South Carolina, but no one ever looked for them. I just got handed over to the foster care system. I used to think about what it would be like living here. I used to wonder about the neighbors, you know. I used to think about being friends with the blond-haired boy next door.

"And the funny thing is, if someone had looked, maybe I would have come here to live and then . . ."

"I really would have been the boy next door." He completed her thought in a whisper.

They stared at one another for the longest moment as strange, miraculous possibilities unfolded.

"Come on. Let's go get some breakfast, and then maybe we can get the car seat out of your car and go find Jenny," he said.

A frisson of panic coursed through Maryanne. "But—"

He put his finger across her lips. His hands were surprisingly warm. "Hush, now. Jenny is a kindhearted woman who knows how to bake a mean apple pie. Her mother died not too long ago, and she truly believes she's alone in this world. Y'all are her family—the only family she's got left. You and Joshua are going to be the best Christmas present she's ever gotten. Trust me on this."

"I'm not good at trusting."

"I know. But we'll work on that." His hand cupped the back of her head, and he leaned down and gave her a soft, gentle, and surprisingly passionate kiss.

Just then the sun peeked over the horizon, and the

black cat meowed and wrapped herself around both of their legs. A rush of relief coursed through Maryanne. She threw her arms around Daniel's neck and hung on.

"Merry Christmas," he whispered against her lips. "I swear to you, Maryanne, this is going to be the first of many, many merry Christmases to come. For both of us."

Dear Reader,

I love Christmas. The gifts are nice, but it's the friends and family gathering, festive food eating, twinkly light stringing, holiday carol singing, and the Christmas tree decorating parts that get me going. I love that once a year an ordinary place is transformed into a magical, other-worldly one.

But I have another special reason for loving the Christmas season. Many years ago I got engaged to my wonderful husband on Christmas Eve. His parents always had their gift exchange on Christmas Eve and we were there, too. I'll always remember his father calling out my name and tossing me a box. He liked to throw the presents so you had to have good reflexes. I opened it while they all watched and there it was. My ring.

He'd already asked, and I'd already said yes, but that made it official when he put the ring on my finger. We were young and didn't have any money, but that was the beginning of our life together. Since then we have celebrated many Christmases together, first with our three children and now with our grandchildren.

I hope you enjoy HAVE YOURSELF A MESSY LITTLE CHRISTMAS!

Best wishes this holiday season,

Molly Cannon

To my beautiful mother, Helen. She always surrounded us with books of every kind, and so for me and my sisters reading was as necessary as breathing. What a wonderful year-round, lifelong gift. I love you, Moo.

Have Yourself a Messy Little Christmas

Molly Cannon

CHAPTER

1

What is it now?" Lincoln had been nose deep in client financial files when a jarring knock on the front door of his house interrupted his concentration. Things at his accounting firm were a little chaotic these days, so he'd been counting on a quiet evening at home to get some work done. He pushed away from his paper-covered dining room table, kicking assorted shoes and old mail out of his way. Opening the door he demanded, "What do you want?"

"Merry Christmas."

Lincoln glared at the woman on his front porch. Her cheerful holiday greeting didn't improve his mood. She was wearing a fur-trimmed Santa hat on top of her bouncy blond hair. Red jingle-bell earrings hung from her ears, making a light tinkling sound when she moved her head. The short red dress she wore skimmed her body invitingly, showing off a terrific pair of legs. Despite his irritation, he'd have to be in a coma not to notice that she was as cute as a bug. And sexy as hell. She smiled and her face lit up—all bright and eager to please. It made him suspicious, and he wondered what she was selling.

He crossed his arms. "Thanksgiving was three days ago. I haven't had time to finish my turkey leftovers. So, I'm afraid this is a no-Christmas zone until at least the middle of December." He didn't care if he sounded like the Grinch. As an accountant he'd seen too many of his clients spend beyond their means every year trying to "buy" a Merry Christmas for those they loved. He wanted no part of the crazy hype.

She nodded agreeably, causing her earrings to jingle-jangle like crazy. "Sir, let me just say that your position is completely understandable."

"Great. I'm glad you understand. Have a nice day." He stepped back and started to close the door, but she was too quick for him.

Her hand shot out, stopping him. She boldly pushed across the threshold and continued her campaign. "I couldn't agree more that the rampant early build-up to the Christmas season is an ever-growing problem."

His eyebrows shot up. "That's quite a speech. Yet here you are on my porch dressed like one of Santa's elves."

She smiled once again. "You're Lincoln Jones, right?"

"That would be me," he admitted cautiously.

"Great." She spread her arms wide and announced, "I'm your early present."

Okay. Now he got it. This was a joke. One of his friends thought it would be funny to send him a woman. They were probably hiding in the bushes to get his reaction. If so, they were in for a big disappointment. "Oh, really? Who sent you? Was it Jake?"

She shook her head. "I don't know anyone named Jake."

"Somebody from the office, then?" He needed to work on his stern boss demeanor if they thought they could get away with this.

She kept smiling and shaking her head, jingling the entire time. "No, your mother sent me. Your mother is Bitsy Jones, isn't she?"

That stopped him cold. "My mother? She sent me a woman?" He straightened, suddenly afraid she might be watching from the bushes.

"I'm not a woman. I'm a service." She held out a business card. "And she's paying for the whole thing."

He took the card warily. "My mother doesn't live here anymore, so if this is a scam you're out of luck." His parents had retired and moved to South Padre Island a few years ago. He'd moved out of his cramped apartment and had been living in the old family house since then.

She continued pushing her way past him and looked into the living room. "Oh my, I can see why she thought you needed me. This place is a mess."

In his opinion she seemed unnaturally delighted by this discovery. He looked around, seeing the place through her eyes, realizing she was right. Piles of newspapers and magazines were stacked here and there. Dishes covered the coffee table, not having made their way back to the kitchen. Shoes and jackets and a variety of clothing were scattered about haphazardly, landing wherever they'd been dropped. Defensively he declared, "I haven't had a chance to pick things up."

"Don't worry. That's perfectly fine." She seemed to be making mental notes, cataloging the depth and breadth of the sloppiness that lay before her.

He was right behind her as she walked farther into the

house. Finally, he'd had enough. "Hold on a minute. What exactly do you do? And what does it have to do with my mother?"

She turned around, holding out her hand for a hand-shake. "Sorry. I'm getting ahead of myself. I'm Dinah Mason, and I own *A Place for Everything*. I'm a professional organizer."

He ignored her outstretched hand. "A professional organizer? My mother stopped telling me when to clean my room a long time ago."

Her hand dropped to her side. "Isn't this her house?"

"Well, yes. My parents own the house, but I live here now, and it's my stuff."

"I understand that, and it's perfectly normal for everyone to get a little protective about their stuff. I promise to be gentle."

He glowered, hoping to get it through her head that nothing had been decided. "I haven't agreed to anything yet, lady."

Calmly she explained, "As I said, the name's Dinah. And maybe you should call your mother to put your mind at ease. Bitsy said she and your father are planning a trip home for the Christmas holidays, and she wanted me to pop in and do my magic. Get the house spruced up and decorated before they arrive. I promise I'll be out of your hair in no time."

His mother's implication that he couldn't handle things on his own cut him to the core. "Well, *Dinah*, she could have just asked me to do that. I can clean a house, you know. I do it every time they come to visit."

"That often?"

He suspected she was being sarcastic. "And on holidays I'm the one who has to climb up in the attic to drag down the Christmas decorations. If they weren't coming home this year I wouldn't even bother putting up a tree."

"Your mama said you don't like attics, but her main concern seemed to be you having your hands full with work right now."

Linc crossed his arms over his chest. "She *told* you I don't like attics?"

"She mentioned something about spiders. Nothing to be ashamed of." She grinned like she enjoyed the idea that they now shared a secret. "The bottom line, Lincoln— Can I call you Lincoln?—is that your mother doesn't want you to worry about any of this. Do you mind if I look around a bit more?" Without waiting for his answer she wandered off toward the dining room.

"Don't touch anything." He couldn't keep the panic from his voice as she approached the table. He let out an undignified yelp when she ignored him and picked up a file. He didn't want anyone barging in and touching his stuff. He breathed a sigh of relief when she moved it an inch to the left and put it back down, but that didn't stop him from hurrying over to block her from rifling through anything else. "I have everything exactly where I want it, so if you could stop."

"I apologize, but it is important that I understand as much as I can about a person's system before I begin to work with them."

In his haste to keep her at a safe distance, he hit a stack of forms with his hip. He closed his eyes and swallowed a curse as they tumbled to the ground, scattering across the floor. He looked around at the mess and with a growl started picking up the papers. "My system may look complicated, but it works just fine." He grabbed a page from her hand and grumbled, "Give me that and don't help anymore." In a nicer tone he added, "Please." He was doing his best to stay polite. Otherwise, he was sure his mother would hear about that, too. But God, this woman was entirely too pushy.

She held up both hands and backed away. "Okay. You win for now, but at least speak to your mother." She handed him another business card. "Unless I hear from you, I'll be back tomorrow morning. Nine o'clock." She headed toward the front door, but then paused. Turning around, she promised, "This is going to be lots of fun, Lincoln. You'll see."

With another of her irritating smiles she walked her cute little self out of the house, leaving him befuddled and fuming. He pulled his phone from his pocket and hit the button to call his mother. She answered on the second ring, but before he could ask her what was going on, she greeted him happily. "Hello, son. Let me guess. You've met Dinah."

"Bitsy Jones hired you?" Dinah's mother seemed impressed. "That's quite a feather in your cap, young lady. I can almost guarantee if she likes your work it will lead to other jobs."

"Thanks, Mom." Dinah sat with her mother at the kitchen table. They each sipped a margarita while her stepfather made his special enchiladas. This was their established pattern whenever they invited her over for dinner. He cooked. They drank and gabbed. "But I won't be working with her. I'll be working with her son Lincoln."

"Oh, he's such a nice young man. He comes into the

bank at least once a week. He's always so friendly and, I might add, awfully good looking, too." Sheila Wright was a manager at Everson Bank and Trust and had her pulse on the happenings around town.

It was true. The man was awfully handsome and yes, her heart had involuntarily taken a giant leap at the sight of him when he first opened his front door. But Dinah frowned and said, "I'll admit he's good looking, but he's been grumpy and disagreeable since the moment I met him."

Her stepfather Warren spoke up. "I'm sure you'll win him over."

"I hope so."

Dinah had moved from Dallas to Everson about a year ago when the company she'd worked at closed its doors. She'd worked as an accessory buyer for Loomis Fine Furniture, and she'd been good at her job, but it wasn't anything she was passionate about. She'd also left Adam, too. He'd been her boyfriend for several years, but they both knew the relationship wasn't heading anywhere, so the split was amicable and probably healthy, too. They'd kept dating out of habit longer than they should have, so nobody's heart had been broken when she moved away. In fact, they still kept in touch, and he'd been very supportive when she'd told him about the new business venture she was launching.

The idea for starting her own business was born when a friend hired her to organize her closet. Nothing made her happier than taking a mess and turning it into order, so turning her passion into a full-time job made sense. And since she'd been unemployed, the timing seemed perfect. Her mother convinced her to move to Everson, and her stepfather found a house she could afford to buy with payments lower than the rent on her loft in Dallas had been.

She'd gone around Everson's town square leaving her business cards everywhere. Things had started out a bit slow, but then Maple Antiques hired her to organize their inventory and that led to other jobs. And after she'd left cards at Binyon's Hardware store, she started getting loads of calls from people wanting help organizing their closets. Since then things had picked up even more, but as her mother said, this job for Bitsy Jones promised to be a real feather in her cap. So she had to do a good job. For that to happen, Lincoln needed to drop the Mr. Cranky act and get with the program.

Dinah showed up at Lincoln's house at nine the next morning, buzzing with anticipation. Just the idea of tackling a house like Lincoln's got all of her juices flowing. From what she'd seen yesterday this place was a genuine, unadulterated disaster. She felt like skipping with joy. Instead she rang the doorbell. And waited.

She listened for the sound of anyone moving around inside. Maybe he'd stood her up in protest. But Bitsy Jones had called her last night and assured her things were all set. She insisted that she'd set her son straight and promised he wouldn't give Dinah any more trouble. No matter what his mother said, it was clear that Lincoln Jones would be a hard nut to crack.

She knocked on the door this time. And waited again. Nothing. She'd finally given up and had one foot down the porch steps when the door flew open behind her.

"Hey, sorry. I was trying to clean up a little before you got here." Lincoln's tall frame filled the doorway. His shirt sleeves were rolled up, showing off his strong fore-arms. He had a dirty plate in one hand and a pillow in the other. A dish towel was thrown over one shoulder and a smear of dirt graced his cheek. None of that hid the fact that he was an attractive man.

Very attractive. He was tall and athletic looking. With dark wavy hair. And those deep dark eyes that might just twinkle if he ever bothered to smile. The man was scrumptious. Just looking at him made her toes curl and her tummy act all wobbly. It had been a long time since she'd had such a strong physical reaction to a man. Mercy, she couldn't afford to get distracted by his looks. She needed to remember he was a client, not a potential date.

"Where's your Santa elf get-up?" he asked as she hurried back across the porch.

She glanced down at her jeans and sensible T-shirt. "I don't work in that outfit. It's only to make the gift presentation festive."

He lifted one eyebrow. "I guess you dress up like a bunny rabbit at Easter time."

She laughed. "I haven't thought about it. Maybe I'll have to get a pair of bunny ears."

He continued staring down at her from his height advantage, blocking entrance into the house. "Oh, I think you should go for the whole shebang. I picture a big fuzzy rabbit outfit with floppy ears. It would be cute."

She was certain he was making fun of her, but she tried not to react. "Okay. Can I come in now?" She felt heat flood her cheeks as he openly studied her.

"Oh, sure." He stepped aside so she could enter.

She took the pillow he was holding. "You really didn't need to clean. I'll take care of everything. In fact, if I see

the way you normally operate I can come up with an organizational program designed specifically for your needs."

"Thanks, Dinah, but I don't want an organizational
program. All I want is to clean the house, get the dang
Christmas decorations up, and make my mother happy."

"Yes, sir. You're the boss."

"Am I?" He didn't sound like he believed her.

"Well, unless your mother gives me a conflicting
directive. She is the one paying me, so . . ."

"That's what I thought. So, where do you want to
start?"

Her eyes darted around, taking stock of all the proj-
ects to tackle. "I need to make some notes first, and then I
promise I'll consult with you before I start tossing things
willy-nilly onto the trash heap."

He glared. "Let's get something straight. Nothing is
going willy-nilly onto any trash heap."

"Relax. I was kidding. You get to make those decisions. In the meantime, just go about your business. Pretend I'm not here."

He backed away, looking like he wasn't at all sure he
should trust her. "I'll be in the dining room working if you
need anything."

"Okay. I'll start in the living room since that's where
the tree will be. Your mother filled me in on her general
decorating scheme."

"Whatever." He grunted and disappeared into the dining room.

She walked into the front room and looked around.
The decor looked like it dated from the seventies. A
plaid sofa and a leather recliner flanked a scarred coffee
table. Despite the outdated furniture the room conveyed

a homey feel. The pictures on the walls, the candles on the television, the hand-embroidered pillows scattered about. She sat down, letting the ambience sink into her skin, imagining it full of people who lived, laughed, and loved together. She didn't know this family, and her first encounter with Lincoln Jones certainly hadn't been friendly, but she had a talent for reading spaces. She'd bet her bottom dollar that she wasn't wrong about this one.

Walking back into the dining room she observed Lincoln hard at work. He was wearing old jeans and a white button-down shirt rolled up at the wrists. He had his head bent over his keyboard and a pair of black framed glasses set on his forehead. She wondered how often he lost those. She smiled thinking she could help him with that, too, if he'd let her.

"Real or artificial?" she asked.

Startled, he looked up and stared at her as if he was trying to place her. His glasses slipped down onto his nose. He adjusted them and asked, "Sorry? What did you say?"

"I was asking about the Christmas tree. Does your family do real or artificial? It makes a difference in my timetable."

He pushed back from the table. "There is an artificial one up in the attic, but since I'm in charge I think we'll go with a real one this year."

"So you do have a little Christmas spirit after all. Or is that just your way of avoiding the attic?" From the scowl on his face she probably shouldn't have mentioned the attic.

"Well, since that's where the decorations are stored, I'll still have to get them down either way, so can we cool it with the attic remarks?"

"Sorry." It probably wasn't in her best interest to provoke him. "So, a real tree it is. That's all I needed to know. I'm moving on to the kitchen."

He made a face. "It's kind of a mess. I didn't get around to cleaning in there. I'll pay you a bonus if you don't tell my mother how bad it is."

She laughed and tried to reassure him. "I'm sure I've seen worse."

He sat back down and was engrossed in his work before she made it out the door.

The kitchen wasn't as bad as she'd feared. The counters were covered with dirty dishes and empty frozen dinner packages. A large trash bag and a few loads in the dishwasher would take care of the biggest problems. She opened the refrigerator and didn't see anything green growing inside; the stove top was clean, but the pantry could use a bit of organizing. Getting the kitchen ready for Bitsy's return would be a simple chore.

She left the kitchen and, with notebook in hand, wandered from room to room. Mostly it was the normal chaos she commonly found among the organizationally challenged. Clothes dropped on every surface. Mail and newspapers tossed about. Odds and ends stashed in places for no apparent reason. Judging by the pile by the front door Lincoln seemed to kick his shoes off the minute he walked into the house. And socks showed up in all sorts of strange places.

She opened a door and found a girl's bedroom, complete with a flowery bedspread and stuffed animals. Linc's sister's old bedroom. Behind another door she found a room that contained weight equipment. Setting up a home office had been one of her goals since she'd found

him working at the dining room table. He'd need a dedicated work space, especially with his family gathering for
the holidays. This room would do nicely. A desk would
fit on the far wall. She moved to the closet and just as she
put her hand on the doorknob Lincoln's voice startled her.

"What are you doing? Stay out of there."

She must have jumped a mile and something in his
voice made her feel guilty. Which was silly. Looking
around was a requirement of the job. "You scared the living daylights out of me. I'm checking out available storage space. "

"Well, this room is fine the way it is." Standing too
close, he placed his body between her and the closet in
question.

"I'm thinking we could set up a home office in here so
you wouldn't have to use the dining room table. Once your
folks get home I assume it will be needed for family meals."

He looked around the room. "You know, that makes
a lot of sense. You could help me do that?" This was the
first time he'd shown any real interest in what she was trying to accomplish.

"Sure. Almost anything will work for a desk, but we
should find a really good office chair. Those dining room
chairs have to be killing your back." She found pleasure
in attempting to anticipate his needs. It was the best part
of her job.

"I have an extra chair at the office and there is an old
desk in the garage. I don't know why I didn't think of this
before." He was actually smiling at her.

"Thinking is what your mother hired me to do." She
walked back toward the closet. "You can store extra office
supplies in here."

Again he blocked her path. "That's okay. I'll bring home what I need from the office."

Clearly he was determined to keep her from opening that closet door. There was something he didn't want her to see, and he was entitled to his privacy. Now her curiosity was piqued, but she waved her hand like it didn't matter and said, "Well, let's go look at that desk."

Linc led the way to the garage. In the far back corner, buried under a stack of boxes, was a walnut desk. He uncovered it and pulled it out to get a good look. "This should work. It's my grandfather's old desk."

Dinah walked around it, pulling open drawers. "It's beautiful. You'll never want to work at the dining room table again."

He smiled. "You're right. Thanks for thinking of this, Dinah."

They dusted it off and together moved it into the weight room.

"I don't know about you, but I'm starving. Can I offer you a sandwich?" Linc asked.

"Oh thanks, but I brought my own lunch."

They sat at the kitchen table. She ate her peanut butter sandwich and drank bottled water. Lincoln ate ham and cheese and drank soda, feeling almost cordial toward her. After lunch he ran to his office and got the chair, and in no time his home office was set up and ready to use.

He carried a stack of folders from the dining room table to his new desk and beamed. "Thank you, Dinah. I don't know what my mother is paying you, but you more than earned your money with this idea."

"I'm glad you like it." She looked at her watch. "I

better go now. I'm meeting some friends to go caroling. You're welcome to join us."

"Thanks, but I'll pass." He leaned against his new desk and crossed his arms across his chest.

She smiled at him indulgently. "Of course, I forgot you don't like Christmas."

"I like Christmas," he insisted.

She shook her head like she didn't believe him. "See you in the morning."

"Okay. I'll see you then." He realized he'd enjoyed the time they'd spent today working hand in hand. It was hard to believe, but he was sort of sorry to see her go.

CHAPTER

2

And then she said, 'This box is for things you want to keep. This box is for things you want to give away. And this box is for everything you want to throw away.'" Linc mimicked Dinah's voice as he tried to explain to his friend Jake what horror his mother had unleashed upon him. In his own voice he added, "Heavy emphasis on the 'throw away' part. We had a tug-of-war over my lucky boxer shorts. She said they should be turned into dust rags. I'll be fortunate if I have a spare T-shirt to call my own by the time she's through."

It had been almost a week since Dinah first showed up on his porch in that Santa outfit. Gone were the bouncy blond curls and the body-hugging dress. Now she showed up every morning with her hair pulled back into a no-nonsense ponytail, wearing pressed work clothes and butt-ugly work boots. After the first day when they'd gotten his home office set up, she'd been relentless—sorting, rooting through, and in general turning his house upside down. Oh, she asked his opinion occasionally, but for the most part he felt like he'd run into a buzz saw.

"Is she cute?" Jake asked.

Linc had asked Jake to meet him after work at Romeo's Pizza. He figured they could have a beer while he vented, but now he gave his friend a hard look. "Forget it. She's not your type."

Jake tipped his chair back. "From your description I'd say she's not your type, either. Easygoing, messy Linc saddled with a neat freak. That's a good one."

"Very funny."

"All I know is I haven't seen you this worked up over a woman since you dated Polly May Olsen. And that was quite a while ago, buddy."

"Please. Polly May turned out to be a crazy woman. I was the happiest man alive when she married Allen Bond and moved to Fort Worth."

He'd dodged a bullet with that lady. She was jealous and clingy and possessive and everything he hated. Since his relationship with her had ended he'd made a point of keeping things casual when it came to dating. And no one in particular had grabbed his attention lately.

Jake nodded. "But Dinah is all you've talked about tonight."

Linc's beer bottle hit the table with a little more force than necessary. "You're missing the whole point. I'm not worked up over *her*. I'm worked up over having someone come in and invade my space. I would have gotten the house cleaned up before Mom and Dad came home."

"You mean you would have called Marla Jean and bribed your poor sister into doing the work for you. Linc, I hate to be the one to break it to you, but you're a total slob."

Linc glared, knowing Jake was right. "What's wrong

with expecting my sister to lend a hand? And whose side are you on, anyway?"

"Let me think about that. Wait. I know. I'm on your mother's side." Jake had grown up across the street from Linc and considered Bitsy a second mother. "I'm no dummy."

"Some friend you are."

"What's the big deal? This Dinah person comes in and gets the house ready for your mother's approval and since you helped, you look like the best son ever. And after that you never have to see Miss Neatnik again. Everybody's happy."

Linc peeled the label from his beer bottle with his thumb. He wanted to hold on to his resentment, but it was getting harder to do. It pained him to admit that Dinah had performed wonders in a short amount of time. Not only that, but he'd started looking forward to her visits. It sounded corny, but her sunny personality brightened his day. Jake didn't need to know that, though. He'd never hear the end of it.

With a grumble he relented. "Okay. You're right." He looked at his watch and then glanced at the front door.

"Do you have to be somewhere?"

"Dinah's meeting me here in a while." He ignored Jake's knowing smile.

"Interesting. I'll get to see what all the fuss is about."

"There's no fuss. We are going next door to pick out a Christmas tree."

"Her services include helping you buy a tree? I can't believe you're complaining." Jake looked up and his eyes widened appreciatively at the blond woman approaching their table.

Without preamble she asked Jake, "What's he complaining about now?"

Linc stood up quickly. "Hey, Dinah. I didn't see you come in."

Jake stood up, too. "Well, hello, Dinah. I'm Jake, and this guy's been singing your praises all night long."

"Really?" Dinah looked at Linc doubtfully, and then turned back to Jake. "It's nice to meet you. Linc's mentioned your name several times."

"Do me a favor. Don't believe everything he says."

Linc scowled as the two seemed to hit it off right away, almost flirting, acting like he wasn't standing right there beside them.

Dinah leaned toward Jake like they were co-conspirators. "Well, don't believe what he says about me, either. He's still in the resistant phase of this operation. It'll take me a while to soften him up."

Jake smiled and winked. "You have your hands full. That's for sure."

Linc interrupted. "If you two are through having fun at my expense, we should get going. We don't want to wait until the trees are all picked over. Jake, old buddy, I'll let you pick up the tab this time."

Jake stuck his hands in his front pockets and rocked back on his heels. "No problem, old buddy. It was nice to meet you, Dinah."

"Same here." She handed him one of her cards. "Just in case you know anyone who needs a hand getting organized."

"Thanks. You two have fun." He winked at Linc and sat down to finish his beer.

Linc hustled her out the door, feeling cranky after her

encounter with Jake. His friend was a good-looking man who could charm a woman with a single glance. Linc usually found his effect on women amusing, but tonight it hit all the wrong notes.

"So, were you complaining about me?" she asked.

"It would be more accurate to say I was complaining about my mother."

She laughed. "That's very diplomatic," she said as they walked out into the warm December night. "Your friend seems nice."

"Jake's a great guy." His tone was at odds with his words, though. She looked perplexed, so he decided to lighten up. "Sorry. All these twinkling lights and carols are getting on my nerves."

"You really don't like Christmas, do you?"

"I never said that." He paused before confessing, "I've just never picked out a tree before."

"I promise it'll be painless." She took his arm and pulled him the short distance to the tree lot.

Ginger's Christmas Trees looked like a winter wonderland. Like the rest of the town square, it was decorated with a million twinkle lights. Fake snowflakes swayed in the breeze and dangled overhead. Piped-in Christmas music reminded shoppers of the season, and the fragrant smell of evergreens filled the air. Trees of every shape and size stood inside the roped-off area, all waiting to be taken home by some loving family.

"Do you like a tall tree?" Dinah took a few steps inside the entrance.

"I guess so. Tall is good. But I don't want it to be all scrawny, either." He picked up a tree and quickly rejected it when he saw the bare spot on one side.

"Here's a nice one." Dinah picked up a spruce and waited for his approval.

He made a face and shook his head.

She wandered over to the flocked trees. "How about purple? Or blue? Oh, look. Pale pink. How about one of these?"

"You're kidding. What self-respecting person would buy a tree covered in fake purple snow? Another perfect example of what's wrong with Christmas."

She laughed. "Sorry. I didn't mean to get you started."

"We are going for a plain old regular green tree. With multicolored lights and icicles. I want the kind of tree we had when I was a kid."

"So, what have you had the last few years?"

"That fake thing in the attic. Mom uses all white decorations, but since she decided to spring this on me I'm going to do the tree my way. I wonder if the old ornaments we had when we were kids are still in the attic."

"And I thought you planned to avoid the attic at all costs."

Before he could answer, one of the lot attendants approached them. Monty Goreville was in his mid-seventies, tough as an old rooster, and somewhere along the line most of his teeth had gone missing. "Hey, Linc, can I help you find a tree?" He graced Dinah with his toothless smile.

"Hey, Monty, we're just looking around." At that moment Linc spotted a tree across the way. "Hold on. I think I see a possibility now." He took off and grabbed the tree, turning it around, checking for bad spots. "This is it," he crowed while doing a little jig.

Dinah smiled like he'd found the golden egg at a goose

convention. He'd begun to notice that her smile did funny things to his insides. It didn't make sense. This short, blond, pushy woman was not his type at all, but she aimed that smile in his direction and he felt the impact all the way down to his toes and back again.

"That is a great tree, Lincoln." She seemed tickled by his success, and it was enough to make him puff up even more.

"We'll take this one, Monty."

Monty picked up the tree and looked at it approvingly. "That there's a Douglas fir, and I'm willin' to bet you found one of the best trees on the lot."

Dinah patted Linc on the arm. "Not bad for your first tree-buying adventure."

"Heck, what can I say? I'm a man with many talents." The touch of her hand on his arm spread a kind of bliss through his chest, and for a moment he got lost looking into her green eyes. Her mouth suddenly seemed perfect for kissing. He leaned in, giving in to the overpowering need to taste her lush pink lips.

Monty cleared his throat to get their attention and the spell was broken. Linc took a deep breath and stepped back.

Monty grinned. "So, kids, if you'll follow me over to the sales counter."

"Thanks, Monty." Linc composed himself as he approached the tall counter. "Evening, Ginger."

"Hi, Linc." Ginger took the tree tag from Monty and rang up the tree on the old-fashioned cash register. "Is this your new girl?" Ginger smiled at Dinah like they were best friends. "I'd heard tell you were squiring some cute blonde all over town."

Lincoln laughed sheepishly and made introductions. "Ginger, this is Dinah Mason. She's my organizational expert. A present from my mom."

Ginger's eyes widened as if she'd never heard of such a thing. As if "organizational" was code for something else, but she nodded her head sagely. "Well, that's real nice. Tell your folks I said hi."

Monty loaded up the tree in the back of Linc's truck. "You're ready to go, and I threw in a bunch of mistletoe for luck." With another wink aimed at Dinah, he added, "Ya'll have a Merry Christmas now." Then he scooted off to help another customer.

"I'll get the tree up in its stand tonight," Linc said. "Then it'll be all ready to decorate by the time you get to the house tomorrow. Does that sound okay?"

"Sounds good. I have to get home anyway and bake cookies for a cookie exchange." Dinah stopped by her car.

"Another one of your never-ending holiday activities?"

She smiled that sunny smile and his world tilted once more. It was all he could do not to walk over and pull her against his body, kiss her, finish what he'd almost started a few moments ago.

She got into her car. "If you're nice I'll bring you a cookie. Good night, Lincoln."

Linc stood watching her taillights disappear down the road. Then he climbed into his truck and headed home. Instead of being annoyed with his mother, he thought about how much he'd enjoyed picking out a tree with Dinah. It felt domesticated, and couple-ish, and all the things that usually sent him running from a woman like his pants were on fire. Tonight, though, the idea hadn't scared him the way it usually did, and he didn't know what to make of the situation. He had to admit he found her awfully attractive. Hell, he'd almost kissed her in a very public place. Maybe it was just that he hadn't gone out with anyone in a serious way that mattered for a long time.

But he couldn't imagine getting involved with someone like Dinah. She was prim and precise, and she'd want to change everything about him. Regulate, smooth down, and even up every jagged corner of his life. He enjoyed his laid-back—and okay, *messy*—lifestyle just the way it was, and no cute blonde with green eyes and legs that went on forever was going to convince him he needed to change. No way, no how. Not in a million years. But he still caught himself humming "Jingle Bells" all the way home.

Dinah unlocked her front door and walked inside. She kicked off her shoes and dropped her purse on the floor where she stood. Lately, she found her orderly thoughts scattered in all directions, and Lincoln Jones was to blame. She wasn't going to sugarcoat it. The man scrambled her brain, and when you were in her line of work a scrambled brain was a real disadvantage.

Goodness, she needed to pull herself together. She picked up her purse and placed it on the shelf by the front door designated for that purpose and then picked up her shoes and carried them into her bedroom, tucking them inside the closet. Putting on her slippers, she walked out to her kitchen and found a pasta dinner in the freezer.

She tapped her foot impatiently, watching her food turn around and around in the microwave. Lincoln had looked like a little kid when he found that tree. It was a great tree, too. Tall and splendid like the man who'd picked it out. Okay, maybe splendid was too poetic. But he was funny and opinionated and sexy as all get-out.

She was finding too much pleasure watching him while he worked. He was so intense, so focused, his concentration so complete, he didn't have time for worrying about silly ideas like putting things in proper places.

With a dreamy sigh she wondered what it would feel like to have that concentration focused on her. If he ever really touched her she might shatter to a million pieces. Lordy, the simple brush of his hand against hers set her nerves to tingling. And tonight, for just a moment, when he'd looked deeply into her eyes at Ginger's, she'd been able to imagine being wrapped in his arms, his mouth crashing down on hers. But the moment passed, thankfully, before she embarrassed herself. Gad, she'd been on the verge of grabbing him and kissing the living stuffing out of him. She really needed to get a hold of herself. This job was too important. A little decorum was in order. Tomorrow she promised herself to act professionally at all times. Mooning over Lincoln was officially forbidden. At least during working hours.

CHAPTER

3

Linc hated spiders. Give him a snake, or a rat, or a charging lion, and he'd be just fine. But an itty-bitty spider turned his spine to jelly. He shuddered as he crawled farther into the attic. He hadn't seen any spiders. Not yet, anyway, but there was plenty of evidence that they were up there lurking. Spiderwebs stretched across the low beams, grabbing at his face and hair. He batted them away and moved forward until he could reach the bin in the far corner. Tucked away behind all of the white-themed decorations his mother had used for the last few years was the one he was looking for. He pulled it toward the attic stairway opening. Something scurried across his path and he let out a mild yelp. He took a breath and slid down the stairs like they'd been greased with shortening.

Dinah was waiting, standing in the garage at the bottom of the ladder ready to help with whatever he found. "Is everything okay? I thought I heard you scream."

"That was a victory cry." He carried the bin to the living room.

"Oh, you found the ornaments." She hurried after him.

He'd stayed up late getting the tree in its stand, and then he'd hung the mistletoe from the entryway light, hoping he might catch Dinah standing beneath it before the day was over.

Then he'd gone to bed and dreamed of Dinah. He'd dreamed this was their house, and their tree, and after it was decorated they made love, rolling in the fallen needles scattered across the floor. In the middle of making love, Dinah had stopped and started making different piles for the needles, deciding which they should keep or throw away. He woke in a sweat.

He'd almost kissed her at the tree lot. It had been a close call. She'd looked so pleased with him and the tree, but Monty interrupted them, or he might not have remembered that he was a client, and so he shouldn't take it personally if she gazed at him approvingly with those sparkly green eyes.

He opened the bin and there they were: the ornaments of his childhood. Colored glass bulbs. Salt dough ornaments made by his mother. His sister's ornaments made from yarn and popsicle sticks. And down in the bottom, one he'd made in school.

"They're wonderful," Dinah said. "I bet your mother will love seeing these again."

"I hope so. I stopped at the drug store last night and bought new lights. Oh, and look what I found." He triumphantly held up a box.

She didn't look impressed. "What's that?"

"Icicles. I bought ten boxes. I think that should be enough. Once everything else is on the tree we'll throw these on last."

"Throw?" She grimaced. "Don't you think we should place them strategically?"

He shook his head. "Absolutely not. Don't even think about it. You take a handful and toss. Wherever they land that's where they stay."

She looked horrified now. "But they'll be all clumped and tangled."

He laughed. "You should see your face. Believe me, it'll be fun."

She didn't sound like she was buying it. "It's your tree. I'll do my best to keep my opinion to myself."

Linc grinned as if he'd won a major battle. "I'll get started on the lights."

"I'll sort the ornaments while you do that."

"Okay." They worked for a while in silence and then he said, "I'm surprised we've never met before. Did you grow up in Everson?"

"No, I moved here last year. My mom and stepdad live here. You probably know them. Sheila and Warren Wright. My mother works at the bank. My stepdad sells real estate."

"Oh sure, I know Sheila. So, is Mason your married name?" He was being about as subtle as a sledgehammer.

She looked confused. "My what? Oh, no. I'm not married."

That was good to know. "What about a boyfriend?" He might as well go for broke.

She laughed. "I'm not married, and I don't have a boyfriend. I've been too busy getting my business going to have time for anything like that. Does that answer all your questions?"

He shrugged. "I don't mean to be nosey. I'm just trying

to get to know you better. You've gotten to dig through my drawers and I hardly know anything about you."

"So, let me ask you a question," she said.

"I don't have a girlfriend, either," he said quickly.

She laughed. "That's not what I was going to ask."

He grinned. "Sorry. What's the question?"

"What do you do for fun? I can usually get a hint when I work with someone's space, but with you I don't have a clue."

"Working is fun for me. I guess that's hard for some people to understand."

She nodded her head eagerly. "I do understand. Nothing makes me happier than taking someplace that's a total wreck and transforming it into a space that operates efficiently."

He smiled. "I feel the same way about numbers. Someone gives me their books and a box of receipts, and I'm in heaven." He'd never explained that feeling to anyone before.

Her smile was sweet when she said, "We sort of do the same thing, then."

"When you put it that way, I guess we do."

Before long the lights were in place, and they worked as a team getting the decorations spread out evenly.

"Which one of these ornaments is yours?" she asked.

He took a funny-looking Santa Claus from the tree. "I made this in my third grade art class."

Santa was made out of paper plates and construction paper. His hat was folded and bent, his beard was shaped from the rippled edge of the plate, and his button nose was falling off. Linc studied it critically, thinking it was pretty good for third grade. "I do my best work in construction paper and glue."

"It deserves a place of honor, for sure," she said solemnly. She reached out to take it from him and her fingers brushed his. He stopped short. It was impossible to ignore the electrical charge that zipped between them. If she'd been any other woman he wouldn't have hesitated. He would have pulled her into his arms, crushing the silly ornament between their bodies, and kissing her right then and there.

She smiled invitingly and her lips parted a bit, enough so he could feel her soft breath on his cheek. Her eyes softened to a leaf green, and he felt his caution crumble and transform into a maddening urgency. He let the ornament fall to the ground.

Then he was kissing her. She tasted like peppermint tea and smelled like cinnamon and pine needles. Her body melded against his, her breasts pressing against his chest. He wrapped both arms around her like he was claiming something rare and long lost. His fingers tangled in her hair, pulling it from that infernal ponytail. Her mouth opened under his and while their tongues dueled, her hands roamed across his back. It wasn't enough. Without another thought, he picked her up and headed down the hall.

They landed on his bed, mouths fused, arms and legs intertwined. There was nothing tidy about the way she got him out of his clothes. She tore his shirt open, and one button popped off and rolled across the floor. His T-shirt followed, landing on the chair beside the bed. She tossed his shoes across the room, knocking a candle off the dresser.

"Oops." She laughed, and he captured the sound, kissing her more deeply than before. He unfastened his pants and she pushed them down his legs before dumping them on the floor.

His hands made quick work of her T-shirt and bra, and the sight of her bare breasts made him still for a moment.

"You're beautiful," he whispered.

"So are you," she told him quietly. Then she grinned and kicked off her shoes so he could remove her jeans and underwear. He pulled her naked body against his and held her tenderly. For the first time, he felt he was exactly where he belonged. Here, with Dinah in his arms. And then the passion washing through his body threatened to sweep him away. He worshipped her body with his mouth and hands, kissing, licking, taking the time to explore every inch of her. Her hands seemed to be everywhere, driving him crazy, touching him with an urgency that threatened to break his control. When he finally pushed inside her it was all he could do to move slowly, to not rush, and to make sure she was right there with him as they reached the crest and rode it together. Slowly, reluctantly, he floated back to earth.

He gathered her close, kissing her, pulling a blanket up to cover them both. Her head nestled against his shoulder, and he thought he would be happy if she stayed there for the next hundred years.

Dinah stretched, reveling in the feel of Lincoln's body next to hers. Her fingers traced the muscles of his chest, down to his flat stomach. She felt him shiver before rolling her underneath him.

"Are you trying to start trouble?" he asked huskily.

She kissed his neck. "Oh, believe me, it's no trouble at all."

He nuzzled the tops of her breasts. "In that case don't let me stop you."

Her hands traveled down his back, down to the firm cheeks of his rear end and up again. She could feel him hardening against her thigh and moved against him, urging him on, welcoming every touch, longing for more. She'd never felt so at ease with a man, while at the same time burning white hot from even the smallest contact. It was glorious. Linc's hand moved to her breast, rolling her nipple between his fingers before sucking it into his mouth. She arched her back, wanting more.

The house phone rang and the shrill noise made them pause. Linc lifted his head and smiled. "I'm going to ignore it."

She smiled, too. "Good idea."

He kissed her and the message machine came on. Dinah froze when Bitsy Jones's voice floated through the room.

"Hello, Lincoln. This is your mother. I hope you aren't giving Dinah a hard time."

Dinah scooted out from under him.

"I wanted you to know we will be leaving on Saturday morning to drive home, and I can't wait to see what she's done to the place. Give me a call when you have time. Bye."

Dinah sat up in bed, grabbing the blanket and pulling it up to cover her body. She felt as if a bucket of cold water had been dumped on her head. How had she let this happen? Bitsy, the woman who'd hired her, was calling her son while Dinah lounged buck naked on his bed. She'd vowed to remain professional, and yet one kiss from Lincoln and she'd practically dragged him down the hall, stripped him bare, and had her way with him.

Lincoln sat up beside her. "Sorry about the interruption. Now where were we?"

Dinah scooted to the edge of the bed, looking around for her scattered clothes. "We were nowhere. I don't know what I was thinking, but this should have never happened."

"What do you mean? Dinah, I'm glad it happened."

She found her T-shirt and pulled it over her head. "Lincoln, I was hired by your mother to do a job, not cavort around with you in the middle of the day." She found her jeans and stuffed her legs into them, not bothering with underwear. She plucked her bra from the nightstand and picked her underwear and shoes up from the floor. "I apologize for my unprofessional behavior. It won't happen again."

Linc stood up. "Dinah, wait." But she was already heading toward the door. He wrapped the sheet around his body and followed her to the front door. "Can't we talk about this?"

"There isn't anything to say. We're through with the tree, and I have other clients I need to check on." Grabbing her purse and jacket she walked barefoot out onto the front porch.

He walked out in just his sheet. "But we haven't done the icicles yet. Don't go."

"Feel free to toss them to your heart's content."

He touched her arm. "I'm so sorry my mother called when she did."

She moved away from him and smiled one of those plastic smiles that never reached her eyes. "It's a good thing she did. As I said, that should have never happened." She left without giving him a second glance.

"Dinah, please."

She could hear the frustration in his voice, but she hurried to her car feeling like the biggest kind of fool.

Dinah drove down the street five miles over the speed limit. For her that was reckless in the extreme. So much for her vow to act professionally. Normally, she wasn't a line crosser, but since she'd met Lincoln Jones she'd had to constantly remind herself there were lines she shouldn't cross. Like the one about not getting involved with a client. But had she listened? No. Like a fool she'd fallen into his bed without an ounce of resistance.

Dinah had told herself his mother was the client, not him, so it was okay to flirt. She'd convinced herself because she liked him and wanted to kiss him with every fiber in her being. When he leaned toward her, her heart started singing "Joy to the World" complete with bells, whistles, and three-part harmony. Just thinking of how he'd rolled her under his big muscular body swamped her with desire all over again. Damn the man.

Her work at the house was finished. The tree had been the last thing on her list. She had no reason to see Lincoln again, so that was the end of the story. The Jones family would have a wonderful Christmas, and she could rest easy knowing she'd helped.

Who was she kidding? She was going to have a miserable Christmas thinking nonstop about Lincoln Jones. Maybe she would take her mother up on her offer to join them on a skiing trip for the holidays.

CHAPTER

4

This is Dinah Mason. I'm away from my phone. Leave a message at the beep."

"Dinah. This is Linc. I could use your help. Please call me. Thanks. Bye."

He sat at the counter at the Rise N Shine staring at his phone. It was the third message he'd left in the last week. He wanted to tell her he was sorry for being such an insensitive jerk, but he didn't want to do it over the phone. Instead he left a message asking whether he should store his wire whisks in the utensil drawer or in the crock on the counter. He didn't give a hang where the damn whisks should go, but he'd assumed she would have a firm opinion. Apparently not, since she never called him back.

Then he'd called a second time and asked about alphabetizing his bookshelf. Did books starting with 'A' and 'The' go under A and T or the next word in the title? He wanted to do it properly, but she didn't seem to care about that, either.

Today's call had been a general, all-purpose cry for

help. If the last calls were any indication she would ignore that, too, but he couldn't help himself. He didn't care that his excuses for talking to her were flimsy.

Who could have guessed he'd become so accustomed to having her around? Hearing her voice, watching her laugh, seeing her fussing over the next project. He missed her arrival at his door every morning at nine on the dot. She'd greet him with a sunny smile and that tidy ponytail, and everything would seem right in his world.

But then he'd blown it. He'd dragged her to bed, plowing past all boundaries, and now she wouldn't give him the time of day. And who could blame her? But he wanted to apologize and, if she'd give him the chance, tell her he was nuts about her.

"How's your lunch, Linc? You've hardly taken a bite. That's not like you, son."

He looked up and Bertie, the diner's owner, stood in front of him. "Hi, Bertie. The food's fine. I just have things on my mind."

"Can I help?" Linc knew Bertie was always on the prowl for good gossip. But she also knew everyone in town.

"Not unless you know where Dinah Mason lives."

"Of course I do. She lives over on Ridgeway in a nice little house her stepdad found for her. I figured you knew since you were squiring her all around town last week. Everyone says you make a cute couple."

He scowled. "I don't think she agrees. I haven't been able to get a hold of her in the last few days."

"Is she back from that ski trip yet?"

He straightened. "She went skiing?"

Bertie nodded. "They went to Colorado, I think."

"Oh. I didn't realize. Thanks for letting me know." He was instantly jealous, wondering who the hell she'd gone away with. Damn it all. Someone as bubbly and bright and pretty as Dinah probably had to fight men off with a stick. That explained why she wasn't answering his calls. She had better things to do.

He paid his bill and walked out of the diner. His parents would be getting into town that afternoon and the holiday festivities would begin in earnest. If only he could stop thinking about Dinah and whoever the hell she was with in Colorado.

Dinah had probably replayed her messages at least ten times. At least the three from Lincoln. Her heart skipped a beat when she first saw his name, but they were calls asking for help. Organizing help. Nothing personal. He didn't even mention the fact that she'd jumped his bones last time she'd seen him.

And that would be a good thing if she wasn't so dejected. She'd spent the whole time in Colorado thinking about him. And not just about the things he'd done to her in bed. The sex had been spectacular, but she also missed the days before that when they'd spent hours discussing every subject under the sun. And he made her laugh like no one else. To her amazement, she'd come to care for him in ways she couldn't have predicted. She missed him. It was as simple as that.

But she wasn't ready to talk to Linc yet. Not about mundane ordinary things like alphabetizing his books. Thankfully, she had plans for the evening that would keep her occupied. Her friends were going caroling again, this time to Everson General Hospital, spreading cheer to those stuck in the hospital during the holidays. She changed into jeans and a red sweater, plunked on her Santa hat, and headed out to meet her friends.

It was Christmas Eve and despite the mess of things he'd made with Dinah, Linc was enjoying having his folks at home. His father had helped him finish putting up the outdoor lights on the house. They'd wrapped the porch rails with garlands and decorated the front door with a fresh wreath. The tree gleamed like a jewel in the front window. It officially looked decked out and ready for the holidays. Inside the house his sister Marla Jean was helping his mother prepare food for the next day's holiday feast. Pies and cakes of all sorts sat cooling on the kitchen counters. He wandered in and tried to sneak a bite. His mother shooed him away, but it was clear she enjoyed his attempt.

"Lincoln Samuel Randolph Patrick Jones, you keep your hands off that pie. It's for Christmas Day. Besides, you'll ruin your appetite. Supper is almost ready." Since he was her first born, she'd had trouble deciding on just a first and middle name, so she'd thrown in a couple of extra ones while she was at it.

He complained good-naturedly and patted his stomach. "Oh, come on, Mom. I'm a growing boy. I need something to keep me going."

She smiled and handed him a chocolate chip cookie. "This will have to do."

Marla Jean snared a cookie for herself and sat down on a kitchen stool. "The house looks great, Linc. I bet you were glad Mom hired some help this year."

"Ya know, sis, I resisted the idea at first, but it turned

out to be one of her best ideas yet. Maybe ever. Dinah deserves all the credit," he stated plainly.

When they'd first arrived home, his mother had been thrilled with the shape the house was in and told him so enthusiastically. Once she got used to the idea that her artificial tree was staying in the attic this year, she even admitted she loved having a real tree in the front living room window.

Bitsy patted her son on the arm. "I plan to send that girl a big thank-you note."

"Maybe we should have her over instead. You can thank her in person." Linc tried to sound casual. He'd heard through the grapevine she was back in town. Even so, Dinah had continued to ignore his calls, but she probably wouldn't ignore his mother's.

Marla Jean spoke up, teasing him. "I wouldn't mind meeting this wonder woman, either. Everyone all over town keeps talking about your new lady friend."

"I'll call her later and set something up," Bitsy promised, and Linc wanted to jump for joy.

"Great idea, Mom."

Milton came in from the garage. "When do we eat? I'm starving."

"Oh, you. Go get washed up, and I'll have it on the table in ten minutes. Are you staying, Marla Jean?"

"No, I need to get home to Bradley, but we will be here bright and early in the morning."

"Okay, see you both then."

Marla Jean left and after they ate dinner Linc's folks said they were going out to play cards with some friends. Linc didn't mind. He had plans of his own. Tonight was the big night. He went into his weight room and walked over to the closet he'd guarded from Dinah and her snooping eyes. Reaching in, he took out a suit and grabbed a bag from the floor. Then he drove to the hospital and found a large meeting room decorated with a big tree, fresh garlands, and a long table holding cookies and punch. Glancing inside he could see it was filled with patients, and the sound of Christmas carols filled the air. Linc waited in the hallway, and as the last notes of the song died away he knew they were ready for him. Ready to make his entrance he peeked around the corner and froze. There was Dinah wearing her Santa hat. His heart raced. He watched as she laughed and chatted with her friends. Everything inside him wanted to run to her, but he didn't. He couldn't. Not then and there. Duty called. Taking a deep breath he took a step into the room. "HO, HO, HO," he boomed. "Merry Christmas!"

After the caroling ended Dinah and her friends made plans to head to Lu Lu's for a drink. As they got ready to leave a great cry went up from the children gathered at the other end of the room. Dinah smiled when they all clapped and cheered as Santa Claus entered the room.

She thought there was nothing sweeter than seeing kids with Santa Claus. Dinah found her jacket and put it on while watching Santa with a little boy on his lap. Santa glanced in her direction and froze for a split second, but the moment passed. She moved closer and something about those dark eyes seemed familiar, but she dismissed the idea immediately. Santa looked a whole lot like Lincoln. But it couldn't possibly be him. He hated Christmas.

Telling her friends she'd catch up to them, she sat down in the back of the room, unable to get the idea out of her head, and before long she was absolutely certain that the man in the red suit and fake beard was Lincoln Jones. The way he held his head, the way he laughed. And especially the way he kept stopping between kids to stare at her. But then his attention would shift, and he'd be totally focused on the child in his lap. He gave each of them a wrapped gift and the nurse would take their picture. Her heart felt ready to bust wide open watching him.

Finally, the kids had each had a turn, and the parents and nurses led them out to return to their rooms. The two of them were all alone in the room at last. She was anxious and overjoyed to see him, but still none of this made sense. Standing up, she walked across the room toward him. "Explain yourself, mister. You don't even like Christmas, and yet here you are dressed like Santa Claus."

His dark gaze never wavered as she approached. "Hey, Dinah. I said I didn't like the blatant commercialization of the holiday. I've seen too many families spend themselves into trouble year after year in an attempt to buy love and happiness. It's bullshit. But I never actually said I didn't like Christmas. You jumped to your own conclusions." Then he shrugged, looking a bit embarrassed while indicating the red suit. "Besides, this is for the kids."

She grinned, pleased by her discovery. "So, how did you get roped into this gig? And where did you get the outfit?"

"I'll have you know this is an old family tradition started by my father. When he retired and moved away I inherited the job along with the outfit. You nearly stumbled across the suit when you tried to open the closet in the weight room. That was a close call. You probably don't realize it, but Santa's identity is a closely guarded secret around these parts."

She laughed. "I couldn't imagine what you were hiding in there, but don't worry. Your secret's safe with me, Santa. And now I know you're nothing but a big softy."

He pulled her onto his lap. "I heard you went skiing."

She should have resisted, but it was so nice to be close to him again. "I did. My mother sprained her ankle, so we came home early."

"Your mother?"

"Yes. I was with my folks."

He smiled so wide she thought his face might break. "That's great. Well, not great. That must suck for your mother." He took a deep breath and confessed, "I thought you'd gone to Colorado with some other guy, and I was jealous."

"You were jealous?" The idea astonished her and happiness blossomed in her chest.

"I know I don't have the right, but I hated the idea of you being off having fun with someone else."

Her green eyes grew misty. "I'm not sure what to say."

"Say you'll let me take you out on a real date. Everyone in town has decided you're my new lady friend anyway. Let's give them something to talk about. Rumor has it we make a cute couple."

"But I'm just the lady hired to straighten your socks. Besides, your mother might not like it." She felt obligated to remind him of the line she'd stepped over.

He dismissed the point she'd tried to make almost before the words were out of her mouth. "My mother loved what you did with the house. In fact, she wants to have you over for cake as a thank-you, but you don't work for her anymore. So, please forget about my mother. She doesn't get a say in this. This is about you and me." His hand cupped her cheek gently.

Yielding to the touch of his hand, she surrendered all objections. "Okay. Let's talk about you and me."

"Go out with me, Dinah." He smiled, and she saw she'd been right about his eyes. They didn't just twinkle when he smiled, they smoldered, and tempted and seduced. "Pretty please."

Knowing her answer was already yes, she asked, "What did you have in mind?"

"Whatever you want—dinner, dancing, parking on Lover's Lane." His wink was an invitation to trouble.

Her hands smoothed the wrinkles of his rumpled red suit. "Why, Santa, are you suggesting something naughty?"

"Yes, ma'am. I am." Pulling her as close as his padded suit would allow, he whispered, "Something very naughty."

"That sounds nice," she said with a sigh.

And this time she didn't hesitate. She grabbed him and kissed the living stuffing out of him.

Dear Reader,

Being a Navy wife, I spent a lot of Christmases in transit. If my husband had the leave available and we had the money, come the holidays, we packed up the car and headed to Oklahoma. One year, stationed in San Diego, I was going to school that semester. I had three finals the week we left for home, along with shopping, wrapping gifts, and packing. Something had to slide.

We left warm seventies' weather for subzero temperatures and wind chills in the negative twenties. Our six-year-old, who'd owned nothing warmer than a jacket and jeans, acquired a new wardrobe along with a great appreciation for cold weather that he nurtures to this day.

After a two-day drive, we arrived back in San Diego early one evening to balmy breezes and shorts weather. Happy to be home again, our son was the first one into the condo, where he skidded to an abrupt stop. "Mom! Dad!" he yelled. "Someone broke into our house!"

Yep, my holiday from cleaning along with the frantic preparation for the trip had left the condo looking ransacked.

These days Christmas means heading to my sister's house in the next town over. Our son is grown with a six-year-old of his own and is still happiest when the temperature drops below twenty, and my house still looks like it's been ransacked. Hey, some traditions are hard to give up.

Merry Christmas to you all!

Marilyn Pappano

Merry Christmas to our troops serving around the globe and to their families, with them or back home missing them. My gratitude is boundless.

Also to the people of my home state of Oklahoma. We've had some tough times this year, but we are strong and resilient. I'm proud to be counted among you.

As always, for my husband, Robert. You're my rock, and I'll love you forever.

A Family for Christmas

Marilyn Pappano

CHAPTER

1

Jared Connors eased through the double doors leading into the community center meeting room at one minute after six. At the front of the room, speaking about gift shopping, holiday meals, and the need for volunteers, stood Joanie Quinton, his office manager for six days. She'd snagged him with that need for volunteers before he'd even had the chance to ask her about community service opportunities.

Catching sight of him, she raised one hand to single him out. "There's a new doctor in town, guys, and we got him. Dr. Jared Connors is from back east, where he attended Harvard and Johns Hopkins, and our hospital was smart enough to make him an offer he couldn't refuse. He's an outstanding pediatrician, and all you have to do to get your kids in to see him is go through me first."

As she paused for the expected laughter, she gestured him nearer. "Come on up, Dr. Connors, and say a few words."

Great. Nothing like being put on the spot. But he

obediently climbed the steps to the dais and took his spot beside her. "Thank you for the introduction, Joanie. I'm anticipating getting to know the city of Tallgrass and enjoying a slower pace than the one I was accustomed to in New York." *You sound like an idiot. What's wrong with "Hi, nice to meet you"?* His face warming, he went on. "I look forward to working with you all in the Prairie Elf—"

Movement at the back of the room caught his attention. An elf had just walked in the door. He blinked, but the slight figure dressed in red and green, complete with pointy hat, didn't go away. She just stood there looking elfish.

He blinked again, trying to remember where he'd lost his power of speech. "Um, in the Prairie Elf Foundation."

"Fundation," Joanie murmured.

"Fundation. Right." Because Prairie Elf wasn't cutesy enough on its own, and the group was about fun and funds, hence the play on words.

There were smiles on the faces looking up at him, along with a few hellos and a round of claps, before they turned away to make conversation. Beside him, Joanie rubbed her glasses on her Rudolph-inspired sweatshirt. "See, that wasn't bad."

He grunted. *Wasn't bad* didn't equate to *good*.

"Now we'll eat dinner before we get down to business. Most of us come straight from work, so we usually bring our own meals, but at least once a month, we have a potluck. You're in for some good cooking, Doc."

Following Joanie to the tables lining the back wall, Jared tried to imagine his parents tolerating the nickname. Howard Connors was a cardiovascular surgeon, Margaret Baxter-Connors a neurosurgeon. Their home base was Boston, although they traveled the world to see select patients. They were surgeons to the rich and powerful, supremely confident and highly respected. If anyone had ever called either of them *Doc*, his parents would have eaten that person for breakfast.

As he and Joanie picked up plates and joined the line, she introduced him to the people around them. He said the appropriate words and stored the names automatically in his head. Memorization was one of his great skills, helping him make an appearance on every Honors list in his educational career.

"Doc, let me make one more introduction before I run off to our PR person." Joanie's smile shifted to the woman across the serving table. "Our elf here is Ilena Gomez. Ilena, this is Jared Connors. Ilena is the heart of Prairie Elf."

"It's my passion," Ilena agreed, nodding at Joanie as Joanie hurried away.

Jared liked women: blondes, redheads, brunettes, and black-haired women, too. In college, he'd even dated a girl with lavender hair. But blondes were his favorite—tall and leggy and sleek, with warm gold hair and perpetually tanned skin that reminded him of tropical beaches—sophisticated and elegant and sinuous and sensuous. Those were the blondes who knocked him off his feet.

Ilena was neither tall nor leggy nor sleek. Her hair was more white than blonde, and her skin looked as if she spent a fortune on super-efficient sunblock and concealing clothes. No way could that whole-face grin pass for sophisticated or the elf outfit for elegant. She was all lush curves in a tiny package, her smile generous, her blue eyes dancing.

He suspected, for an instant, that she could also knock him off his feet, and that wasn't necessarily a good thing. He hadn't moved halfway across the country to get involved in a serious relationship.

"So what brings you to Tallgrass?" Ilena asked as she spooned food onto her overloaded plate.

Truthfully, he hadn't come there so much as he'd fled something else: the position his parents had arranged for him with the country's most prestigious pediatrics partnership. If he was going to practice an insignificant specialty, they'd reasoned, the least he could do was practice with the significant people in the field.

Of course, he couldn't give that answer unless he wanted to sound like the awkward teenager his parents still believed him to be. "Oklahoma has a serious shortage of rural doctors, so I signed up." Pissing off his parents, embarrassing his siblings, and feeling a little better about himself, all in one shot.

"Funny. I don't think of Tallgrass as rural." Ilena dished a heaping spoonful of casserole onto her plate. He identified diced tomatoes and green onions, but not much else. "I grew up in a town in South Texas that had a hundred eight people. We got our gas, our mail, our news, and our food all at the same place. *That* was rural." Ilena scanned the table, then balanced her overflowing plate in both hands. "Where did you come from?"

"New York."

As they moved along the table, he took a bit of one dish, then another. Except for the garden salad, everything looked heavy and indulgent: lots of cheese, rich sauces, and dressings. It was the kind of food that never made an appearance on the Connors' dinner table. His father didn't merely talk the talk. Jared, his brother, and his sisters had been eating a heart-healthy diet since they'd traded the bottle for real food.

He reached the end of the table first, then looked around for a seat. The others had already filled two tables and part of another and were deep in conversation. He felt the way he had at camp the summer the swimming instructor had pushed him off the dock into ten-foot-deep water before he was ready. *Sink or swim*, the girl said with a laugh, and he'd done the first several times before managing the second.

A green-and-red hat bobbed into his line of vision. "Come on," Ilena said, nudging him with her elbow. "We'll sit over there."

He followed her to the end of the third table, then sat across from her. His plate looked anemic compared to hers. Where did she put all that food?

They settled in, spreading paper napkins, putting plastic utensils on their plates, choosing bottles of water from the small ice bucket in the center of the table. She took a bite of pasta salad, another of baked beans, a third of cream-cheese-and-ham-stuffed tortilla, then sighed happily as if her initial burst of hunger had been satisfied. "So, Doc. Go ahead. You know you want to ask."

Slowly Jared chewed and swallowed savory meat loaf with a caramelized tomato glaze before meeting her gaze. "Ask what?"

"Why the weird costume?"

At least she knew dressing as an elf for a meeting wasn't exactly normal. "Okay," he said evenly. "Why the weird costume?"

"What weird costume?" Her laugh sounded like a set

of crystal chimes that had hung outside his window at their summer home on Nantucket. Their tinkle had lured him to sleep on many a warm night.

Her expression sobered, but there was still a general sense of pleasure about her. "What we do here is serious business, but people need to laugh. And it's no weirder than people wearing antlers on their heads or most of the Christmas sweaters this time of year. Besides, the jingle bells make my baby laugh."

Baby. Something rose inside him, not a surge or a swell, just a small, strange bit of... He didn't even know what to call it. Dismay? Disappointment? It drew his attention automatically to her left hand, but it was bare of rings. Didn't mean anything. His parents had been married more than forty years, and they didn't wear wedding rings. Too much hand scrubbing and gloving to bother, they said.

But he'd always thought a wedding ring, and the commitment it represented, was worth the bother.

"Boy or girl?"

"Boy. Six months last week. John."

"Does he have an elf costume, too?"

"He does. And a snowman and a Santa and a little hooded coat with ears that makes him look like a fat sleepy bear."

"Is he with your husband tonight?"

"No." Another emotion he couldn't easily identify flickered through her eyes, though her expression didn't change. "Juan was killed in Afghanistan a year ago, so it's just John and me."

The information caught him off guard. Sure, a lot of his patients in the city had come from single-parent homes, and some of those missing parents were dead. That was natural. Death happened. It happened more often in a community tied to the military, as Tallgrass was to Fort Murphy.

But those patients' parents were professional relationships. Jared couldn't think of anyone among his friends and family who'd lost a spouse at such a young age. "I'm sorry."

That generous smile curved her mouth again. "We get along. All my best friends are widows. Except for Carly, who got married just before John was born. And Therese is getting married as soon as Keegan gets out of the Army. And Jessy. Hmm, I guess only half my best friends are widows." She took a moment to eat more—honey-glazed ham, tabouli, chicken and fat dumplings that glistened with gravy. "Is there a Mrs. Connors?"

"Only my mother, though she answers to Doctor instead of Mrs. And my sister-in-law, but she kept her maiden name, since her oncology practice was already established when she got married."

"So you come from a family of doctors."

A family who called themselves physicians, surgeons, or whatever their specialty, so people wouldn't mistake them for the garden-variety MD. "Mother, father, brother, two sisters, sister-in-law, brother-in-law, and a niece in her first year of medical school." He wasn't bragging. Just giving the facts.

"I'm impressed. My dad was a farmer, my granddad was a deputy sheriff, and my great-granddad made moonshine."

"Moonshine?"

"Yeah. Hootch. White lightnin'. The kind of stuff you brew illegally out in the backcountry."

The words sounded so strange coming from her pretty, innocent, happy elf's face that Jared did something he hadn't done in a long time. He laughed out loud.

"What do you think of Dr. Connors?"

Ilena wrapped foil over the empty dish that had contained her cornbread salad before meeting Joanie's inquisitive gaze. The doctor had left a few minutes earlier, walking out with the reporter from the Tallgrass newspaper who gave the fundation as much coverage as he could. "He seems nice."

"He is. Cosmopolitan-sophisticated-nice. I mean, can you imagine him wearing a Santa costume or something like that?" She gestured toward Ilena's outfit. "Dress shirt, trousers, tie—that's all I've ever seen him in."

"And you've seen him—what? Five or six times? At work?"

"Yeah, well, Doc Sheldon used to come in straight from the fields in overalls and knee-high rubber boots. And Doc Patrick never dressed up, not once in the decade he was here. We're never gonna get this one out of those preppy clothes. Still, if I were twenty years younger..." Joanie's smile was sly. "Hey, you *are* twenty years younger."

Although the idea of getting Jared out of those clothes all but demanded a sassy response, Ilena shook one finger at her. "No matchmaking for the elf. Santa's rules, and you wouldn't want to tick him off this close to Christmas, would you?"

"No, of course not. But Christmas will be over in three weeks. Then the rules don't apply."

With a laugh, Ilena said good night and headed

out the door, huddling deeper into her coat when she pushed through the exit and the prairie wind hit her. "O-Oklahoma, where the damn winds have to come sweeping down the plain," she sang off-key, wishing she'd traded the elf hat for the wool one stuffed in her coat pocket.

"So the song's true."

Startled, she lifted her gaze from the curled toes of her shoes and saw Jared standing beside a pricey low-slung car. There was something expectant about his casual stance, as if he'd been waiting for her. He wasn't shivering inside his jacket, and his hair merely fluttered in the breeze. He was definitely handsome in that rich, upper-crust, privileged way she associated with New England and old money.

"That part of it is, definitely. Sometimes I think it can sweep *me* across the plains. Not that I'm a lightweight. I'm short but solid." And freezing. The quiet purr of his car enticed her with visions of hot air blasting from vents. She beeped open her door, set the dish and her bag on the passenger seat, then started the engine before facing him again. "You must be used to cold weather back east."

"We get our share." He shifted his weight from foot to foot, then shoved his hands into his pockets. "If you're not in a hurry to get home, is there someplace we could get a drink?"

Ooh, the handsome man wants to have a drink with me. The handsome, brand-new-in-town, stranger-in-a-strange-land who probably didn't like sitting in restaurants alone.

She cocked her head to the side, studying him. When he lifted one brow, she explained, "I'm trying to imagine you in Bubba's, Buddy's, or Bronco's. Those are three of our popular spots." Mostly cowboys and oil field workers frequented Bubba's, with soldiers and uniform groupies preferring Bronco's. Plenty of Buddy's customers were still in suits for their after-work drinks, but she couldn't quite place Jared among them. "Maybe you should define 'drink.' Cocktail, wine, beer, coffee, pop, hot cocoa…"

"Coffee. Cocoa." His shrug was elegant, made more so by the cashmere of his coat. "I don't drink if I'm working the next day."

"Good policy." She hardly ever drank at all. As a result, she was a very cheap date, Juan had teased. Half a glass of wine, and soon enough, her clothes were coming *off.* "I have the perfect place. Three Amigos on East Main. Have you seen it?"

Of course he nodded. A person would have to be blind to miss the orange, lime, and red building plunked in the middle of the shopping center parking lot.

"I'll meet you there." With a wave, she climbed into the truck and sighed as heat surrounded her. It was wonderful what a difference forty degrees could make.

And the prospect of time alone with a sexy man.

On the way to the restaurant, she called Mary Epps—neighbor, friend, and John's surrogate grandmother—to clear her plans. Naturally, Mary encouraged her to stay as long as she liked. Although she had been single herself for nearly twenty years following an ugly divorce and intended to die that way, she thought Ilena needed to stay open to the idea of another man in her life.

With a glance at the headlights in her rearview mirror, Ilena acknowledged that she'd always been open. Losing Juan had broken her heart, not her spirit. She had too much love to give. She liked being part of a couple, snuggling in bed, fighting and making up and making love. She wanted more babies. It would have been perfect if she'd been able to have all that with Juan, but loving someone else could be perfect, too.

"Big thoughts for a first date," she chided herself as she steered into the turn lane in front of Tallgrass Center. Not even a date, really. A date required planning, while this was a spur-of-the-moment coffee invite. But it was the closest she'd gotten to a date since the last one with Juan, so she would count it.

Besides, although she'd fallen in love with Juan about ten minutes after meeting him, and thought muscular, dark-skinned, and dark-eyed was sexy as hell, she'd always had a soft spot for tall, lean guys with blue-black hair and Irish blue eyes. Even if they came from New York.

She claimed the parking space nearest Three Amigos' door, waited for Jared to approach, then slid out of the truck. Together they hustled across the lot, heads ducked into the wind. He opened the heavy door for her—aw, she loved little courtesies—and once again comforting warmth welcomed them.

The hostess gave a double-take, probably appreciating a new, handsome face, then she proved Ilena wrong. "For a moment there, I thought it was Tuesday again. Nice to see you on this lovely Thursday night. Follow me, please."

As soon as they were seated at a table for two in a dimly lit corner, Ilena shrugged out of her coat, then swiped off the hat and bounced it with a jingle. "You get credit for being seen in public with me wearing this. But hey, when you've got the tunic, the tights, and the pointy shoes, the hat doesn't matter so much."

"What? I don't seem the kind of person who would appear in public with a beautiful woman?"

She tried to hold in her snicker but couldn't call it successful. She loved compliments, but she didn't believe most of them. Charming men said charming, if untrue, things. "A woman, sure. An elf, no."

"But here I am. I proved you wrong." A slight smile crossed his features, just reaching his eyes. "You mentioned you're from Texas. How long have you lived in Tallgrass?"

"Four years. Juan was on his second deployment when he died. I thought about going home, but I had just found out I was pregnant, and I'm a lot closer to his family in Tulsa than my own. Plus, my margarita girls are here so John has more aunties than he knows what to do with."

Once again he raised one brow in question. It was a very elegant brow. "Your margarita girls?"

"A bunch of us meet here every week. The Tuesday Night Margarita Club, also known as the Fort Murphy Widows Club. It started as a support group, and now we're the best friends ever. I don't know how I would have gotten through the last year without them."

He didn't seem to know quite what to say, but she was used to that. Death was a difficult subject for most people, including, apparently, some doctors.

She slid the flip-through drink menu in the middle of the table his way. "I hear that everything they make here is good, but the only thing I can personally recommend besides the iced tea is the dessert coffee. It's brown sugar, cinnamon, cloves, cocoa, and whipped cream, and it's incredible."

"Is there coffee in it, too?" he asked drily.

She smirked at him. Never let it be said that a sexy guy could fluster her. She'd learned at an early age that she was what she was: smart, competent, simple, and, at times, silly, klutzy, and a bit of an airhead. *What you see is what you get.* People loved her, or they didn't, and she was okay with that.

She would bet people loved him. What wasn't to like, besides his accent that was a little too East Coast for her tastes? Time and his new neighbors would dilute that. Maybe he was a little preppy with his clothes, but he wore the look well. He was a pediatrician willing to work in rural Oklahoma, and he'd volunteered for the Prairie Elf Fundation, God love him.

In fact, as he gave the waitress their order for two dessert coffees, the thought occurred to Ilena that maybe she wouldn't discourage Joanie's matchmaking efforts after all. She wanted to fall in love again, and the only way to do that was to meet guys. The odds that Jared would be that guy were slim, but someone would be. She knew it in her heart.

Besides, wouldn't it be fun finding out if Jared *might* be the one?

CHAPTER

2

Friday was another cold day, the sky clear, crisp, thin white clouds sharp against an even sharper blue. The wind rustled dead leaves and trash across the street ahead of Jared's car, and people hurried along the downtown sidewalk, traveling between offices, restaurants, and shops. When he had a few hours, he intended to check out the antique shops. His mother might appreciate Oklahoma more if he found a gift from its early days for her collection.

But today wasn't the day. He'd closed the office at four, taking advantage of the slow clinic days while they lasted, and now he was on a mission. Back home, he would have a hundred stores to choose from. Better than that, he would have a dozen or so people to delegate the job to and would go into work Monday morning to find it all completed.

"You're not in New York anymore, Doc," he murmured as he turned into the parking lot of the best shopping destination in Tallgrass for civilians: Walmart.

He parked as far from the entrance as was possible, then hiked across the lot, entering at the garden center.

The patio was filled with lighted, moving outdoor decorations that made him cringe, along with live Christmas trees. Their fragrance was muted but stirred a yearning for the Maine cottage where the Connors family spent Christmas Day. This would be the first Christmas he'd ever missed, but he couldn't go back so soon. Family dinner wouldn't be worth the pressure.

Inside the store, he located a display of artificial Christmas trees: all sizes and shapes, some pre-lit, some so skinny they were just short of pathetic. The best one was six feet tall, its tag said, but stuffed into a box that was only five feet tall. With his hand resting on top, he looked it up and down, wondering if there was any chance it was vacuum-packed: cut away the box and, poof, the tree resumed its normal shape.

"In case you haven't figured it out, this box isn't fitting in that itty-bitty car of yours."

Ilena stood a few feet away, wearing a dress and boots, her hair mussed from the cap that occupied the kid seat of her cart along with her coat and gloves. A child seat, the kind that converted for a car, filled the bottom of the cart, and from it peered a round brown face, solemn eyes, and a Santa-themed pacifier. John Gomez looked nothing like his mother. Everything like his father?

Tough competition.

Jared forced his gaze from the baby to Ilena. "I hadn't thought of that," he remarked as he studied her. The dress was emerald green, quite possibly the best color in the world for her white-blond hair and fair skin. It ended above her knees, where black tights led into black boots. Together, the outfit conspired to hide her lush curves inside straight falls of fabric and leather.

"Lucky for you, I happen to have an SUV with plenty of room for a tree. What are you putting on it?"

That simply, she offered to deliver his package, even though it was surely out of her way. Could she also be persuaded to keep him company while he put up the tree? Maybe have dinner with him afterward? Keep him from spending one more night alone in his room at the B&B?

Her question registered belatedly, and he gestured toward the sample tree. "Don't you think it has an air of simple elegance the way it is?"

Grinning, she shook her head.

"Of course not. I bet you think it needs at least a hundred ornaments on it."

"A hundred?" She snorted. "That wouldn't even be a start for an Ilena Elf tree. The decorations are over here."

He left the tree and followed her and John across a few aisles. The dress didn't fit nearly as snugly as he would like, but it hinted at womanly curves, softness and warmth and welcome. Each time he saw her, he felt a little more in need of warmth and welcome.

"Is the tree for your house?"

"Don't have one yet. It's for the office."

"Little hands and climbers, so nothing breakable." She asked more questions that hadn't occurred to him—color preference, theme, tree skirt, icicles—and in no time had boxes and packages stacked in every bit of cart space John wasn't occupying. They returned for the tree-in-a-box, then went to the checkout line. As Jared began unloading items, she shrugged into her coat, hat, and gloves, then tucked a quilt over John before hefting his seat from the cart. "Why don't you get rung up, and I'll meet you outside?"

She was halfway to the door, him watching her, before he remembered to respond. "Sure. Thanks."

At the manual door, she turned to shove it open with her back, grinned at him, then disappeared among the cringe-worthy animated decorations.

"You didn't come here to have a relationship," he muttered.

Yeah, and you didn't come to be a monk, either. Your contract is for two years. If you can be celibate for two years, you've got bigger problems than a pretty woman, buddy.

Distantly in his head, he heard his father saying, *My lawyer can get you out of that contract. We'll make a donation, add a bonus, persuade someone without your connections to do it.* Like it was okay to weasel his way out of an obligation, to expect someone else to treat the common patients. Like he was too important to treat rural kids' fevers, give them shots, and examine the bruises and bumps of their lives.

Jared's jaw tightened. He'd signed the contract, and he would fulfill it. He would take care of these Oklahoma kids, most of whose families couldn't possibly assemble enough wealth and power to qualify for attention from any of the other Connors physicians, and he would be happy doing it.

The checker, wearing a Santa hat that contrasted badly with her vivid orange hair, gave him the total, followed with a perfunctory "Merry Christmas." Balancing the carton across the top of the cart, he pocketed his receipt, then headed out the door and to the SUV idling at the curb. Ilena was bundled up at the back.

"I'm glad you got a tree," she said as she lifted the cargo door. "Everyone should have one."

"Let me guess. Yours has been up since Thanksgiving."

He lifted the box in, shoving it to the left where the rear seat was folded down. Curiosity piqued by the noise, John twisted in his car seat to look, babbling softly. Definitely his daddy's boy.

Ilena cocked her head to the side. "The main tree, yeah. We put up John's tree a week before and the one in my bedroom the week before that. The tree in the kitchen stays up year-round, but it's not really a Christmas tree. We decorate it for all holidays and birthdays."

Four trees for two people. Anyone else, he would have thought that was overkill, but it seemed just right for Ilena.

"I've never put up a tree before," he admitted as he transferred the last of the bags. "At our house, it magically appeared on December first and disappeared on January first. My mother's holiday designers were convinced they didn't need my help."

"Wow. I didn't realize there was a job to be had decorating other people's trees. I could do that. Though I doubt people who can afford holiday designers would appreciate my taste."

Probably true. *Elegant* and *sophisticated* were the bywords in Dr. Margaret Baxter-Connors' house. While he could think of a lot of words to describe Ilena, *elegant* and *sophisticated* weren't among them.

Pretty. Guileless. Sweet. Confident. Pleasant. Happy. Sexy in an innocent elf/mama way. Great legs. Great ass. Great boobs.

"Are you good with your hands?"

Shaking out the image of his last thoughts, he looked at his hands: familiar, steady, strong. Capable hands. "I've done surgery with them."

"Pish." She waved her own hand in the air between them,

clad in black suede, small and delicate and also steady and strong. "Anyone can do surgery. There's an art to decorating a tree. Lucky for you, John and I have nothing on our schedule this entire evening. You pick a time, and we'll be there."

When fate gives a gift, grab it with both hands. "How about now?"

The delight that was always evident in her features deepened as a broad smile curved the corners of her generous mouth. "Sounds great. Let me go home and change, and we'll meet you there. Good?"

The prospect brought his own smile, and for a moment he just stood there, looking goofy—no, looking happy—before he remembered to answer. "Good."

Just about the best *good* ever.

Juan had been handy in just about every way possible. He'd already had crazy-good mechanical skills, and the Army had taught him more. Ilena's dad could fix any piece of farm machinery, no matter how decrepit it was, and wring another few years of life from it. Ilena herself was pretty good with a hammer, climbing on roofs, crawling under vehicles, or doctoring animals that outweighed her twenty to one.

Jared's hands were healing hands. Tree-assembling? Not so much. Oh, but it was fun watching him try.

She and John sat on a couch in the reception area, decorated to appeal to both parents and kids. John wasn't interested at the moment, but maybe someday he'd be a patient here. Right now he got his care at the Army hospital on post, but when Ilena remarried, that benefit would stop.

Wouldn't it be nice to have a baby doctor in the family, especially when she planned to have more babies?

With a grunt, Jared took a few steps back. "Okay. I straightened and bent and fluffed. That's as close as it's going to get to a real tree." He frowned at her. "You do realize real trees aren't perfect, either. A few bare spots are going to happen."

"It's Christmas, Jared. Christmas trees *are* perfect." And his had been, too, for about ten minutes. She'd just been enjoying the sight of him, stretching, bending, fabric pulling tightly over muscles and planes, running elegant fingers through his hair when she said, *No, no, it's not balanced.*

"So it's good?"

She looked from him to the tree, mounted on a low coffee table and scooted into a corner, then back at him—hair mussed, preppy clothes a little mussed, too—and she smiled. "It's very good."

His quick, perfect smile showed he had no clue that she was talking about him. "So now we get rid of the box, then I sit with John while you decorate it."

"Oh, no, no, no, no. I've done this dozens of times. You need the experience, and the best way to get it is to do it. John and I will advise you."

His frown came back as he studied the boxes and bags filling every flat surface around the tree. "Shouldn't we take it one step at a time? I mean, look, I put together a very good tree. I can attempt the decorations next year."

Aw, she adored a man who bargained. She sometimes even compromised with them. But not yet. "When you're doing something new, it's better if you immerse yourself completely in it. You know, like learning another language and speaking nothing else until you're fluent."

"Even if I worked all day and I'm hungry?"

Hearing the *h* word, John stuffed two fingers in his mouth and started sucking. Ilena felt a tug of hunger, too. They were all like Pavlov's dogs. "Even if. But we can break for dinner."

Jared started toward the check-in desk. "I can order something in."

"Or we can go out."

"Joanie brought menus from every restaurant in town."

"Or we can go out," Ilena repeated. "Don't you want to see what Tallgrass has to offer? Meet some people? Try something new?"

He shoved the tree box that he'd tossed aside earlier into a corner, then ruefully said, "Everything since I left New York is new."

It was hard being a stranger in a different universe from the one he'd left behind. Ilena remembered the initial alienation she'd felt after trading her tiny hometown for Fort Lewis, Washington, three days after she and Juan got married. New place, new life in general, Army life in particular, nothing familiar . . .

Shifting John to her hip, she pushed to her feet, a little grunt escaping. "I hope my boy walks early because in a few months, I'm not gonna be able to lift him. Get your coat, Jared. Serena's is a nice new experience. The food's great, the people are wonderful, and everyone goes there eventually."

She bundled the baby, then herself. Before she could pick him up again, Jared's long elegant fingers curled around the seat handle. Smiling—John really was a chunk—she took her purse and diaper bag and led the way outside to her truck.

Within fifteen minutes, they were seated in a booth

at the downtown restaurant, John's carrier snugged into a high chair at the end of the table. It had taken five minutes to reach Serena's entrance, the other ten to reach the booth, trading greetings and introductions all the way. She loved the intimacy of the small town and its people who had welcomed her and made a place that would always be home, no matter where she lived.

She wasn't sure Jared was embracing the friendliness—the nosiness—quite as readily, but, like the tree, he was trying.

Serena's specialty was home cooking, the heart attack–inducing kind. Ilena always ordered her winter favorite—stew with tender chunks of beef, carrots, potatoes, plus mushy soft cloves of garlic and a little crunch from celery—so while Jared studied the menu, she prepared a bottle for John, then lifted him from his seat. He grinned, showing his single tooth, and waved his little fists in the air, telling her how yummy the bottle looked and how he was famished in words that all sounded like *Hrble mrble drble.*

It didn't sound any worse than her early attempts to speak Spanish.

Before she could settle him in her arms, Jared laid his menu aside. "Can I feed him? If you don't mind?"

Ilena went still, leaving John's feet dangling. In that first moment she'd found out she was pregnant, she'd had startlingly clear visions of Juan cradling John in his arms, giving him a bottle, stroking his little cheek, looking at him with such awe and adoration. John's *abuelito* had held him adoringly and fed him, but it wasn't the same.

She slid the baby into Jared's capable hands, gave him the bottle, then dug in her bag for a burp cloth, but instead of passing it over, she curled her fingers in it tightly. Jared held John with all the ease she would expect of a pediatrician, but there was, oh, so much more to it than that. Curiosity. Tenderness. A softening of Jared's edges. And, yeah, a little bit of awe, to match the awe growing inside her.

When the waitress came for their order, she gave the two males a look and said, "Aw, sweet," before sneaking a wink in Ilena's direction. "Beef stew with cornbread?"

Ilena nodded, and Jared took his gaze from John long enough to say, "Make that two." After the waitress left and there were only the sounds of John's sucking between them, Jared quietly asked, "Would you do it again if you knew how it would turn out?"

"Do what?"

"Marry a soldier. Get pregnant when he's going off to war."

Under the table, she touched her ring finger, bare for a long time. She'd slipped off the band a few months after Juan's funeral, strung it on a chain, and worn it close to her heart another few months. Now it rested in her treasure box with other important mementos of her life.

"He wasn't a soldier when he asked me to marry him, but I knew he would become one, and that couldn't have stopped me. Some things are too right to say no. As for John..." She smiled at her son, still milking the nearly empty bottle while his eyes slowly fluttered shut. "My boy was a happy surprise. I guess our good-bye sex was too much for the birth control to do its job."

Was that a little bit of a blush darkening his cheeks? Aw, she adored a man who could still blush at the mention of sex. "So what about you, Jared? You want kids?"

CHAPTER

3

Kids? Jared thought three was a good number. *It's a start,* she said before casually dropping the words *six, seven, or more.* She asked if he'd been married. He told her more about his parents—Dr. Dad and Dr. Mom, she called them—and his siblings. She told a few stories about her grandfather the deputy sheriff arresting his father the moonshiner. The things she said were important, even the unimportant ones, and the sound of her voice lulled him into a comfort he hadn't felt in . . . well, ever that he could recall, helped along by the solid weight of the baby sleeping in his arms.

Jared hated for dinner to end, certain that when they walked out of the restaurant, the slap of cold weather would chase away the coziness, the comfort, the intense satisfaction that seeped through him.

It didn't.

They returned to the office, and while John slept, they decorated the tree. The ornaments were nothing like the Lladró pieces that nestled in precisely determined placements on the Connors tree, but the finished project had a homey warmth about it that made the Connors tree sterile in comparison. It was the kind of tree toddlers could gather around without fear, the kind that could survive a pet.

A family kind of tree.

After he placed a delicate angel on top—blond hair, fair skin, blue eyes; coincidence?—he stepped back to study it. Ilena turned off the overhead lights and joined him. She smelled of baby and vanilla and Christmas and something light and flowery that made him think of warm weather, sunny skies, and long, sultry nights, and heat radiated from her slender body. Even without a smile, contentment enveloped her. She'd gone through hell, but she'd come out the other side with hope and a deep appreciation for life. It was a very appealing part of her.

Then he breathed deeply again and corrected himself: every part of her was appealing.

"You did good for your first time." She tilted her head to smile up at him, but her smile slowly faded, and instead she studied him a long moment. He wondered what she saw, what emotion was in his eyes and face, if she knew he wanted to pull her closer, if she could tell he suddenly wanted to kiss her, right this minute, and maybe not stop.

She raised one impossibly delicate hand, cupping her palm to his cheek, sending heat flooding through him, then pivoted toward him, lifting onto her toes and touching her mouth to his.

Oh, yeah, she knew.

He slid his hands over her shoulders, the curve of her breasts, her narrow waist, and the flare of her hip, lifted her against him, held her so they touched everywhere from head to toe, and he pushed his tongue into her mouth. In response she gave him a faint nip, swallowed a laugh, then sighed as he stroked her tongue with his, as his fingers slid beneath her sweater to caress the skin above the waistband of her jeans. Soft. She was soft. Delicate. Womanly. So powerfully appealing.

Although her touch was light as a feather, he felt the instant her fingers made contact, even through his shirt. It was the blast of heat that sent a shiver through him, the zing of awareness, the intense greed that flared inside him. More. He wanted more.

But he didn't get more. With another languid sigh, Ilena pulled away, sinking from the tiptoe position, resting her forehead against his chest for a moment. His pulse was pounding in his ears; he wasn't sure but thought he heard her murmur something before she backed away. *Wow.*

One surprise kiss, a couple of moments, one erection...yeah, *wow.*

"Let's store all the ornament packages in the tree box," she said, turning away to scoop up empty cartons.

He thought about catching her arm, pulling her back, and kissing her again, but all he did was retrieve the big box and move it closer. They worked in silence by the light of six hundred multi-colored bulbs. When they finished, he expected her to grab John and leave, but she sat on the sofa beside him, resting one hand on his chair, patting the empty cushion to her right in wordless invitation. The leather made a quiet *whoosh* when he sat down.

"You're the first man I've kissed since Juan."

She didn't need to tell him that. He'd known. "You're the first woman I've kissed since—"

Though he stopped short, she finished for him. "Since

you left New York?" With a grin, she bumped her shoulder against his.

"Longer than that." Long enough that he'd have to think to remember that last kiss. But Ilena was the first woman who really meant something. The first woman who tempted him to think long-term—five, ten, twenty years down the line. The first woman who felt impossibly right, though, for the life his parents had planned for him, he couldn't imagine anyone more totally wrong.

"It was nice," she said, and never had the word *nice* sounded so big and special. "I'd like to do it again. But right now I need to get my boy home and bathed and in bed. We're going to Tulsa tomorrow to shop and have lunch with Juan's family."

Some emotion settled low in his gut, something he wouldn't name, but he didn't like the discomfort. She'd told him she was close to Juan's family. Of course she visited them. Of course she made certain they got to see his baby regularly. And of course there were photos of him, conversations about him, memories and love they'd shared for him. He'd been her husband. Jared wouldn't expect anything else.

But that something in his gut thought it might be easier to get involved with a woman whose contact with her husband's family had ended when the marriage had.

How selfish did that make him?

He turned on the main lights. She switched off the tree lights. He pushed the box down the hall and into an exam room. She dressed for the cold and picked up John. He put on his own coat and gloves and followed her outside. The air was frigid enough to turn their breath to frost the instant it left their bodies, and when the quilt slipped from John's face, he opened his eyes and fixed his cranky expression on Jared while Ilena buckled him into his car seat.

When she straightened, job done, he touched one finger lightly to John's cheek. "See you later, buddy." Then, to Ilena, he said, "Thank you for the help."

"Thanks for letting us help. I love decorating. And thanks for dinner." She closed the door before starting around to the driver's side. "Hey, you want to have a home-cooked meal Sunday? Cooking after church is a tradition even if my boy is more interested in chewing on his fingers than food. Want to join us?"

Sunday dinner. It sounded like everything his family had never been. Who was he to tinker with tradition? Besides, it seemed only fair, if she was spending tomorrow with Juan's family, that they would spend the next day together. "I'd be happy to."

"Good." Her smile broadened, and she repeated the word as if it needed a little emphasis. "Good. I'll see you at one Sunday."

A Sunday dinner that didn't end until a follow-up late-evening supper. A Monday meeting of the Prairie Elf Fundation. Tuesday lunch since Ilena's evening plans with the Tuesday Night Margarita Club took precedence over everything except John. Now it was Wednesday afternoon, and Ilena and Jared had both taken off early for a driving tour of Tallgrass's better neighborhoods.

You're having a romance! Jessy had exclaimed over dinner last night.

I certainly hope so, Ilena responded. If all this time together, talking nonstop or not at all, and all these kisses and incredibly special moments just being together didn't add up to a romance, she didn't know what did.

She still thought of Juan a hundred times a day. She still said *I love you* to him in her heart every night. She still felt his loss deeply, but she felt new possibilities, too. And a few times, when John did something cute or something funny happened, her first thought was *I can't wait to tell Jared* instead of Juan. She could feel guilty and sad about it, but Juan understood. She knew he was up there in heaven cheering her on.

"Okay, we've seen the rich parts of town and the cookie-cutter subdivisions," she said as he stopped at the gates of the newest such collection. "I can show you the historic areas, or you could always buy land and build your own place."

"What about condos?"

She blinked, images of sleek, glass-and-steel, high-tech high-rises filling her mind, places far too modern and upscale for Tallgrass. "We've got lots of apartments, but I don't know of any condos."

"Except when I was home with my family, I've always lived in condos." His smile was thin, his gaze distant. Thinking of the life he'd left behind? Maybe missing it a little? "Show me the old stuff."

His parents' house in Boston was old. So was the one in Nantucket. And the one in Maine. One couple, four children, three homes, all within a few hours of each other. *Rich people*, her father would say and shake his head. *They're different.*

But differences could be overcome. She'd always believed that. Look at her and Juan. And she still believed it. Look at her and Jared. She really wanted there to be a *her and Jared*.

Pushing down the niggling in her stomach, she directed him to the oldest neighborhood in Tallgrass. The stately houses rose two or three stories, built of sandstone or brick, homes to the bankers, oilmen, and the most successful of the early merchants. The structures were probably simple compared to the places Jared had called home, but she loved them with their big porches and expansive lawns, wrought-iron fences, and especially the sense that they would be there forever.

Low dark clouds obscured the sun before it had set, dropping the temperature sharply. Snug in the luxury car with its heated leather seats, Ilena shouldn't have noticed, but a little chill had settled over her, forcing a falsely cheerful tone to her voice. "See anything you like?"

He glanced over. "You." Then he dragged his hand through his hair. "Maybe I'll stay at the bed-and-breakfast a while longer."

"Sounds like a plan," she said. Not one she would choose for herself. Room service and housekeeping were great, but she loved having a place of her own. Her room in her parents' farmhouse, the tiny cheap apartment she and Juan had shared when they first married, the standard quarters they'd occupied in Tallgrass, and her current house all had one thing in common: they were *home*. It was more than a place; it was a state of mind. Roots. Stability. But roots didn't just anchor people. They tied some people down and made them feel trapped, stuck in a place they didn't want to stay.

Jared had never said he wanted to stay in Tallgrass.

She didn't want to think about living anywhere else, so she wouldn't. Simple, huh?

He slowed for a stop sign before looking her way. "What now?"

"How about dinner at my house, then we go back out to look at the Christmas lights? One of the churches on the west side of town does an incredible display." It grew by ten thousand lights a year, they boasted, and she envisioned taking John there when he was ten for a display that could be seen from space.

He echoed her earlier words with a grin that chased away every last bit of the chill inside her. "Sounds like a plan."

CHAPTER

4

On Saturday morning, when Jared followed Ilena and John into the high school cafeteria, he realized immediately what Joanie had meant at the elf meeting when she called it wrapping day. The tables that normally held raucous kids were filled with a few thousand miles' worth of gift wrap and tape, and mountains of gifts were stacked in a long row at one end. "Wow. Haven't you people heard of gift bags? They're way easier."

"Oh, yeah, and can't you just see the joy in the kids' eyes as they tear into a gift bag to see what Santa brought them?" She rolled her own eyes, looking adorably elfin in her amusement. "Haven't you ever ripped open wrapping paper with sheer delight, Jared?"

"I've never done anything with sheer delight," he said, tossing his coat on a chair, then helping her out of hers, revealing her tight jeans and equally snug sweater. "But I'd like to rip the wrapping off of you. That would qualify."

Giving him a sly look, she nudged her body against his. "You show how good you are with your hands today, and

I'll show you how good I am with mine tonight." Then she surprised him by blushing, her cheeks almost matching the red of her sweater. Snatching John out of his seat, she scurried off to say hello to some of the volunteers, giving him a look over her shoulder that was both shy and seductive. The combination could kill him.

Forcing in a breath, he turned his attention to the gifts again. They filled pallets and boxes and spilled out of sacks: toys, books, clothing, plenty of stuffed animals and warm coats. "That's a lot of gifts."

"And only about half of our wish list." Joanie stopped on her way past. "There are a lot of families in need."

"Will you get enough?"

"We trust that we will. We've never had to turn anyone away empty-handed yet."

We, we, we. Would he ever feel that much a part of the fundation, or the town, or anything? Given his reluctance to look for a house...

It had been his suggestion to check out the various neighborhoods on Wednesday, to get an idea of where he might live the next few years. But when it had come to actually considering a particular house or even a certain area, he just couldn't do it. He couldn't picture himself in any of those houses, in any of those neighborhoods. It seemed too... permanent.

"People are as generous as they can afford to be at the holidays," Joanie went on. "We don't worry until the last twenty-four hours."

Jared admired her spirit as she walked away. If he were in charge, he would be panicked enough to start calling his parents, his siblings, and their famously successful surgeon friends to badger donations.

His cell beeped in his pocket. It could have been Morse code for *speak of the devil.* He considered silencing it, then looked at Ilena and thought what she would say about that. Pulling it out and heading for the exit instead, he greeted his mother with as much cheer as he could fake.

"Are you still in Smallgrass, or have you come to your senses?"

Dr. Mom isn't big on hellos, is she? Ilena's voice laughed in his head, the delicate tinkling-chime sound, and his nerves eased a bit. "I'm still here."

"Are you bored yet?"

"How could I be bored? I've just opened my own practice. I'm seeing patients. I don't have to take call, I haven't had a single emergency, and I'm not answering to anyone but myself." *Mental apologies to Joanie, whose managerial style included ordering him about at work.*

"Diagnosing strep, checking boo-boos, giving inoculations. How could you be anything but bored? Don't you miss civilization?"

He opened his mouth to say, *No, of course not,* but the words didn't come. Sure, the pace was slower; he'd expected that. New doctor in town, building a practice from scratch, during the holidays, no less. People had to know he was there before they could bring their kids to him. And he'd had more patients this week than last. When flu season really hit, he'd have plenty more.

But he was bored sometimes.

"Mom, I knew Small"—he winced—"Tallgrass was going to be a big difference. I like it. I like the people." Two, in particular.

"Which you'd tell me even if you hated it because you

never could admit you'd made a mistake. Have you found a place to live?"

He leaned against a wall across the corridor from a glass case crowded with sports trophies. "Not yet. I did decorate a Christmas tree for my office."

"Oh, Jared, that's what staff are for. You're a classic case of avoidance. If you don't commit to something as simple as a house, then you don't have to commit to the town." Noise rumbled in the background, then she said, "Your father said his offer to buy out the contract still stands."

Was he avoiding commitment? No, no way. He was just... busy. Still adapting. A little reluctant. That was all. "Tell Dad thanks, but I'm fine. In fact, I've got to go, but I'll send you my address as soon as I have it. Love you." Before she could respond, he hung up.

Wrapping Christmas presents was one of Ilena's favorite holiday routines. Close behind it was watching specials on TV with mugs of hot cocoa, freshly made treats, and a fire warming the room with its wood-smokey fragrance. This year her new favorite thing was sharing those things with John snoozing in her arms and Jared's strong arms wrapped around them both.

He made her second Christmas without Juan so much more bearable.

He shifted positions and grunted. "I didn't realize gift-wrapping could be harmful to your health."

"It can be when you spend half a day doing it. I'd offer to rub your back, but my arms are full." She'd already offered to do more: *You show how good you are with your hands today, and I'll show you how good I am with mine tonight.* Her cheeks warmed at the boldness of it. Not that she'd ever been shy about asking for what she wanted, but propositioning Jared was a whole different issue from doing the same with Juan.

"He's got to go to bed sometime."

Heavens, how did the room get so much warmer with that simple observation? She felt as if she were dressed for a polar chill in the Saharan desert, only the heat was coming from inside out. She'd swear even her hair was radiating fire.

"Well..." Sounding husky, she cleared her throat. "It *is* nearly an hour past his bedtime. And I think it would be okay to skip his bath tonight. Don't you agree, Dr. Pediatrician?"

"It's not like he's done a lot of running around since his bath last night." Jared sounded husky, too, and seemed to pulsate with tension even though he'd gone very still.

She drew a breath, squeezing air into her lungs. Were they really going to do this? Oh, she wanted it with every taut muscle, hypersensitive nerve, and fiber of her being. She didn't care that it had been longer for her than for him, or that the last man she'd been with was Juan. She didn't worry about how pregnancy had changed her body. She wouldn't consider the chance of getting her heart broken. She wanted this. Wanted *him.*

It was so easy. Shut off the television. Carry John into his room. Lay him on his back in the crib and stroke his cheek gently when he roused. The red and green lights on his foot-tall Christmas tree cast a warm glow over him, and its ornaments—stars to guide him, angels to watch over him, puppies to make him laugh—shone in the dim light.

"I love you, my baby. I'll love you forever. No matter how long, no matter wherever," she whispered as she gave him one last pat. A silly rhyme, but special to her because it was the last thing John heard from her every single night.

Jared waited at the door, arms folded across his chest, handsome and comfortable but with an edge that strained his features, giving him a needy, primal look. As she approached him, she felt the urge to give her own primal growl.

The roar would come later.

Her bedroom was just down the hall, the headboard visible through the doorway. She'd shared that bed with Juan, but not the room, not this house. But he wasn't a ghost to banish. Just a precious memory to lock away for a bit while she made more precious memories.

The lights on her own tree were white, tiny round globes, and so were the ornaments, angels of every type. Her favorite sat at the top, wild blond curls, wearing a dyed burlap dress, with a thin gold ribbon for a halo and a white cowgirl hat. Red cowboy boots peeked from underneath the dress.

Jared pushed the door but stopped before it closed. She appreciated the thought, though it wasn't necessary. When John cried in the night, he did it with great passion.

And his mama was about to do something with great passion, too.

He picked up a photo of her and Juan from the dresser top. "You were very happy."

"We were. We made the best of what we were given. Now I'm going to make the best of what—" She caught herself before *we* slipped out again. It was too soon to talk about feelings, emotions, potential, futures, love. "What I'm given."

Jared set the picture down, then studied her. "You're more beautiful than any angel in this house."

"Aw..." The way he looked at her made her feel beautiful. Desirable. It gave her the courage to close the distance between them, to place her hands on his chest, and to brush her mouth across his. Her intent was to tantalize, and judging by his harsh breath and the rigidity of his body, she'd succeeded.

They made short work of their clothes on the way to the bed, constantly touching even when the wrinkle of plastic indicated he'd retrieved one or more condoms from his trousers before kicking them aside. The fabric of the spread was cool against Ilena's skin, chased away the instant Jared laid his body over hers and sought her mouth for a sweet, needy, hungry kiss.

Great passion, her own voice echoed, barely audible above the pounding of her heart, the sizzling of her blood, the ragged breathing that rasped from both of them. It had been so long since she'd felt this kind of passion. For everyday life, sure. For John, absolutely. But for a man... Mercy, she'd missed it.

He touched her, kissed her, made her grateful to be alive, and she did the same to him, stroking taut muscles, kissing flat nipples, sending waves of sensation rippling across his belly. When her fingers wrapped around his erection, age-old emotions rose inside her: satisfaction, awe, need, completion. When he settled between her thighs and slid inside her, she was in a perfect daze. This act, this time, this man, this woman...*Primal*.

There was no roar when she climaxed—she really

wasn't the roaring sort—but desperate whimpers of hunger and shuddering gasps of completion. Her entire body strained against Jared's, her fingers clenching his shoulders, her mind reduced to nothing but feeling.

Feeling incredible.

Jared's harsh breaths followed immediately, as if the frenzy of her finish propelled him to his. His eyes were squeezed shut, his features sharp and angular in the soft light, and his body rigid, until a guttural groan ripped through him and, an instant later, he collapsed against her.

She stroked his damp hair, let his rasping breaths tickle her ear, and tucked the moment away in her memory forever. There were things a woman never forgot, and falling in love with Jared Connors was definitely one of them.

CHAPTER

5

Jared had had better weeks. In the two since his first night with Ilena, the flow of patients through his office had slowed to a trickle. If not for the financial aid his contract guaranteed from the local hospital and the town, there was no way he could keep the office open after a few more such weeks. It was the holidays, Joanie said. *People are busy. They'll come soon.* He was sick of the B&B but no closer to finding a place to live, and the newness of Tallgrass had worn off.

He missed New York. He missed his condo and his friends and his familiarity with the city. He missed not having to be in charge. Having his own clinic and practicing rural medicine sounded better in theory than they were turning out to be in reality. He was out of his element and feared he always would be.

But he still had Ilena and John. That made everything else bearable.

It was the Saturday before Christmas, and he, Ilena, and John had spent another marathon day gift-wrapping.

Like before, his back ached. It was a satisfying discomfort, though, this feeling that he'd done good. It was sad that he'd practically reached thirty without experiencing it more often.

It was cold outside, dark early thanks to the low-hanging clouds. Snow had begun to fall on the way back from the high school, thick flakes drifting lazily to the ground. A white Christmas, reporters were forecasting, a prospect that made Ilena dance with joy. She was in the kitchen, fixing dinner, and Jared and John shared the rug in front of the fireplace, lying on their bellies, studying each other. The kid was cute, round, solemn but willing to show off his lone tooth in slobbery smiles. When Jared stroked his cheek, John grabbed his finger and started to chew before he lost his balance and tumbled onto his side.

"You getting another tooth, buddy?" Jared stood and was swinging John onto his hip when his cell phone beeped. Expecting the sound of his mother's voice, he answered reluctantly, then was surprised to hear a much lower rumble.

"You remember Perry Cookson?" Dad wasn't much on hellos, either.

"Pediatric surgeon in New York. Sure." Also a medical school friend of his parents and a golfing buddy whenever they could hook up. Three facts that made Jared's gut tighten. "Why?"

"I saw him at a conference yesterday. He's willing to take you on board to do general care, then get you into a surgical residency. All you have to do is call him. You can't turn this one down, Jared. You can still take care of kids, but you'll have the chance to do some real good. Though the residency doesn't start until July, you can work in the clinic until then. What do you say?"

Jared's first thought: New York. The one place he thought of as home.

Second: *Stop finding jobs for me. I have one, and I'm already doing real good.*

Third: Ilena and John. Would they go with him? Could he leave them behind?

Last, and maybe most important: he didn't want to do surgery. Jared swallowed hard and gently removed John's chubby hand trying to pull his phone away. "I have an obligation here, Dad."

"We can take care of that."

Of course. His parents had the influence and the money to take care of everything that got in their way. "How much would it cost to buy out my contract?"

"I haven't had my lawyer look into it, but it's manageable." His father's voice was a shade triumphant. "I told you before, cash and someone to take your place, and they'll jump at it. They didn't hire *you*, Jared. They just wanted any warm body who managed to finish medical school."

That stung. He'd always known his parents didn't think highly of his career choices. He'd just hoped they would eventually accept them. Apparently, too much to ask.

Bouncing John to distract him, Jared said, "So I should... what? Tell the folks here, 'Hey, something better came along. I'm heading back to the city before the end of the year'?"

"Well, your mother would hope before Christmas. Everyone will be at the cabin by Monday."

John stretched, arms reaching over Jared's shoulder, mouth broadening in the grin reserved for only one person. He babbled a few syllables that would soon become *Mama* as Jared turned to face Ilena standing in the doorway, stiller, paler than usual. It was the first time he'd seen her without a hint of pleasure on her face.

His gut knotting even tighter, he muttered, "I'll call you back, Dad."

She folded her arms across her middle, her gaze burning him like the hot blue flames produced by a Bunsen burner in the lab.

"That wasn't what it sounded like," he said lamely.

"It sounded like you wanted to know how to buy out your contract. That something better had come along. That you're planning to go back to the city in the next week. If it wasn't that, then what was it?" Her voice, usually layers of happiness, joy, and gratitude, was flat, her tone accusing.

He took a few steps toward her, but stopped again. "One of Dad's friends offered me a job and his pull to get into a surgical residency in New York next summer. I didn't ask him to do it. I didn't say I was interested."

"You didn't say you weren't interested."

"This isn't the first time Dad and Mom have interfered, Ilena. I told you, they wanted me to become a surgeon and to stay on the East Coast. But I didn't do either. I did the residency I wanted, and I signed a contract here."

"One that you could buy your way out of." Reaching for her, John started to fuss, and she closed the distance, swooping him into her arms before retreating again. "I thought you were committed to this job, Jared, to the people here, to the idea of giving back. I thought you were dedicated to filling a need, not just passing time until something better comes along. Is that why you haven't moved out of the bed-and-breakfast? Why you haven't had your personal stuff shipped? Because the only needs you're dedicated to filling are your own?"

That stung, too, worse than his father's comment. Dad was Dad—gifted hands, not so much on bedside manner. But Ilena...she *knew* him. She loved him, or so he'd thought.

His spine stiffened, a muscle in his jaw twitching. "That's not fair. Okay, Tallgrass wasn't quite what I expected. It's been a little harder adapting. But I signed that contract, and my only intention has been to honor it every single day of those two years."

She shifted John to the other side, looking small and fragile and hurt, and quietly asked, "What about after those two years?"

Jared didn't mean to shrug. It seemed careless, something his father did all too often when he just didn't care. "Maybe I would like it enough to stay. Or maybe—" He dragged his fingers through his hair. "Maybe I would go back to the city with the knowledge that I'd done what I set out to. I'd stood up to my parents."

Her fair skin went paler. "So this has been your little rebellion. Taking the job, joining the fundation, helping the poor common people, and knowing it's pissing your parents off."

"I didn't mean that, Ilena." He closed the distance, reaching out to brush a strand of white-blond hair from her face. "I came here—"

For exactly those reasons. To prove he could find his own job, run his own life, and, especially, to spite his parents. "I never said I was here permanently. This whole venture is new to me. I knew I'd stay the two years, but after that..." If he'd really liked it, he might have stayed longer, but honesty forced him to admit that he'd never viewed it as anything more than temporary in his mind. He'd lived his entire life on the East Coast. If he'd looked ahead into the future, that was where he saw himself—definitely not for two years, but probably in five.

She stepped back to put space between them. "What about John and me?"

"You would love New York."

The flare of her nostrils let him know immediately that was the wrong thing to say. "Really? What led you to that decision? My growing up in a south Texas wide spot in the road? My staying in Tallgrass after Juan died? My sophistication and elegance and burning desire to escape small-town life for the big city?"

Acid churned in his stomach, and the aches in his spine were spreading up and through his brain. How had they gotten into this conversation? They should have been sitting down to eat by now, talking about nothing and laughing at John's messes. They would have cleaned up together, bathed John, lit a fire, and watched TV, and before too long, they would have put the baby in his room and entertained each other in Ilena's.

"You were an Army wife," he said helplessly. "You moved several times with Juan. It's part of life."

Moments ticked by as she stared at him. Her mouth in a thin line, she quietly said, "I *am* an Army wife. One who's not leaving Tallgrass for New York City."

Her message was pretty clear. She'd given up home, job, and friends for Juan, but she wouldn't do the same for Jared. She connected with Juan, even dead, more than with Jared.

The stomach acid calmed, the headache easing. He couldn't feel anything for the icy numbness inside him. It allowed him to nod, to speak politely—"I'd better go"—and to turn and walk away. He got his coat and gloves from the closet and walked outside into the snow, hoping he stayed this numb for a long, long time.

Only once in her life had Ilena awakened on Christmas Eve without feeling as giddy as a child—last year, when she'd just buried a piece of her heart. This time the rest of her heart had merely been broken. She had survived heartache before and would do it again.

Besides, it was John's first Christmas, and though he wouldn't remember, she intended to make it the best ever. Even if her heart *was* broken.

With a sigh, she adjusted her elf cap, the jingling bells drawing John's gaze. He wore his own elf costume, a one-piece snuggly in red and green, the stuffed toes curling up and sewn with bells. He had his own cap, too, but had yanked it off and alternated between waving it to ring the bells and stuffing it in his mouth to gnaw on. Teething was no fun.

Joanie joined them at the table near the decorated tree, cooed at John, then gave Ilena a critical look. "The doors are opening in one minute. Put on that big elf smile."

Ilena bared her teeth, and Joanie drew back. "Hey, you don't want to scare the kiddos. Where's your Christmas spirit, elf?"

"It ran off." Not quite true. It had walked out her door Saturday night and she hadn't seen it since. But she had a talent for finding the good amidst the bad. Surely she could fake it long enough for a drib of it to become real.

Joanie's gaze darted away as the big double doors at the far end of the community center gymnasium swung open, then she hugged Ilena. "Smile for the kiddos, hon, and we'll talk afterward, okay?"

Ilena grudgingly bobbed her head, and Joanie took off.

She moved John in his seat to a table against the wall as other volunteers began to join her. There would be a brief welcome, then songs, sweet treats, and snacks. After a visit from Santa, the fundation and its extra help would hand out gifts and all the makings for the traditional dinner. Everyone pitched in then, but right now Ilena was on treats duty.

The noise level in the gymnasium tripled as excited kids and their parents poured through the doors. No matter what else was wrong, the sound of happy kids always lightened Ilena's mood. When the first wave hit the treats table, she was smiling wobbly, but soon enough it became a real grin. Only the Grinch could be immune to the children's joy.

Grinch made her think of Jared, and for a moment her smile wobbled again. She chatted with her margarita girls—Fia, Jessy, and Bennie—and sang a few carols though singing wasn't one of her talents. Every few minutes she checked on John, always finding someone else fussing over him even when he dozed. There was only one exception, when Jessy interrupted her conversation with the baby to announce, "Ilena, this kid needs to be sanitized, sterilized, and antibacterialized. Damn, I've smelled cow poop that wasn't this bad. Does he do that often?"

"Every day. You'd better get used to it. We're all going to teach our kids to want only Aunt Jessy to change their diapers." Slinging the diaper bag over her shoulder, Ilena picked up John and headed for a more distant table, half hidden behind a wall of collapsed bleachers. Talking in a baby voice, she freed John's lower half from the outfit and took care of business. Her nose wrinkled as she tied the soiled diaper into a scented plastic bag, then tossed it into a garbage can. Jessy might have overreacted, but not by much.

"How can such a pretty boy be so stinky, huh?" she whispered as she dressed him again, kissing his feet, nuzzling his belly, pressing her face against his soft black hair. For a moment she stayed there, her heart full enough to overflow and empty enough to hurt. She drew a breath smelling of lavender soap, baby detergent, and wipes before straightening. "Everything's going to be all right, *mijo*. You and me—that's all we need. We'll take care of each other and be the best family ever. Deal?"

"Um, Ilena?" The voice coming from around the corner of the bleachers was Fia's, sounding a bit wary. "You need to come out here."

"In just a minute. We're almost finished." She started to double-check all the snaps and flaps of John's outfit, but Fia spoke again.

"No, you need to come now."

Curious because Fia was never bossy, Ilena hefted John and the bag, then circled the end of the bleachers, where her feet stopped of their own accord. When Jessy took the baby from her, she hardly noticed. When she slid the bag strap off Ilena's arm, Ilena let her maneuver her like a mannequin. She couldn't help, couldn't think, couldn't do anything but stare.

There was an elf standing at the treats table. A tall, lean elf with blue-black hair and Irish blue eyes, wearing a green coat, gold tights, and curled-toe black shoes. His hat was conical, green with a gold stripe, and the expression on his face was priceless. Kids gaped, adults whispered, and the margarita girls waited, their excitement as palpable as Jared's discomfort.

Ilena's own response was simpler. She blossomed. Her eyes grew damp, her heart healed, and her Christmas joy returned in abundance. Wiping her clammy palms on her tunic, she moved closer.

His first words surprised her. "Go ahead. You know you want to ask."

Her smile formed slowly, and the tightness she'd lived with the last two days disappeared. "Why the weird costume?"

"What weird costume?" He moved to the end of the table, where nothing separated them but space. "I wanted to bring your gift."

The box he offered was jewelry-sized. From the intake of breath behind her, she knew her friends were hoping for an engagement ring. So was she.

She was half right. There was a silver ring inside, and attached to it were three keys. She stared at them, a lump forming in her throat.

After swiping her hand across her eyes, she found Jared standing right in front of her. His long index finger touched the first key. "The key to the SUV I just bought." He touched the second. "The key to the house I just bought." Then the third. "The key to the clinic I just bought."

Not rented, not temporary. *Bought.* He was committing to his practice, to the town, to a life here—to *her*—and that was so much better than an engagement ring.

"I didn't know what I was doing here when I came here, Ilena." His voice was hoarse, pitched so only she could hear. "I didn't know what to expect, how to adapt, if I could ever fit in. There are things I miss about New York, I admit, but I can live without them. What I can't live without is you and John. Anyplace in the world will be home as long as I'm sharing it with you two."

That was what *home* was all about—the people living

there with you. Ilena had been blessed to find that home with Juan, with her margarita girls, with John, and she was doubly blessed to find it with Jared.

She slid her arms around his waist and tilted her head back. "I love Tallgrass—this town has been home to me more than any other place I've lived—but despite what I said, I could leave for a good reason. And you, Jared, are a very good reason."

His strong, capable, healing hands cupped her face. "Thank you." His mouth brushed hers. "But how could I ask you to leave the perfect place for a family? You and John and me, and maybe one or two babies more."

Her eyes fluttered as he left a trail of kisses—sweet, innocent, indecently hot kisses—along her jaw. "Maybe four or five more," she murmured, but he chose that moment to stop kissing her. She looked up at him, his elf hat tilted endearingly to one side, and found him staring intently at her.

"Maybe," he agreed. "I love you, my darling. I'll love you forever. No matter how long, no matter wherever." Then he grinned, a big happy grin that perfectly suited his green-and-gold elf costume. "Will you marry me, Ilena?"

Her throat tightened, and she had to force out the words. "Jared, I love you. Of course I'll marry you." Cupping her hands to his cheeks, she rose onto tiptoe for another lovely, sweet, hungry kiss. Dimly, in the back of her mind, she heard Bennie speak.

"Anyone the least bit surprised that Ilena's in love with an elf?"

"Not me," Jessy said, and Fia echoed, "Not me."

Not me, either. Like she'd said, Ilena had been blessed.

An Excerpt from *He's So Fine*
by Jill Shalvis

For a guy balancing his weight between the flybridge of his boat and the dock, thinking about sex instead of what he was doing was a real bonehead move. Cole Donovan was precariously perched on the balls of his feet above some seriously choppy, icy water. So concentrating would've been the smart move.

But he had no smarts left, which was what happened when you hadn't had a good night's sleep in far too long—your brain wandered into areas it shouldn't.

Sex being one of those areas.

He shook his head to clear it. It was way too early for those kinds of thoughts. Not quite dawn, and the sky was a brilliant kaleidoscope of purples and blues and reds. Cole worked with a flashlight between his teeth, his fingers threading new electrical wire through the running lights on the stern. He only had a couple hours before a group of eight was coming through for a tour of the area.

That's what Cole and his two partners and best friends did—they hired out themselves and their fifty-foot Wright

Sport boat, chartering deep-sea fishing, whale watching, scuba diving...if it could be done, they did it. Sam was their financial guy and boatbuilder. Tanner was their scuba diving instructor and communications expert. Cole was the captain, chief navigator, mechanic, and—lucky him—the face of Lucky Harbor Charters, mostly because neither Sam nor Tanner was exactly a service-oriented person.

They'd had a warm Indian summer here in the Pacific Northwest, but October had roared in as if Mother Nature was pissed off at the world, and maybe in need of a Xanax to boot. But business was still good. Or it had been, until last night. He and Tanner had taken a group of frat boys out, and one of the idiots had managed to kick in the lights running along the stern, destroying not only the casing but also the electrical.

Cole could fix it—there was little he couldn't fix. But as he got down to it, a harsh wind slapped him in the face, threatening his balance. He kicked off the dock so that he was balanced entirely on the edge of the stern. Still not a position for the faint of heart, but after seven years on oil rigs and two more running Lucky Harbor Charters, Cole felt more at ease on the water than just about anywhere else.

He could smell the salt on the air and hear the swells smacking up against the dock moorings. The wind hit him again, and he shivered to the bone. Last week, he'd been out here working in board shorts and nothing else, the sun warming his back. Today he was in a knit cap, thick sweatshirt, cargo pants, and boots, and he was wishing for gloves like a little girl. He shoved his flashlight into his pocket, brought his hands to his mouth, and blew on his fingers for a moment before reaching for the wires again.

Just as they connected, there was a sizzle and a flash, and he jerked, losing his footing. The next thing he knew, he was airborne, weightless for a single heartbeat...

And then he hit the icy water, plunging deep, the contact stealing the air from his lungs. Stunned, he fought the swells, his heavy clothes, himself, eyes open as he searched for the flames that surely went along with the explosion.

Jesus, not another fire. That was his only thought as panic gripped him hard. He opened his mouth and—

Swallowed a lungful of seawater.

This cleared his head. He *wasn't* on the oil rig in the gulf. He *wasn't* in the explosion that had killed Gil, and nearly Tanner as well. He was in Lucky Harbor.

He kicked hard, breaking the surface, gasping as he searched for the boat, a part of him still not wholly convinced. But there. She was there, only a few feet away.

No flames, not a single lick. Just the cold-ass swells of the Pacific Northwest.

Treading water, Cole shook his head. A damn flashback, which he hadn't had in over a year—

"Omigod, I see you!" a female voice called out. "Just hang on, I'm coming!" This was accompanied by hurried footsteps clapping on the dock. "Help!" she yelled as she ran. "Help, there's a man in the water! Sir, sir, can you hear me? I'm coming. *Sir?*"

If she called him "sir" one more time, he was going to drown himself. His dad had been a *sir*. The old guy who ran the gas pumps on the corner of Main and First was a *sir*. Cole wasn't a damn *sir*. He was opening his mouth to tell her so, and also that he was fine, not in any danger at all, when she took a flying leap off the dock.

And landed right on top of him.

The icy water closed over both of their heads, and as another swell hit, they became a tangle of limbs and water-laden clothing. He fought free and once again broke the surface, whipping his head around to look for the woman.

No sign of her.

Shit. Gasping in a deep breath, he dove back down and found her doing what he'd been doing only a moment before—fighting the water and her clothes, and herself. Her own worst enemy, she was losing the battle and sinking fast. Grasping the back of her sweater, Cole hauled her up, kicking hard to get them both to the surface.

She sucked in some air and immediately started coughing, reaching out blindly for him and managing to get a handful of his junk.

"Maybe we could get to shore first," he said wryly.

Holding on to him with both arms and legs like a monkey, she squeezed him tight. "I've g-g-got y-y-you," she stuttered through already chattering teeth, then climbed on top of his head, sending him under again.

Jesus. He managed to yank her off him and get her head above water. "Hey—"

"D-don't panic," she told him earnestly. "It's g-g-gonna be o-o-okay."

She actually thought she was saving him. If the situation weren't so deadly, Cole might have thought some of this was funny. But she was turning into a Popsicle before his very eyes, and so was he. "Listen, just relax—"

"H-hang on to m-me," she said, and...dunked him again.

For the love of God. "*Stop* trying to save me," he told her. "I'm begging you."

Her hair was in her face, and behind the strands plastered to her skin, her eyes widened. "Oh, my God. You're trying to commit suicide."

"What? *No*." The situation was ridiculous, and he was frustrated and effing cold, but damn, it was hard not to be charmed by the fact that she was trying to save him, even as she was going down for the count herself. "I'm trying to keep you from killing me."

The flashback to the rig fire long gone, Cole treaded water to keep them afloat as he assessed their options. There were two.

Shore or boat.

They were at the stern of the boat, much closer to the swimming platform than to the shore. And in any case, there was no way his "rescuer" could swim the distance. Though Cole was a world-class swimmer himself, he was already frozen to the bone, and so was she. They needed out of the water...fast.

With a few strokes, he got them to the stern of the boat, where he hoisted his would-be rescuer up to the platform, pulling himself up after her.

She lay right where he'd dumped her, gulping in air, that long, dark hair everywhere. Leaning over her, he shoved the wet strands from her face to better see her and realized with a jolt that he recognized her. She lived in one of the warehouse apartments across from Lucky Harbor Charters.

Her name was Olivia Something-or-Other.

All he knew about her was that she hung out with Sam's fiancée, Becca; she ran some sort of shop downtown;

she dressed in a way that said both "hands off" and "hot mama"; and he'd caught her watching him and the guys surfing on more than one occasion.

"Y-y-you're bleeding," she said from flat on her back, staring up at him.

Cole brought his fingers to the sting on his temple, and—perfect—his fingers indeed came away red with his own blood. Just a cut, no less than he deserved after that stupid stunt of shocking the shit out of himself with the wiring and then tumbling into the water. "I'm fine." It was her he was worried about. Her jeans and sweater were plastered to her. She was missing a boot. And she was shivering violently enough to rattle the teeth right out of her head. "You're *not* fine," he said.

"Just c-c-cold."

No shit. "What the hell were you thinking?" he asked, "jumping in after me like that?"

Her eyes flashed open, and he discovered they were the exact same color as her hair—deep, dark chocolate.

"I th-th-thought you were d-d-drowning!" she said through chattering teeth.

Cole shook his head. "I didn't almost drown until you jumped on top of me."

"What h-h-happened?"

"I was working on the electrical wiring and got shocked and fell in."

"S-s-see? You needed help!"

He absolutely did not. But arguing with her would get them nowhere, except maybe dead. "Come on, the plan is to get you home and warmed up." Rising to his feet, he reached down and pulled her up with him, holding on to her when she wobbled. "Are you—"

"I'm f-f-fine," she said, and stepped back to look down at herself. "I l-l-lost my favorite b-b-boot rescuing y-y-you."

She called that a rescue? "Can you even swim?"

"Y-y-yes!" She crossed her arms over her chest. "A l-l-little bit."

He stared at her in disbelief. "A *little bit*? Seriously? You risked your life on that?"

"You were in t-t-trouble!"

Right. They could argue about that later. "Time to get you home, Supergirl."

"B-b-but my b-b-boot."

"We'll rescue the boot later."

"We w-w-will?"

No. Her boot was DOA—dead on arrival. "Later," he said again, and grabbing her hand, he pulled her across the platform, through the stern. He needed to get her off the boat.

She dug her heels in, one in just a sock, one booted.

"What?" he asked.

Still shivering wildly, she looked at him with misery. "I d-d-dropped my ph-ph-phone on the dock."

"Okay, we'll grab it."

"Y-y-yes, but I d-d-didn't drop my keys."

"That's good," he said, wondering if she'd hit her head.

"Y-y-you don't get it. I th-th-think I lost my k-k-keys in the w-w-water."

Well, shit. No keys, no getting her inside her place. This wasn't good. Nor was her color. She was waxen, pale. They couldn't delay getting her out of the elements and warm. "Okay, plan B," he said. "We warm you here on the boat." Again he started to tug her along, needing to get her inside and belowdecks, but she stumbled against him like her limbs weren't working.

Plan C, he thought grimly, and swung her up into his arms.

She clutched at him. "N-n-not necessary—"

Ignoring her, he got them both into the small galley, where he set her down on the bench at the table. Keeping his hands on her arms, he crouched in front of her to look into her eyes. "You still with me? You okay?"

"Y-y-y—" Giving up, she dropped her head to his chest.

"Not okay," he muttered, and stroked a hand down the back of her head and along her trembling frame.

Truth was, he wasn't much better off. His head was still bleeding, and his shoulder was throbbing. He had nothing on her, though. She was violently trembling against him. Easing her back, he got busy. First he cranked the heater, then he opened their linens storage box, pulling out towels and blankets, which he tossed in a stack at her side. "Okay," he said. "Strip."

An Excerpt from *Own the Wind* by Kristen Ashley

His cell rang and Parker "Shy" Cage opened his eyes.

He was on his back in his bed in his room at the Chaos Motorcycle Club's Compound. The lights were still on and he was buried under a small pile of women. One was tucked up against his side, her leg thrown over his thighs, her arm over his middle. The other was upside down, tucked to his other side, her knee in his stomach, her arm over his calves.

Both were naked.

"Shit," he muttered, twisting with difficulty under his fence of limbs. He reached out to his phone.

He checked the display, his brows drew together at the "unknown caller" he saw on the screen as he touched his thumb to it to take the call.

"Yo," he said into the phone.

"Shy?" a woman asked; she sounded weird, far away, quiet.

"You got me," he answered.

"It's Tabby."

He shot to sitting in bed, limbs flying and they weren't his.

"Listen, I'm sorry." Her voice caught like she was trying to stop crying or, maybe, hyperventilating, then she whispered, "So, so sorry but I'm in a jam. I think I might even be kinda...um, in trouble."

"Where are you?" he barked into the phone, rolling over the woman at his side and finding his feet.

"I...I...well, I was with this old friend and we were. Damn, um..." she stammered as Shy balanced the phone between ear and shoulder and tugged on his jeans.

"Babe, where are you?" he repeated.

"In a bathroom," she told him, as he tagged a tee off the floor and straightened, waiting for her to say more.

When she didn't, gently, he prompted, "I kinda need to know where that bathroom is, sugar."

"I, uh...this guy is...um, I didn't know it, obviously, but I think he's"—another hitch in her breath before she whispered so low he barely heard—"a bad dude."

Fuck.

Shit.

Fuck.

He nabbed his boots off the floor and sat on the bed to yank them on with his socks, asking, "Do I need backup?"

"I don't want anyone..." she paused. "Please, don't tell anyone. Just...can you please just text me when you're here? I'll stay in the bathroom, put my phone on vibrate so no one will hear, and I'll crawl out the window when you get here."

"Tab, no one is gonna think shit. Just give me the lay of the land. Are you in danger?"

"I'll crawl out the window."

He gentled his voice further and stopped putting on his boots to give her his full attention.

"Tabby, baby, are you in danger?"

"I ... well, I don't know really. There's a lot of drugs and I saw some, well, a lot of guns."

Shit.

"Address, honey," he urged, and she gave it to him.

Then she said, "Don't tell anyone, please. Just text."

"I'll give you that if you keep me notified and often. Text me. Just an 'I'm okay' every minute or so. I don't get one, I'll know you're not and I'm bringin' in the boys."

"I can do that," she agreed.

"Right, hang tight, I'll be there."

"Uh ... thanks, Shy."

"Anytime, Tab. Yeah?"

He waited, and it felt like years before she whispered, "Yeah."

He disconnected, pulled on his last boot, and stood, tugging on his tee as he turned to his bed. One of the women was up on an elbow and blinking at him. The other was still out.

As he found his knife in the nightstand and shoved the sheath into his belt, he ordered, "Get her ass up. Both of you need to get dressed and get gone." He reached into the nightstand and grabbed his gun, shoving it into the back waistband of his jeans and pulling his tee over it. "You got fifteen minutes to get out. You're not gone by the time I get back, I will not be happy."

"Sure thing, babe," the awake one muttered. She lifted a hand to shove at the hip of her friend.

Jesus.

Slicing a glance through them he knew he was done.

Some of the brothers, a lot older than him, enjoyed as much as they could get, however that came, and they didn't limit it to two pieces of ass.

He'd had that ride and often.

It hit him right then it went nowhere.

He'd never, not once, walked up to a woman who looked lost without him and became found the second she saw him. Who leaned into him the minute he touched her. Who made him laugh so hard, his head jerked back with it. Whose mouth he could take and the world melted away for him just as he made that same shit happen for her.

And he would not get that if he kept this shit up.

He jogged through the Compound to his bike and rode with his cell in his hand.

She texted, *I'm okay*, and Shy took in a calming breath and turned his eyes back to the road.

She texted again. This time, *I'm still okay*, and, getting closer to her, Shy felt his jaw begin to relax.

A few minutes later she texted again. This time it was *I'm still okay but this bathroom is seriously gross*.

When Shy got that, after his eyes went back to the road, he was flat-out smiling.

She kept texting her ongoing condition of *okay*, with a running commentary of how much she disliked her current location, until he was outside the house. He turned off his bike and scanned. Lights on in a front room, another one beaming from a small window at the opposite side at the back. The bathroom.

He bent his head to the phone and texted, *Outside, baby*.

Seconds later he saw a bare foot coming out the small window and another one, then legs. He kicked down the stand, swung off his bike, and jogged through the dark up the side of the house.

He caught her legs and tugged her out the rest of the way, putting her on her feet.

She tipped her head back to him, her face pale in the dark.

"Thanks," she said softly.

He, unfortunately, did not have all night to look in her shadowed but beautiful face. He had no idea what he was dealing with. He had to get them out of there.

He took her hand and muttered, "Let's go."

She nodded and jogged beside him, her hand in his, her shoes dangling from her other hand. He swung on his bike, she swung on behind him. A child born to the life, she wrapped her arms around him without hesitation.

He felt her tits pressed to his back and closed his eyes.

Then he opened them and asked, "Where you wanna go?"

"I need a drink," she replied.

"Bar or Compound?" he offered, knowing what she'd pick. She never came to the Compound anymore.

"Compound," she surprised him by answering.

Thank Christ he kicked those bitches out. He just hoped they followed orders.

He rode to the Compound, parked outside, and felt the loss when she pulled away and swung off. He lifted a hand to hold her steady as she bent to slide on her heels, then he took her hand and walked her into the Compound.

Luckily, it was deserted. Hopefully, his room was, too. He didn't need one of those bitches wandering out and fucking Tab's night even worse.

"Grab a stool, babe. I'll get you a drink," he muttered,

shifting her hand and arm out to lead her to the outside of the bar while he moved inside.

Tabby, he noted, took direction. She rounded the curve of the bar and took a stool.

Shy moved around the back of it and asked, "What're you drinking?"

"What gets you drunk the fastest?" she asked back, and he stopped, turned, put his hands on the bar and locked eyes on her.

"What kind of trouble did I pull you out of?" he asked quietly.

"None, now that I'm out that window," she answered quietly.

"You know those people?" he asked.

She shrugged and looked down at her hands on the bar. "An old friend. High school. Just her. The others..." She trailed off on another shrug.

Shy looked at her hands.

They were visibly shaking.

"Tequila," he stated, and her eyes came to his.

"What?"

"Gets you drunk fast."

She pressed her lips together and nodded.

He grabbed the bottle and put it in front of her.

She looked down at it, then up at him, and her head tipped to the side when he didn't move.

"Glasses?" she prompted.

He tagged the bottle, unscrewed the top, lifted it to his lips, and took a pull. When he was done, he dropped his arm and extended it to her.

"You can't get drunk fast, you're fuckin' with glasses," he informed her.

The tip of her tongue came out to wet her upper lip and Jesus, he forgot how cute that was.

Luckily, she took his mind off her tongue when she took the bottle, stared at it a beat, then put it to her lips and threw back a slug.

The bottle came down with Tabby spluttering and Shy reached for it.

Through a grin, he advised, "You may be drinking direct, sugar, but you still gotta drink smart."

"Right," she breathed out like her throat was on fire.

He put the bottle to his lips and took another drag before he put it to the bar.

Tabby wrapped her hand around it, lifted it, and sucked some back, but this time she did it smart and her hand with the bottle came down slowly, although she was still breathing kind of heavy.

When she recovered, he leaned into his forearms on the bar and asked softly, "You wanna talk?"

"No," she answered sharply, her eyes narrowing, the sorrow shifting through them slicing through his gut. She lifted the bottle, took another drink before locking her gaze with his. "I don't wanna talk. I don't wanna share my feelings. I don't wanna *get it out*. I wanna *get drunk*."

She didn't leave any lines to read through, she said it plain, so he gave her that out.

"Right, so we gonna do that, you sittin' there sluggin' it back and me standin' here watchin' you, or are we gonna do something? Like play pool."

"I rock at pool," she informed him.

"Babe, I'll wipe the floor with you."

"No way," she scoffed.

"Totally," he said through a grin.

"You're so sure, darlin', we'll make it interesting," she offered.

"I'm up for that," he agreed. "I win, you make me cookies. You win, you pick."

He barely finished speaking before she gave him a gift the likes he'd never had in his entire fucking life.

The pale moved out of her features as pink hit her cheeks, life shot into her eyes, making them vibrant, their startling color rocking him to his fucking core before she bested all that shit and burst out laughing.

He had no idea what he did, what he said, but whatever it was, he'd do it and say it over and over until he took his last breath just so he could watch her laugh.

He didn't say a word when her laughter turned to chuckles and continued his silence, his eyes on her.

When she caught him looking at her, she explained, "My cooking, hit and miss. Sometimes, it's brilliant. Sometimes, it's…" she grinned "…*not*. Baking is the same. I just can't seem to get the hang of it. I don't even have that"—she lifted up her fingers to do air quotation marks—"*signature dish* that comes out great every time. I don't know what it is about me. Dad and Rush, even Tyra, they rock in the kitchen. Me, no." She leaned in. "*Totally* no. So I was laughing because anyone who knows me would not think cookies from me would be a good deal for a bet. Truth is, they could be awesome but they could also seriously suck."

"How 'bout I take my chances?" he suggested.

She shrugged, still grinning. "Your funeral."

Her words made Shy tense, and the pink slid out of her cheeks, the life started seeping out of her eyes.

"Drink," he ordered quickly.

"What?" she whispered, and he reached out and slid the tequila to her.

"Drink. Now. Suck it back, babe. Do it thinkin' what you get if you win."

She nodded, grabbed the bottle, took a slug, and dropped it to the bar with a crash, letting out a totally fucking cute "Ah" before she declared, "You change my oil."

His brows shot up. "That's it?"

"I need my oil changed and it costs, like, thirty dollars. I can buy a lot of stuff with thirty dollars. A lot of stuff *I want*. I don't want *oil*. My car does but I don't."

"Tabby, sugar, your dad part-owns the most kick-ass garage this side of the Mississippi and most of the other side, and you're paying for oil changes?"

Her eyes slid away and he knew why.

Fuck.

She was doing it to avoid him. Still.

Serious as shit, this had to stop.

So he was going to stop it.

"We play pool and we get drunk and we enjoy it, that's our plan, so let's get this shit out of the way," he stated. Her eyes slid back to him and he said flat out, "I fucked up. It was huge. It was a long time ago but it marked you. You were right. I was a dick. I made assumptions, they were wrong and I acted on 'em and I shouldn't have and that was more wrong. I wish you would have found the time to get in my face about it years ago so we could have had it out, but that's done. When you did get in my face about it, I should have sorted my shit, found you, and apologized. I didn't do that, either. I'd like to know why you dialed my number tonight, but if you don't wanna share that shit, that's cool, too. I'll just say, babe, I'm glad you did. You need a safe place just to forget shit and escape, I'll give it to you. Tonight. Tomorrow. Next week. Next month. That safe place is me, Tabby. But I don't want that old shit haunting this. Ghosts haunt until you get rid of them. Let's get rid of that fuckin' ghost and move on so I can beat your ass at pool."

As he spoke, he saw the tears pool in her eyes but he kept going, and when he stopped he didn't move even though it nearly killed him. Not to touch her, even her hand. Not to give her something.

It killed.

Before he lost the fight to hold back, she whispered, "You are never gonna beat my ass at pool."

That was when he grinned, leaned forward, and wrapped his hand around hers sitting on the bar.

"Get ready to have your ass kicked," he said softly.

"Oil changes for a year," she returned softly.

"You got it but cookies for a year," he shot back.

"Okay, but don't say I didn't warn you," she replied.

He'd eat her cookies, they were brilliant or they sucked. If Tabitha Allen made it, he'd eat anything.

Shy didn't share that.

He gave her hand a squeeze, nabbed the bottle, and took off down the bar toward the cues on the wall.

Tabby followed.

They were in the dark, in his bed, in his room in the Compound.

Shy was on his back, eyes to the ceiling.

Tabby was three feet away, on her side, her chin was tipped down.

She was obliterated.

Shy wasn't even slightly drunk.

She'd won four games, he'd won five.

Cookies for a year.

Now, he was winning something else, because tequila didn't make Tabitha Allen a happy drunk.

It made her a talkative one.

It also made her get past ugly history and trust him with absolutely everything that mattered right now in her world.

"DOA," she whispered to the bed.

"I know, sugar," he whispered to the ceiling.

"Where did you hear?" she asked.

"Walkin' into the Compound, boys just heard and they were taking off."

"You didn't come to the hospital."

He was surprised she'd noticed.

"No. I wasn't your favorite person. Didn't think I could help. Went up to Tack and Cherry's, helped Sheila with the boys," he told her.

"I know. Ty-Ty told me," she surprised him again by saying. "That was cool of you to do. They're a handful. Sheila tries but the only ones who can really handle them are Dad, Tyra, Rush, Big Petey, and me."

Shy didn't respond.

"So, uh...thanks," she finished.

"No problem, honey."

She fell silent and Shy gave her that.

She broke it.

"Tyra had to cancel all the wedding plans."

"Yeah?" he asked quietly.

"Yeah," she answered. "Second time she had to do

that. That Elliott guy wasn't dead when she had to do it for Lanie, but still. Two times. Two weddings. It isn't worth it. All that planning. All that money..." she pulled in a shaky breath "...not worth it. I'm not doing it again. I'm never getting married."

At that, Shy rolled to his side, reached out, and found her hand lying on the bed.

He curled his hand around hers, held tight, and advised, "Don't say that, baby. You're twenty-two years old. You got your whole life ahead of you."

"So did he."

Fuck, he couldn't argue that.

He pulled their hands up the bed and shifted slightly closer before he said gently, "If he was in this room right now, sugar, right now, he wouldn't want this. He wouldn't want to hear you say that shit. Dig deep, Tabby. What would he want to hear you say?"

She was silent then he heard her breath hitch before she whispered, "I'd give anything..."

She trailed off and went quiet.

"Baby," he whispered back.

Her hand jerked and her body slid across the bed to slam into his, her face in his throat, her arm winding around him tight, her voice so raw, it hurt to hear. His own throat was ragged just listening.

"I'd give anything for him to be in this room. *Anything*. I'd give my hair, and I *like* my hair. I'd give my car, and Dad fixed that car up for me. I *love* that car. I'd swim an ocean. I'd walk through arrows. I'd *bleed* for him to be here."

She burrowed deeper into him and Shy took a deep breath, pressing closer, giving her his warmth. He wrapped an arm around her and pulled her tighter as she cried quietly, one hand holding his tight.

He said nothing but listened, eyes closed, heart burning, to the sounds of her grief.

Time slid by and her tears slowly stopped flowing.

Finally, she said softly, "I dreamed a dream."

"What, sugar?"

"I dreamed a dream," she repeated.

He tipped his head and put his lips to the top of her hair but he had no reply. He knew it sucked when dreams died. He'd been there. There were no words to say. Nothing made it better except time.

Then she shocked the shit out of him and started singing, her clear, alto voice wrapping around a song he'd never heard before, but its words were gutting, perfect for her, what she had to be feeling, sending that fire in his heart to his throat so high, he would swear he could taste it.

"*Les Mis*," she whispered when she was done.

"What?"

"The musical. *Les Misérables*. Jason took me to go see it. It's very sad."

If that was a song from the show, it fucking had to be.

She pressed closer. "I dreamed a dream, Shy."

"You'll dream more dreams, baby."

"I'll never dream," she whispered, her voice lost, tragic.

"We'll get you to a dream, honey," he promised, pulling her closer.

She pressed in, and he listened as her breath evened out, felt as her body slid into sleep, all the while thinking her hair smelled phenomenal.

Shy turned into her, trapping her little body under his and muttering, "We'll get you to a dream."

Tabby held his hand in her sleep.

Shy held her but didn't sleep.

The sun kissed the sky and Shy's eyes closed.

When he opened them, she was gone.

An Excerpt from *Inn at Last Chance*
by Hope Ramsay

The bitter January wind had blown in a cold front. The clouds hung heavy and somber over the swamp. There would be rain. Possibly ice.

Jenny Carpenter wrapped a hand-knit shawl around her shoulders and gazed through the kitchen window of the house she'd bought last August. The tops of the Carolina pines bent in the wind. The weatherman said it was going to be quite a storm, and Allenberg County had already had one ice storm this year—on Christmas Eve. It was now just two weeks past New Year's Day.

She turned away from the window toward the heart of her house. Her kitchen restoration was nearly finished. Yellow subway tiles marched up the backsplash behind the Vulcan stove. An antique pie safe occupied the far wall. The curtains were gingham. Everything about this room was bright and cheerful, in sharp contrast with the weather outside.

Jenny closed her eyes and imagined the smell of apple pie cooking in her professional baker's oven. This kitchen would rival the one Savannah Randall had installed at the old movie theater in town. She smiled. Savannah's strudel was good, but Jenny's apple pie had still won the blue ribbon at the Watermelon Festival last summer. She could almost hear Mother sermonizing about pride, and her smile faded. She turned back toward the window.

She couldn't remember a colder January. And Jenny hated even the mild winters that usually visited South Carolina. Today she had good reason to hate the season. Winter was getting the best of her.

She'd hired a crew to cut back the overgrowth on either side of the driveway, but they had called to say that they wouldn't be out today, and probably not tomorrow. The movers weren't going to show up today, either, which meant Mother's antique furniture would spend yet another night in the commercial storage space where it had been sitting for five years. Without furniture Jenny would have to postpone her plans to move in at the end of the week. Finally, Wilma Riley, the chair of the Methodist Women's Sewing Circle, had called five minutes ago all atwitter because there was ice in the forecast.

The sewing circle had graciously volunteered to help Jenny sew curtains for the bedrooms and sitting room. The fabric bolts—all traditional Low Country floral designs— were stacked in the room that would soon be the dining room. But as Wilma pointed out, the gals were not coming all the way out to the swamp on a stormy day in January. So today, Jenny might be the only one sitting out here sewing.

It wasn't just the weather that had her second-guessing herself. She'd taken a huge risk buying The Jonquil House. The old place wasn't anywhere near downtown. If she'd been able to buy Charlotte Wolfe's house, her bed-and-breakfast would have been located near the middle of things. And she would probably already be in business, since Charlotte's house was in perfect condition.

But Charlotte had changed her mind about selling. She'd returned from California with her son, Simon. And Simon had married Molly Canaday, and they were all living happily in Charlotte's beautiful house.

So Jenny had bought The Jonquil House, which was way out on Bluff Road, near the public boat launch on the Edisto River—a prime location for fishing and hunting. And you couldn't beat the view from the porch on a summer's day. She hoped to attract business from fishermen and hunters and eco-tourists anxious to canoe the Edisto or bird-watch in the swamp.

The Jonquil House had the additional benefit of being dirt-cheap, since it had been abandoned for years. But Jenny had to spend a lot of cash to shore up the foundation, replace the roof, and update the plumbing and electrical. Not to mention installing her state-of-the-art kitchen. Still, the purchase price had been so ridiculously low that, on balance, Jenny was financially ahead of where she would have been if she'd bought Charlotte's house.

And if all went well, The Jonquil House would be open for business by March first, just in time for the jonquils to be in full bloom. There were hundreds of them naturalized in the woods surrounding the house. No doubt they had been planted by the Raintree family, who had built the house more than a hundred years ago as a hunting camp and summer getaway.

Those jonquils were the reason she'd chosen yellow for her kitchen walls. She couldn't wait to take pictures of her beautiful white house against the backdrop of the dark Carolina woods, gray Spanish moss, and bright yellow daffodils.

That photo would be posted right on the home page of the inn's website, which was still under construction, too.

She was thinking about her breakfast menu when there came a sudden pounding at her front door. Her new brass knocker had yet to be installed, but that didn't seem to bother whoever had come to call.

In fact, it sounded like someone was trying to knock the darn door down.

She hurried down the center hall, enjoying the rich patina of the restored wood floors and the simple country feeling of the white lath walls. Maybe the movers had changed their minds, and she'd be able to get Mother's furniture set up in the bedrooms after all.

She pulled open the door.

"It's about damn time; it's freezing out here." A man wearing a rain-spattered leather jacket, a soggy gray wool hat, and a steely scowl attempted to walk into her hallway. Jenny wasn't about to let this biker dude intimidate her, even if he was a head taller than she was.

His features were stern, and his nose a tad broad, as if it had been broken once. Several days' growth of slightly salt-and-pepper stubble shadowed his cheeks, and his eyebrows glowered above eyes so dark they might have been black. If he'd been handsome or heroic looking, she might have been afraid of him or lost her nerve. Handsome men always made Jenny nervous. But big guys with leather jackets and attitudes had never bothered her in the least. She always assumed that men like that were hiding a few deep insecurities.

"Can I help you?" she said in her most polite, future-innkeeper voice.

"You damn well can. I want a room."

"Um, I'm sorry but the inn isn't open."

"Of course it's open. You're here. The lights are on. There's heat."

"We're not open for business."

He leaned into the door frame. Jenny held her ground. "Do you have any idea who I am?"

She was tempted to tell him he was an ass, but she didn't use language like that. Mother had beaten that tendency out of her. It didn't stop her from thinking it, though.

When she didn't reply, he said, "I'm the man who sold you this house. I would like, very much, to come in out of the rain."

"The man who—"

"The name's Gabriel Raintree. My family built this house. Now let me in."

She studied his face. Gabriel Raintree was a *New York Times* bestselling author of at least twenty books, several of which had been made into blockbuster horror films. His books were not on her reading list. And she wasn't much of a moviegoer.

She'd never met Mr. Raintree. The sale of The Jonquil House had been undertaken by his business manager and attorney. So she had no idea if this guy was the real Gabriel Raintree or some poser. Either way she wasn't going to let him come in. Besides, the house was not ready for guests. The furniture had not even arrived.

"I'm sorry. The inn isn't open."

His black eyebrows lowered even farther, and his mouth kind of curled up at the corner in something like a sneer. He looked angry, and it occurred to Jenny that maybe she needed to bend a little. The minute that thought crossed her mind, she rejected it. She had inherited a steel backbone from Mother, and this was a good time to employ it. She wouldn't get very far as an innkeeper if she allowed herself to be a doormat.

"I need a place to stay," he said, "for at least three months. I'm behind on my deadline."

Three months. Good Lord, she wasn't running a boardinghouse. But then, she supposed that if anyone could afford three months' lodging at a B&B it would be someone like Gabriel Raintree.

The income would be nice. But she wasn't ready for any guests.

"I'm very sorry. The inn won't be open until March. If you need to stay in Last Chance, there's always the Peach Blossom Motor Court. Or you could see if Miriam Randall will take you in. She sometimes takes in boarders."

"Damn it all, woman, this is my house." He pushed against the door, and Jenny pushed back.

"Not anymore," she said.

He stopped pushing and stepped back from the threshold. By the deep furrows on his brow, she could only surmise that he was surprised anyone would stand in his way. She slammed the door on him to punctuate her point. Then she twisted the bolt lock and took a couple of steps back from it, her heart hammering in her chest.

Gabe stood on the porch breathing hard, trying to control his anger and a dozen other emotions he didn't want to feel, chief among them a deep, gnawing loneliness.

The hollow feeling had been with him for a long time—even before his breakup with Delilah years ago. And now, this place and the memories it raised made the loneliness feel deep and wide, like a gaping chasm. There was something dark and frightening down in the depths of that empty place. Something monstrous.

He leaned on the porch railing and looked around at the familiar scene. His younger self had been happy and carefree here. Christ, it had been a long, long time since he'd felt that way.

And The Jonquil House was perfect for what he needed right now, a quiet place almost entirely off the grid where he could wrestle with his writer's block and escape from his mistakes. Hiding out here in the middle of nowhere seemed like a good idea. He'd have solitude. He could be alone with his demons.

But a tiny little innkeeper stood between him and what he needed. It was worse than that—she hadn't even recognized him.

He let go of a short bark of laughter. He should be happy. In Charleston, he couldn't walk down a street without someone, usually dressed like a Goth, accosting him and wanting a piece of him.

He stared at the closed door. He was an idiot if he let that woman bruise his ego. Besides, he'd come here to hide out. And she'd just convinced him it was the perfect place for that singular activity.

He surveyed the overgrown drive, memories filling his head. Twenty-five years ago he would have been greeted by Zeph Gibbs, the hunting guide and caretaker. Lottie Easley would be back in the kitchen cooking up hoppin'-john and corn bread and fried okra. He could almost taste Lottie's cooking.

And he longed to see their faces. But they were ghosts now. Especially Luke, the brother he'd lost twenty-five years ago in a hunting accident.

Ten-year-old Gabe had been there the day Luke died, but Gabe had no memory of what had happened that awful day. Those memories were locked behind a barrier as high and thick as Hadrian's Wall.

His heartbeat echoed inside his empty chest. He had worshiped his older brother, and Luke's death had changed everything.

He moved down onto the porch step and let the rain fall on his head and shoulders. It was quiet here. Peaceful. Precisely the kind of place he needed to get back in touch with his muse. The kind of place he needed to write the damn book that had been eluding him for almost a year. The kind of place where a lonely man could simply be left alone.

The muscles of his neck and shoulders tensed in frustration. If the inn wasn't going to open until March, he'd have to come up with another plan.

But he didn't want a plan B. He wanted to come back here. Something in his gut told him that this was precisely the right place to be.

The rain was picking up, and sleet was beginning to mix with it. The roads were going to get bad before too much longer.

Either way, he'd have to stay the night at the seedy motel in town. But tomorrow, when the storm had passed, he'd come back out here and negotiate. The little innkeeper had her price. Everyone did.

Tomorrow he'd buy back The Jonquil House.

The wipers smeared the light from the motel's sign as Gabe pulled his Lexus SUV into the parking lot. Peach blossoms blinked on and off, like opening flowers, but the neon was burned out in a few places, so that the sign read "each Bosom Moo," which Gabe found vaguely hilarious, given the motel's reputation.

He remembered the motel from his boyhood. It hadn't looked nearly so run-down twenty-five years ago.

He sat in his car for a long moment, the wipers thumping a syncopated counterpoint to the recording of Bach's Brandenburg Concerto Number 1 coming from his top-of-the-line sound system.

Maybe he should turn around and head toward Columbia. Columbia might be a sleepy southern capital, but they had hotels there. Nice ones, with room service. He might be able to hide out in Columbia. Of course, he'd have to be careful not to go out to eat or walk the streets or any of those things. There were a lot of people in Columbia, and some of them were sure to recognize him. Someone would tweet about him. And his editor would come looking for him. And his crazy fans would find him and hound him.

But here, he was just one of the Raintree boys, come back to town after a long hiatus. If he wanted to be a hermit living out at The Jonquil House, the people here would let him be. Last Chance was full up to the brim with eccentric people and no one thought anything about it.

Besides, the fishing was better here.

He almost smiled at the thought, and then he remembered that it was the dead of winter and he'd pretty much freeze his ass off if he went fishing. And of course, he hadn't been fishing in years. But if he lived here, he might take it up again.

He weighed his options as he watched the icy rain splatter on his windshield. In the end, the sleet made the decision for him. The Lexus might have four-wheel drive, but that was next to useless on black ice.

He checked in, took one brief look at the run-down furniture in the room, and then headed back out into the weather. There had to be a café or something where he could get himself some dinner.

It occurred to him that he'd almost never eaten out when he'd come to visit this place as a boy. Lottie had done the cooking. He'd have to find himself a cook, once he bought The Jonquil House back.

Just thinking about Lottie's corn bread had his stomach growling. He hadn't eaten since this morning, and he was feeling a bit light-headed. His blood sugar was low.

He reached for the roll of Life Savers he always carried and popped one into his mouth. It was cherry flavored.

He stood on the concrete pad under the roof overhang that protected his room door from the rain. It wasn't a long walk from here into the heart of downtown Last Chance, but the ice was building on the sidewalks fast. The road, on the other hand, had been treated with sand and salt.

So he took a chance and drove the SUV slowly back into downtown. He found a parking spot in front of The Kismet movie theater. The old movie palace looked pretty good, especially compared with the run-down motel.

Looking up at the marquee, it finally hit him that it had been a quarter century since he'd set foot in this little town. *Lethal Weapon* had been the last movie he and Luke had seen in this old movie theater. Luke died three days later, on the Saturday before Easter.

The memory caught him unaware. He tried not to think too much about Luke.

Maybe that was the missing puzzle piece. Maybe that was why he'd awakened yesterday and knew that he had to return here. Who knew.

He climbed out of his car and stood for a long time under the marquee. It wasn't a first-run theater anymore, and that hardly surprised him. The signs on the front door said it was only open on Friday and Saturday nights. These days the movies came with dinner attached.

A light was burning in the theater's lobby. He took a step toward the glass doors and peered in. The place was much as he'd remembered. A gifted carpenter had created a masterpiece when he'd set his hand to The Kismet's lobby. It was awash with Moroccan motifs and Moorish archways. Gabe cocked his head to get an angle on the ceiling, but it was too dark. Once upon a time, the ceiling had been painted like a night sky with twinkling stars.

The theater was worthy of historic registry status, and it warmed him in some odd way to know that it hadn't been left to molder.

A moving shadow just beyond the candy counter momentarily startled him, until he remembered that the owner of The Kismet had always kept a cat—a black one. The shadow danced again, casting itself eerily against the walls. Gabe cupped his hands around his face to get a better look.

A black man with gray hair, wearing a pair of faded overalls and carrying a toolbox, stood up from behind the candy counter.

Gabe took a step back, his heart pounding. He would know that man anywhere. That face was from out of the distant past. Why had he assumed that Zeph Gibbs was dead and gone?

The hairs on the back of Gabe's neck rose, and the icy night got a little more frigid—cold enough to freeze him right where he stood while something hot and evil writhed in his gut.

The door opened. Zeph stepped out of the theater and stopped in his tracks. Time seemed to slow down as their gazes met and clashed.

"Gabe?" Zeph cocked his head.

"It's me."

"Lord a'mighty, what are you doin' here?"

It wasn't exactly a hearty welcome, but that didn't surprise Gabe for some reason he couldn't exactly articulate. Zeph had been a big part of his boyhood. This man had taught him to shoot a BB gun and bait a hook and walk quietly in the woods. And yet seeing him once again after a quarter century brought no joy.

"Hello, Zeph." There seemed to be a torrent of words locked up inside him, but the simple greeting was all he could manage. Christ on a crutch, he had some strange feelings about Zeph.

Gabe had turned Zeph into a villain named Zebulon Stroud in the novel titled *Black Water*. And *Black Water* had taken Gabe to the top of the *New York Times* bestseller list. *Black Water* was also the first of Gabe's novels to be made into a feature-length motion picture. Danny Glover had won an Oscar for his portrayal of the villain. Zeb Stroud was one of those characters people remembered, like Hannibal Lecter.

"You need to leave," Zeph said.

"That's going to be hard with all this ice."

"Tomorrow then, when it melts."

"Look, Zeph, about the character in *Black Water*, I sure don't want you to take it—"

"This has nothing to do with that story. I'm not mad at you for that. But you can't stay here."

"I can't stay here? Why not? I know The Jonquil

House has been sold, but I can certainly book a room at the motel. In fact, I have."

"Why are you here?"

"I was thinking about buying The Jonquil House back from that little woman who owns it now."

"You can't. You have no business being in this town. Not now. Not ever."

This confused him. "Why not?"

"You know good and well why it's a bad idea to come back here." Zeph turned and locked the theater door.

Gabe couldn't think of one good reason why he shouldn't stay. But he understood why Zeph wouldn't be happy about his being here. After all, Zeph was responsible for Luke's death. The man probably didn't want Gabe hanging around reminding him of that tragedy all the time. Granddad had never forgiven Zeph.

But Gabe could.

"Look, Zeph, I'm not my grandfather. I don't blame you for what happened. I'm not here to rub your nose in it."

Zeph turned around. He didn't say a word, but he pressed his lips together as if he was trying damn hard not to say something ugly.

Gabe stuck out his hand. "I forgive you."

Zeph stood there staring at Gabe's outstretched hand as if he had been speaking in tongues or something. "What are you talking about, boy? You and I both know that's not why I want you to go."

"Then why?" He lowered his hand.

Zeph's eyes unfocused for a moment. It made him look a little wild eyed and crazy, like Zebulon Stroud. Staring into those black eyes was more than unsettling. The bad guy in *Black Water* had been a psychopathic killer.

But of course Zeph wasn't like that at all. Luke's death was an accident.

"You don't remember, do you?" Zeph said.

"I don't remember what?"

Zeph shook his head. "Lord have mercy," he said, then blew out a long breath that created a cloud of steam.

"You mean about Luke?" Gabe said. "No I don't remember exactly what happened. Afterward, you know, I went to see a therapist, and she told Granddad that it was just as well that I didn't remember. But now I'm starting to think maybe that was bad advice. What happened, Zeph? You're the only one who can tell me."

"You should go back to Charleston. Don't come here turning over rocks. You might not like what you find underneath."

And with that, the man who'd once been Granddad's hunting and fishing guide turned on his well-worn boot and strode off into the storm.

An Excerpt from
Flirting with Forever
by Molly Cannon

She hadn't bothered with a bathing suit.

Irene floated in her swimming pool, letting the hot Texas sun lull her into a lethargic daydream state. She closed her eyes and listened idly to the chirping birds and the chattering squirrels. Peace and quiet.

Exactly what she needed.

No one could see her way up here on her hillside home. The front of the house looked down on the small town of Everson. She could stand on her front porch and watch the traffic move through the streets, but the back of her house was completely private, backing up to an undeveloped area of small hills and trees. No, she was quite safely out of view, drifting languidly in her own private world.

The rumbling sound of a small plane overhead disturbed her tranquility. As she shaded her eyes it flew closer and then buzzed directly overhead. She made no attempt to cover herself. In fact she was tempted to sit up and wave. She had never been known for her modesty, and if some bozo pilot was out for a joyride he might as well enjoy a cheap thrill. But she didn't react at all, instead deciding she wasn't going to let the uninvited visitor ruin her day. She watched as the plane tilted its wings, in a way of a greeting it seemed, and then circled around heading in the direction of the small airfield on the outskirts of town.

In a flash she realized exactly who was flying that noisy, intrusive airplane. Theo Jacobson. She knew he was coming back to town. According to his brother Jake, he was due back in town for the wedding sometime this week. It was just like him to make a splashy return, arriving like some winged warrior mocking her from on high.

Good, she thought defiantly. Let him have a good look. He should get an undisguised eyeful of the woman he hadn't wanted all those years ago. The woman he hadn't bothered to acknowledge since. He broke her heart and never looked back. A big fluffy cloud wafted by, momentarily covering the sun. She trailed a hand through the relaxing water, but it suddenly felt too cold. She slipped off the float and pulled herself from the pool. A terry cloth robe lay draped across a lounge chair, and she picked it up, wrapping it around her chilly body. With one more look at the now empty blue sky, she opened the back door and went inside her house.

"Welcome to the Rise N Shine. My name is Nell, and I'll be your server today."

Theo looked up at the waitress standing by the booth at the back of the local diner. She was willowy and tall with a ponytail of thick red hair trailing down her back. Her expression was carefully polite.

"Well hello, Nell." He added a smile to soften the

impact of his wild and wooly appearance. He knew he must look like a grizzled mountain man who'd just stumbled back into town after a long, cold winter's hibernation. That wasn't too far from the truth. His full dark beard and unruly mess of long black hair were a testament to the untamed months he'd just spent running backcountry tours up in Alaska. As soon as he'd landed he'd called his brother to let him know he'd arrived and then called Everson's only taxi to take him into town. He was starving, so he'd had Bo Birdwell drop him at the diner. Later this afternoon he'd meet up with Jake and Marla Jean.

The smile must have helped because she smiled back. "Are you ready to order?"

"Sure, I'll have the meat loaf and mashed potatoes. And a side of mustard greens." He took a quick glance at the menu and then refocused his blue eyes on her again. "And I think I'll try some of that peach pie, too. What do you think?"

"Good choice. My mom makes the best meat loaf in the world, and her peach pie is my personal favorite."

"Okay, then. That's good enough for me. I'm hungry enough to eat a bear. So, Bertie's your mother?" He nodded toward the Rise N Shine's owner loudly holding court at the front counter.

"She sure is. And I was just telling her we should add bear to the menu." They both laughed in the way people do when they're flirting rather than because something is actually funny. "Are you new in town?"

"Actually, I'm just passing through. I'll be here for a week or two, and then I'm taking off again to parts unknown." He gestured out the window indicating the far horizon.

She peered out the window and then looked back at him. Moving closer, she said, "Parts unknown. That sounds mighty adventurous."

He leaned closer, too, like he had secrets to share. "It certainly can be, Nell. I'm Theo Jacobson, by the way."

Her eyes widened. "Jacobson? Wait a minute. As in Jake Jacobson?"

"The very one. He's my big brother. I'm here for his wedding."

She held the order pad against her breast as she studied him more closely. "I knew you looked familiar. Underneath all that hair, that is."

He grinned. "So you know Jake?" He wasn't surprised. Everson was a small town after all.

"Of course. And Marla Jean, too." She gave his shaggy head of hair another once-over. "Maybe you should stop off at her place for a haircut."

His future sister-in-law owned the local barbershop. "Are you suggesting I look uncivilized?" He leaned back in the booth with an unrepentant grin.

She raised her eyebrows, fully flirting now. "Uncivilized isn't necessarily a bad thing, Theo Jacobson. I was just thinking you might be worth asking out if I could see what you look like under all that shaggy growth."

He was thinking Nell was pretty damn cute. He wouldn't mind spending some time getting to know her better while he was in Everson. He wouldn't mind that one little bit. After all, he was here to have a good time. Enjoy the wedding. Help Jake with some jobs. Keeping it all easy and uncomplicated.

Which was why he'd been out of his mind to buzz Irene Cornwell's house on the way into town. Because he certainly didn't plan to spend the short time he was here reflecting on the time in his life that included her. Some things were better left in the past where they belonged. But the last time he was in town she'd ignored him completely, didn't even give him the passing courtesy she'd extend to a stranger, and he could admit he'd let it get under his skin. It chafed, and festered, and bugged the hell out of him. He was determined not to let her get away with doing that again. Not that he expected her to run and jump into his arms. He didn't want that, either. A simple hello or nod of the head would do.

But the image of her floating buck naked in her swimming pool would be hard to forget. As soon as he'd spotted her he'd reacted with something close to physical pain and an old, ancient longing that he thought had died out a long time ago. His body didn't seem to get the message that she was off limits now. With effort he refocused on the woman standing in front of him. "Are all the women around these parts as bold as you, Nell?"

She laughed. "Hold your horses, mister. Let's not get ahead of ourselves. I haven't asked you out yet, have I? And I better go put in your order." She winked and turned to go.

He watched her walk back toward the front of the diner, taking his time, admiring the way her waitress uniform skimmed tightly over her perky little butt. This visit to Everson might turn out to be a lot more fun than he'd expected.

"Well, well. If it isn't the best man."

As Theo made his way through the gate and into the backyard of the Hazelnut Inn a soft feminine voice hit him like a nasty punch to the gut. He'd recognize that voice anywhere. Irene Cornwell. He must have been thinking about her so much that she'd materialized right in front of him like a magic trick gone wrong. Shit. Irene Cornwell. Fully clothed this time. Double shit. And she was actually speaking to him this time. Mission accomplished. He could check that off his list. Not just a hello or a nod of her head, but an entire sentence. For some reason it didn't feel like a victory. It felt like he'd jumped out of his airplane without a parachute. Free-falling, waiting for the impact that was sure to follow. But he wasn't about to let her see him sweat, so he slapped a cocky grin on his face and said, "Well, if it isn't Irene Cornwell. How the heck have you been, Ree?"

She sat at an outside patio table with a thick file folder open in front of her and a pair of big, black-framed sunglasses shoved on top of her head. Her long, dark hair was caught up in a messy bun that he guessed was her attempt at looking serious. He allowed himself a minute to stare. She was still the most beautiful woman he'd ever seen, but he would be careful to keep that opinion strictly to himself. Seeing her from a distance had been bad enough. But now, here she was close enough to touch. He was determined not to even consider that idea. Not even if someone offered him a ten-foot pole.

Her smile was bright and brittle. "No one calls me Ree anymore, Theodore. And I'm fine, thanks."

He laughed thinking how easy it was to get a rise from her. "No one but you ever called me Theodore, and that was only when you were mad at me. I hope you're still not mad at me after all this time."

"Don't be silly." She waved her hand as if she thought he was being ridiculous. "Of course not."

He dropped into the chair across from her. "I'm glad to hear that, and this is great. We're actually sitting here having a conversation. Last time I was in Everson you pretended I didn't exist." He kept smiling like he was tickled pink by their unexpected reunion.

Her chin lifted regally. "I don't know what you're talking about." He didn't push it when she changed the subject. "Jake will be glad you made it home for the wedding."

He looked at his watch. "Yeah, I'm supposed to meet him and Marla Jean here at four."

She nodded to the back door of the inn. "They're inside talking to Etta about the food for the wedding reception, but they should be out any minute. We need to finish going over the details of the ceremony."

"We?" He couldn't think of any reason she'd be involved in the wedding.

She closed the folder on the table and held out her hands in a "look at me" gesture. "Haven't you heard? I'm their wedding planner."

An involuntary bark of laughter escaped his throat. But she looked completely serious, so he asked, "You? A wedding planner? Since when?" Even to his own ears it sounded like he was accusing her of some sinister crime.

She crossed her long legs to one side. "Actually, it's a fairly recent development. It came to me in a flash. When the Inn opened and I found out Etta planned to hold weddings here, I thought it sounded like something I'd be good at doing."

"You don't say? You don't need the money, do you? So what? You just happened to have some extra time on your hands?" He didn't try to hide his skepticism.

"Something like that." She stuck out her chin, looking

like she was ready to engage in a battle over the subject. "Why do you find that so peculiar?"

"No reason. Don't go getting all defensive, Ree. Forget I said anything." He shrugged as if it didn't really concern him.

He could tell she wasn't ready to forget it, though. "I'm not defensive, but you obviously have a strong opinion on the subject. So, please, share. I'm simply dying to hear what you have to say."

Theo knew he'd be smart to keep his mouth shut, but he plunged ahead anyway. "Okay, and don't take this the wrong way, but it seems to me that a certain respect for the institution of marriage should be necessary in order to do a good job as a wedding planner."

The look she gave him clearly let him know his sarcasm had been noted. "Okay, and don't take this the wrong way, but I'll have you know my respect for the institution of marriage has increased by leaps and bounds since you knew me, Theo. Besides, you remember how I love a good party. A wedding and the reception aren't that much different."

He was about to stick his foot farther into his mouth by saying that her feelings must have improved once he was out of the picture, but he was saved when he spotted Jake and Marla Jean coming out the back door. They were talking about the advantages of a sit-down dinner versus the simplicity of a buffet.

Marla Jean was saying, "I don't want people to think we're being cheap, Jake."

"No one will think we're cheap. But a buffet is less stressful. Less wait staff to hire. People can help themselves," Jake said. "Don't you agree, Irene?"

Before the words were completely out of his mouth, Marla Jean spotted Theo. She ran toward him in a full sprint and jumped into his arms. "Theo, you're actually here. Oh, Jake, look, it's Theo."

Theo laughed as he caught her in mid-jump and spun her around. "That's the way I like to be greeted. You sure you're marrying the right brother, Marla Jean?"

Jake reached the two of them just as Theo set Marla Jean's feet on the ground. "Take your hands off my future wife, little brother."

Theo turned and grabbed Jake in a bear hug. "I'm glad she's going to make an honest man out of you, Jake. It's about time." His big brother meant the world to him. Growing up, Jake had been the one person he could count on to love and support him with no questions asked. Seeing him happily married to Marla Jean was a cause for real celebration.

"Now that you're here, everything is going to be absolutely perfect," Marla Jean said.

"Once Jake asked me to be his best man, you know nothing could have kept me away," Theo assured her.

"With all the stops you had along the way, we weren't sure exactly when you'd get here, though. I was so happy when Jake told me you landed this morning. I couldn't believe it when he said you were flying your own plane all the way from Alaska."

"Oh, really? You flew in this morning?" Irene asked from her patio chair. "I think I saw your plane."

Theo smiled widely. So, she realized it was him flying over her house. "It's a nice view from up there."

He watched her chin jut out as she declared, "Nice? I've heard it's nothing short of spectacular."

Marla Jean turned to Irene. "Have you met Theo, Irene?"

"As a matter of fact, Theo and I are old friends." Irene stood up and walked over to the group.

Jake looked at Theo in surprise. "Is that so? How come I didn't know that?"

Old friends. Such a catch-all phrase, such a generic inadequate term for what they'd been. But now was not the time or place to squabble over how to define their past. "Yeah, Ree and I go way back. You remember when I got that job working at the Piggly Wiggly after school. Ree was a checker while I was a lowly grocery sacker."

Jake looked from one to the other. "That grocery store was over in Derbyville. You lived in Derbyville, Irene? I never realized that, either."

She nodded. "I grew up there. But I couldn't wait to escape to the big city. I moved to Dallas right after high school."

Jake narrowed his eyes like he was sensing a deeper undercurrent. "And so did Theo."

Theo nodded. "Yep. That was a long time ago, though. A lot of water under the bridge."

"In all your visits you never mentioned you knew Irene," Jake said suspiciously.

Theo wished they would all just drop the subject. He glanced at Ree who seemed completely unmoved by the conversation. On the other hand he felt like he was teetering on the edge of a cliff, scrambling to get his feet back on solid ground. "It just never came up, and, well, our paths haven't crossed much since those days."

Marla Jean swatted Jake's arm. "Quit being so nosy, Jake."

Theo smiled at Marla Jean gratefully. "Yeah, Jake, we all have a few secrets in our deep, dark past." He was talking to Jake, but he looked directly at Irene while he spoke.

Irene met his eyes and lifted her chin as if she was ready to challenge any version of things he might offer. Abruptly, she turned and marched back to the patio table. She grabbed the wedding folder and announced, "I hate to interrupt this walk down memory lane, folks, but we should head over to the pavilion and walk through the ceremony. We have a lot of ground to cover before it starts getting dark." She started off down the backyard path without waiting to see if they would follow.

"We're coming." Marla Jean grabbed Jake's hand, and they bounded after her like puppies let off their leash. Theo found their enthusiasm for the upcoming wedding to be downright heartwarming. He planned to concentrate on their happiness while he was here, and as much as possible, ignore the woman who had broken his heart without a backward glance all those years ago. That might have been easier to do if the recent picture of her wet, naked body hadn't been seared permanently into his brain.

An Excerpt from
A Love to Call Her Own
by Marilyn Pappano

Monday mornings came too damn soon.

Jessy Lawrence rolled onto her back and opened her eyes just enough to stare at the shadows the sun cast across the bedroom ceiling. It was high in the sky. Ten o'clock, maybe eleven. In the four weeks since she'd lost her job, she'd been sleeping in late. Why not, with no more annoying alarm clock beeping at 6:45? No more dressing up, putting on makeup, smiling for customers who annoyed her so much that she wanted to smack them. No more caring whether she was late or if she looked more ragged than she should or if anyone noticed—like that nosy hag, Mrs. Dauterive—she was having a tough day.

It should have been heaven.

If possible, she was more miserable than before.

After her eyes became accustomed to the sun's glare, or what there was of it peeping around the edges of the blinds, she turned her head carefully to the nightstand and bit back a groan. It was twelve twenty-one. Officially afternoon. She'd slept away the whole morning.

She should shower. Brush that god-awful taste from her mouth. Put some drops in her eyes so they didn't feel so puffy. Get something to eat—proteins, vegetables, carbs, fruit. She'd been subsisting on junk food and booze so long that she couldn't remember the last time she'd had a real meal.

She should get dressed, too, walk down the street, buy a copy of the Tallgrass newspaper, and check out the help-wanted section. She needed a job. A sense of purpose. A reason to get out of bed in the morning ... or afternoon, as the case may be. She didn't need the money. Bless Aaron and the United States Army, his life insurance would cover her expenses for the next few decades even if she did nothing but loll on the couch.

What she did need was a reason for living. It was two years and eight months too late to crawl into Aaron's grave with him, and she didn't deserve to be there anyway. He could have done so much better than her if he'd survived his last two weeks in Afghanistan.

But he hadn't survived, and she had, and here she was, wasting her life. It was shameful.

She sat up, her head pounding, and slowly eased to her feet. The shuffle to the bathroom jarred every pain sensor in her head and made her stomach do a queasy tumble. Once inside, she peed, turned the shower to hot, then faced herself in the mirror. She wasn't a pretty sight.

Her red hair stood straight up on top, a counter to the flattened frizz that cradled the sides of her head. At some point in the last day or two, she'd put on makeup, then failed to remove it before crawling into bed. Shadow smeared and mascara smudged, giving her eyes a hollow, exaggerated look. Deep circles underneath emphasized their emptiness. Indentations from the pillow marked her cheek and forehead, and her usual healthy glow had gone gray and pasty.

It was a wonder small children didn't run away at the sight of her.

Only because small children didn't frequent the places she did.

Steam was forming on the mirror when she sighed, turned away, and stripped off her tank and shorts. She took a long shower, scrubbing herself once, twice, closing her eyes, and letting the stinging water pound into her face. By the time she was ready to get out, it had turned cold, bringing shivers and making her teeth chatter.

Four weeks since she'd been fired from the bank—all because some snotty teenage brat with a sense of entitlement could dish it out but couldn't take it—and she hadn't told anyone yet. Not that there were many people to tell, just the margarita girls, her best friends. None of them banked at Tallgrass National. Like her, they were all Army widows, and like her, they kept their accounts at the Fort Murphy Federal Credit Union.

She should have told them at the first Tuesday Night Margarita Club dinner after the dismissal happened. She liked to think she would have, except all the earthshaking going on in their lives was the good kind: weddings, babies, mad love, and lust. They didn't get fired from their jobs, they didn't keep secrets or prove themselves to be colossal losers like Jessy did. If they knew all her failings, they would lose respect for her, and she would lose the most important people in her life. Better that she stay quiet a while longer.

God, how she wished she could talk to someone.

For the first time in years, she mourned the family relationships she'd never had. They lived in Atlanta: mother, father, two sisters with husbands and children who got regular gifts from their Aunt Jessy but wouldn't recognize her if she break-danced in front of them. She couldn't recall the last time she'd gotten an affectionate hug from her mom or a word of advice from her father. She'd been such a disappointment that she was pretty sure, if asked, Prescott and Nathalie Wilkes didn't even acknowledge the existence of their middle daughter.

She got dressed, finger-combed her hair, then wandered through the empty apartment with its high ceilings and tall windows to the kitchen. A quick look in the refrigerator and freezer showed nothing but a few bottles of water, condiments, and some frozen dinners, age unknown. The pantry held staples: rice, pasta, sugar, plus a lonely can of pinto beans and some packets of instant mashed potatoes. The cabinets were empty, as well, except for a box of oatmeal and another of instant pudding. Like the childhood poem, her cupboards were bare.

Except for the one below and to the left of the sink. *Out of sight, out of mind,* the old saying went, but the bottles in that cabinet were never far from her mind. That was her problem.

She needed food, real food, healthy food. Though she wasn't much of a cook, she could learn. She could fill a few of her empty days with taking care of herself: eating properly, exercising, cleaning, detoxing herself. It was a momentous project, but she was worth the effort, right? And what else did she have to do?

She would start with shopping, she decided, grabbing her purse and keys and heading toward the door before she could talk herself out of it. She was a champion shopper, though she preferred to look for killer heels and cute outfits and Bobbi Brown makeup. She could handle a sweep through Walmart, maybe even grab a burger at the McDonald's just inside the door, and at this time of day, she wouldn't risk running into any of her margarita sisters. They would all be working, as they believed her to be.

After locking up, she took the stairs to the street level, stepped out into the warm May afternoon, and stopped immediately to rummage in her purse for a pair of dark glasses. Cars passed on Main Street, a few steps ahead, and a few shoppers moved past, running errands on their lunch breaks or grabbing a meal at one of the nearby restaurants. Jessy loved living right in the heart of downtown Tallgrass, on the second floor of a sandstone building that dated back to Oklahoma's statehood. She loved the busyness of the area during the day and the quiet at night, her only neighbors few and far between in other converted spaces.

Her car was parked down the alley in a tiny lot shared by the owners of Serena's Sweets next door and a couple other businesses. She drove to First Street, then headed south to Walmart, stoically ignoring the bank at the intersection of First and Main as she passed. They'd replaced her with ease—people with the skills to be customer account reps weren't hard to come by, else Jessy couldn't have done the job—and after electronically sending her final paycheck, they were done with her. Not even Julia, the account rep she'd known best, had bothered to contact her.

Walmart was always busy, even in a military town

where service members and their families had the option of the post exchange and the commissary. She parked at the far west end of the lot, figuring she could use the exercise and a little fresh air, since among the many things she couldn't remember was the last time she'd seen daylight. She felt a tad like a vampire—had looked like one, too, in the mirror before her shower.

Determination got her into the store and all the way to the back, where she started with bottled water. Municipal water in Tallgrass tasted like it came from one of those shallow ponds that cattle stood in on hot summer days. She added milk, two-percent, though she wasn't sure for what. But healthy diets included dairy products, right? She tossed in a twelve-pack of Greek yogurt and added fake egg blend, turkey bacon, whole-grain bread— whatever caught her attention as she trolled the aisles.

She was standing in front of the jarred pasta sauces, remembering the spaghetti sauce Aaron had taught her to make—ground beef, tomatoes, mushrooms, onions, and just a bit of sugar—when a crash jerked her attention to a woman fifteen feet away. A jar of pizza sauce lay splattered on the floor around her, its bright red spotting her jeans like blood, and she was clenching her cell phone tightly to her ear.

Such a look on her face.

Jessy went hot inside, then a chill spread through her. She knew that look. Dear God, she'd *lived* that look. She still wore it in her nightmares, still saw it at times in her mirror. That awful, heart-stopping, can't-breathe, can't-bear-it look of shock and pain and anger and grief and pure, bitter sorrow.

The nearest shopper edged her cart away from the

woman while sneaking looks. Other customers and a few stock boys barely old enough to shave stared at her outright as she sank, as if in slow motion, to the floor, a wail rising out of her, growing with anguish until it scraped Jessy's skin, uncovering her own barely-scabbed-over anguish.

This shouldn't be happening here, and it damn well shouldn't be happening with Jessy. Therese—she was motherly, loving, kind. Carly, too. Ilena, Marti, Lucy, and Fia could empathize and offer comfort with the best of them. Jessy didn't comfort. She didn't reach out. She couldn't handle her own emotional messes without turning to the bottle. She certainly couldn't get involved in a stranger's emotional messes.

But no one was helping the woman. No one was trying to move her off the glass-shard-littered floor, giving her any assistance or, barring that, any privacy. Jessy knew too well what it was like to grieve alone. She'd done it for eighteen months before she'd met her margarita sisters.

She knew in her heart that this woman had just found out she could be a margarita sister, too.

Her first step was tentative, her stomach knotted, her chest struggling for air. Too soon she was beside the woman, though, sobbing amid the broken glass and splattered sauce as if she, too, were broken. She was older, probably in her fifties, gray roots just starting to show in her brown hair. Her clothes were casual but well-made: faded jeans in the hundred-dollar price range, a cotton shirt whose quality shone in its very simplicity, stylish leather sandals. Dior clouded the air around her, mixing with the scent of tomatoes and basil, and the gems on the fingers that still clenched the cell phone were tastefully impressive.

Jessy noticed all those things to delay that first touch, that first word. What did you say to a person whose world had just shifted so dramatically that it might never be normal again?

Trying to channel Therese, Carly, Ilena, Jessy crouched beside the woman, touched her, and said, "I'm so sorry." Three totally inadequate words that made her feel almost as low as the jerks gawking from both ends of the aisle.

"Patricia? Patricia, are you there?" The tinny question came from the cell phone.

Gently Jessy pried the phone free and raised it to her ear. "Hello?"

"Who is this?"

"A friend of Patricia's. What did you tell her?"

"Oh. I thought she was alone. At least, she was when she left her house." The voice belonged to a man, old, smug, with a touch of whine. It brought back long-ago memories of visits from Nathalie's parents, a hateful old woman and a spiteful old man. "I told her there's two Army officers all dressed up in their finest lookin' for her. I bet it's about her husband George. He's in the war, you know. Over in—"

Jessy disconnected and pocketed the phone. Despite the Army's best intentions, things sometimes went wrong with casualty notification calls: no one home but kids who called their parent in a panic, nosy neighbors who couldn't resist being the first to pass on bad news. She'd received her call at work, just about this time of day on a Wednesday, back from lunch and summoned into the bank president's office to face a weary chaplain and a solemn notification officer. *We regret to inform you . . .*

Army wives knew that soldiers on their doorsteps

never brought good news, especially during wartime. Just the sight of that official government-tagged vehicle in the driveway, those dress uniforms, those somber expressions, was enough to break their hearts before they started beating again, slowly, dully, barely enough to sustain life, or pounding madly until it felt like it might explode.

Everyone in the margarita club had been through their own notification, and every one remembered two things about it: the unbearable grief and those five words. *We regret to inform you ...*

"Come on, Patricia," she said quietly, wrapping her arm around the woman's shoulders. "Let's get you off the floor. Let's find someplace quiet."

Unexpected help came from one of the young stockers. "The manager's office," he volunteered, taking hold of Patricia's arm and lifting her to her feet. "It's up at the front of the store."

Jessy paused to take the woman's purse from her cart—her own bag hung messenger-style over her head and shoulder—then the three of them moved haltingly down the aisle. By the time they reached the end, a heavy-set guy in a shirt and tie was hurrying toward them, a dark-haired woman on his heels. The manager, she presumed, and likely an assistant. Maybe she could turn Patricia over into their care and get back to her shopping. Get those awful memories back into the darkest corners of her mind.

But Patricia was holding on to her like they were best friends, turning a stricken look on her. "Please don't go ... You know ... don't you?"

Jessy claimed sometimes that she could recognize a

drunk from a mile away. Could a newly widowed woman recognize someone who'd been through it before?

Her smile was a grimace, really, but she patted Patricia's hand, feeling like the biggest fraud that ever lived. "I know," she admitted. "I'll stay."

Dalton Smith gave the palomino colt one last assuring pat, then headed toward the house. The animals were all cared for, including the colt who'd opened a laceration on his leg, so now it was time to feed himself before he went to work on the tractor sitting uselessly inside the shed. The hunk of machinery was as cantankerous as its owner and broke down a lot more. He ought to give in and buy a new one, or at least new to him.

But in this economy, ranchers didn't pay the bills by giving in, not without a hell of a fight first. Besides, he'd been working on old hunks since he was ten. Ranching 101, his dad had called it.

When he cleared the barn, the first thing he noticed was Oz, the stray who'd adopted him, stretched out in a patch of lush grass. He lay on his back, head tilted, tongue lolling out, all four legs in the air, letting the sunshine warm his belly. When he'd come limping down the driveway, the shepherd had been painfully scrawny and covered with fleas and ticks. Five weeks of regular meals had turned him into a new dog. His coat was thick and shiny, his ribs no longing showing through his skin. He had retired his herding instincts, suckered Dalton into giving him a cushy new home, and was making the most of it.

The second thing Dalton saw was the dusty RV parked behind his truck. He groaned, and Oz opened one eye to look at him. "Some watch dog you are," he muttered as he passed the dog. "You could've at least barked."

Not that he really minded a visit from his parents. Since they'd retired to South Texas six years ago, they'd spent more than half their time traveling the country in that RV, and any time their route wandered near Tallgrass, they dropped by. His dad helped with chores, and his mom filled his freezer with home-cooked meals. There wasn't a piece of equipment made that David couldn't fix or a house that Ramona couldn't make feel like home.

It just took a bit of effort for Dalton to make himself sociable.

Unfazed by his criticism, Oz jumped to his feet and fell into step with him, heading for the back door. As Dalton pried his boots off on the top step, he scowled at the dog. "You're gonna wish you'd warned me. Mom doesn't allow animals in the house." He might have bought the house from his folks, but that didn't make it any less Ramona's house.

The first thing he noticed when he walked inside was the smells. The house never stank; he wasn't that bad a housekeeper. It just sometimes smelled a little musty from the dust accumulated everywhere. At the moment, though, it smelled of beef, onions, jalapeno peppers, sugar, and cinnamon, and it made his mouth water. How many times had he come home to the aromas of hamburgers, Spanish fries, and cinnamon cookies in the oven? Hundreds.

Dad was sitting at the kitchen table, reading glasses balanced on the end of his nose, the Tallgrass newspaper open in front of him, and Mom stood in front of the stove, prodding the sliced potatoes, onions, and peppers in a pan filled with hot Crisco. She looked up, smiling brightly.

"Sweetheart! I thought I was going to have to send your father looking for you. I hope you haven't eaten lunch yet because there's way too much food here for just your dad and me."

Before Dalton could do more than hug her, her gaze shifted lower to Oz. "Didn't I already tell you once that you couldn't come in?"

As Oz stared back, Dad spoke up. "Ramona, you're the queen of the house on wheels parked out there, not this one. If Dalton doesn't mind having him in here, then you don't get to mind, either." He folded the paper and laid it aside as he stood. Tall, lanky, his face weathered from years working in the sun and wind and cold, he looked the way Dalton expected to look in thirty years. "How are you, son?"

No handshakes for David. He was a hugger. It used to drive Dillon, Dalton's twin, crazy, being twelve, sixteen, eighteen, and getting hugged by his dad in front of everyone. Knowing that was half the reason Dad did it was enough to make it bearable for Dalton. Noah, the baby, never minded it at all. He was more touchy-feely than the rest of the family combined.

"Good," Dalton replied as Oz defiantly pushed past Ramona and went to his water dish. "I wasn't expecting you guys."

"Don't worry, we're just passing through." Mom spooned the Spanish fries onto paper towels to drain, then tossed in a second batch. "Our friend, Barb Watson—do you remember her? She and her husband Trey stopped by here with us a few years back. Anyway, Barb died yesterday, so we're heading home for the funeral."

"Sorry." Dalton went to the sink to scrub his hands.

"It's such a shame. She was only eighty-three, you know, and she got around as well as I do. She was too young to die—"

In an instant, everyone went still in the room, even Oz. Mom's face turned red, and her hands fluttered as if she could wave away the words. "Oh, honey...I didn't mean..."

To remind him of his wife's death. No one in the family talked about Sandra, not because they hadn't loved her or didn't miss her, but because it had always been so hard for him. It had been four years this past January—four years that his grief and anger and the secret he'd guarded had made tougher than they had to be.

She'd been a soldier, a medic, on her second combat tour when she'd died. Twenty-seven years old, way younger than his parents' friend Barb, bleeding out in the desert thousands of miles from home. Losing her had been hard enough. Knowing she'd died in war had made it worse. Finding out she'd chosen to die had damn near killed him, and keeping that knowledge from everyone who'd loved her had almost finished the job.

What had eaten at him the most? The heartbreak of losing her so young? The ache in his gut that she hadn't trusted him? The anger that she hadn't given him any say, hadn't cared a damn about what he wanted? Most days he wasn't sure, but at the moment he thought maybe it was the guilt every time he lied by omission to the family. Her parents, her sisters, his parents and Noah—they all believed she was a hero, tragically killed doing the job she loved, saving fellow soldiers. They believed she would have done *anything* to come home to them.

They didn't know she'd lacked the courage to come

home. They didn't know she'd chosen to die in that damned desert and leave them forever.

And though it hurt soul-deep, Dalton intended for them to never find out. He wished like hell he didn't know. He would make damn sure their families didn't.

"It's all right, Mom. I know what you meant." Shutting off the faucet, he dried his hands on a dish towel. He took care to rehang it perfectly straight on the rod, then slipped his arm around his mother's shoulders. "Oz and I are starving. Are those burgers about ready?"

Benjamin Noble was dictating notes in the small workspace outside the exam rooms that made up his pod of the clinic when the office manager came around the corner. He paused, wasting a moment trying to decipher the look on her face. Luann was competent, capable, and faced crises on a regular basis without so much as a frown, but this afternoon the smallest frown narrowed the space between her eyes.

"Dr. Noble, you got a call from a Jessy Lawrence. She asked you to call your mother. Said it's urgent."

She offered him a pink message that he hesitated to take. His cell phone was on vibrate, as it always was while he saw patients, but he'd felt it go off three times in the last half hour. Jessy Lawrence's name had shown up on caller ID, but since he didn't know anyone by that name and she'd left no voice mail, he'd ignored it.

"Urgent" messages from Patricia were common enough, given their relationship, that this one didn't concern him. It could mean she wanted a diagnosis of her cough over the phone or information about hormone replacement therapy, despite his polite reminders that he was an orthopedic surgeon. It could mean she'd made the acquaintance of a friend's children or grandchildren and wondered about her own or that she was feeling a rare moment of remorse.

Remorse that had come way too late.

"Thanks, Luann. I'll take care of it when I get a chance." He pocketed the number, breathed deeply to clear his head, then picked up the dictation where he'd left off. His exam rooms were filled with patients, and they'd run out of chairs in the waiting room an hour ago. Clinic days were never good days for dealing with his mother.

Honestly, he couldn't imagine a good day for dealing with his mother.

Twenty years ago she'd walked out on the family. She hadn't just left his father for another man. She'd left all of them—Dad, him, and his sisters. Ben had been fifteen, old enough and busy enough with school to not be overly affected, but Brianne and Sara, eleven and nine, had missed her more than any of them could handle.

Not the time to think about it. He put on a smile and went into room one. "Mrs. Carter, how'd you do with that last shot?" Picking up the needle his nurse had waiting, he sat on the stool and rolled over in front of the patient on the table. She was fifty-five—Patricia's age—and had severe osteoarthritis in her right knee, bone grating on bone. The injections weren't a cure but helped delay the inevitable surgery. Though she'd recovered beautifully from the total knee replacement on her left, she was hoping to put off a repeat of the brutal rehab as long as she could. He didn't blame her. It was human nature to put off ugly things, the crinkle of paper in his pocket reminded him.

He positioned the needle, deftly pushing it in, and was depressing the plunger when his cell phone vibrated again. His hand remained steady. Whether giving shots, inserting appliances to strengthen badly fractured bones, or sawing through the femur or tibia to remove a diseased knee, his hands were always steady.

The nurse blotted Mrs. Carter's knee and applied a Band-Aid while they exchanged the usual chatter—*Don't stress the joint for twenty-four hours, call me if you have any problems, see you in six months if you don't*—then he returned to the workspace to dictate notes again. There he pulled out the cell and looked at it a moment.

He routinely told his patients to call him if they had any problems, but that courtesy didn't extend to his mother. Granted, his patients didn't abuse the privilege—most of them, at least. There were a few for whom hand-holding was part of his job, but when Patricia was needy, she did it to extremes.

He was still looking at the phone when it began to vibrate. Jessy Lawrence again. He might ignore her, but she apparently had no intention of remaining ignored. Since he had no intention of being stalked around his office by a stranger on a smartphone, he grimly answered. "This is Benjamin Noble."

There was that instant of silence, when someone was surprised to get an answer after repeatedly being sent to voice mail, then a husky, Southern-accented voice said, "Hey, my name is Jessy Lawrence. I'm a—a friend of your mother's over here in Tallgrass."

He'd heard of the town, only an hour or so from Tulsa, but he couldn't remember ever actually having been there. "I didn't know she was back in the state."

Another moment's silence. She clearly thought it odd that he didn't know where his mother was living. When Patricia had left them, she hadn't made much effort to stay in touch except when guilt or selfishness pushed her, and he'd learned not to care.

"She is," Jessy said at last. "If you've got a pen, I'll give you her address. Ready? It's Three Two One West Comanche—"

"What is this about, Ms. Lawrence?"

"I'm sorry, Benjamin—Dr. Noble. There's no easy way to say this. Your stepfather was killed in Afghanistan. Your mother just found out. She needs you."

A bit of shock swept through him, momentary surprise, the instinctive reaction a person felt upon hearing of someone's death. Though he'd met George only three times—at his, Brianne's, and Sara's high school graduations—Ben could feel regret that the man had died, that Patricia now found herself a widow.

But not a lot of regret. Patricia's loss couldn't possibly equal what he and his sisters had gone through when their father died. Rick Noble had stayed when Patricia left. He'd loved them, taken care of them, been both father and mother to them, and losing him had broken their hearts.

And it was Rick's own heart, broken when the love of his life abandoned them for another man, that had led to his death at forty-six. Yet Patricia expected Ben to mourn that man's death? To drop everything and rush to her side to be with her?

That wasn't going to happen.

"Give her my condolences, Ms. Lawrence. If you'll excuse me, I've got patients waiting."

"But—"

He hung up, returned the phone to his pocket, then on second thought laid it on the counter beneath a stack of charts before heading to room three. Out of sight, out of mind, the old saying went. He hoped it held true today.

Patricia, Jessy had learned in the past hour, was Patricia Sanderson, wife—now widow—of Colonel George Sanderson. He'd been in the Army twenty-nine years and would have been promoted to general or retired by the end of thirty. Patricia had been in favor of retiring. She'd grown tired of traveling from assignment to assignment and never wanted to face a moving van and a stack of cartons again.

And she had a bastard of a son.

Immediately Jessy regretted that thought. She was proof that not all parent/adult child relationships were healthy. She hadn't spoken to her own parents in years and had had LoLo Baxter, the casualty notification officer, inform them of Aaron's death. They hadn't called, come to Tallgrass for the funeral, sent flowers or even a damn card. That didn't make her a bitch of a daughter.

It had just made her sorry.

"Is that coffee about ready?" LoLo came into the kitchen, bumping against Jessy deliberately on her way to choose a cup from the wooden tree. The major had the toughest job in the Army: telling people their loved ones had died. The first time—delivering tragic news, watching the surviving spouse collapse, getting dragged into the grief—would have destroyed Jessy, but LoLo had done it countless times with grace and great empathy.

She'd made the worst time of Jessy's life a little easier to bear, and Jessy loved her for it.

"I talked to the son," Jessy said as LoLo poured the coffee, then sipped it and sighed. "He said, and I quote, 'Give her my condolences.'"

LoLo didn't appear surprised. She'd seen families at their best and their worst. *The stories I could tell,* she'd once said. Of course, she hadn't told them. Was there someone she did share with? Someone who helped eased her burden and made it possible for her to continue doing her job?

Jessy didn't know. Though all the margarita sisters knew LoLo, none of them knew anything about her personal life. She was compassionate, kind, supportive, and a mystery.

"Any other kids?"

"Two daughters, both in Tulsa. She doesn't have their phone numbers, and I doubt the doctor's going to cough them up." Jessy fixed her own coffee, with lots of sugar and creamer, then peeled an orange from a bowl on the counter. She hadn't gotten anything to eat yet, and her stomach was grumbling. She glanced toward the doorway. Down the hall in the living room, Patricia was sitting with the chaplain, their low voices punctuated time to time by a sob. She lowered her own voice. "Her son didn't know she was living in Oklahoma."

"Any other family?"

"No one on George's side besides some nieces and nephews she doesn't really know. Her sister lives in Vermont, her brother in Florida. They're both currently on vacation in Canada and will try to come for a few days before the funeral. They've both got kids, so they're going to contact them."

LoLo leaned against the counter, cradling the coffee

cup, and studied Jessy solemnly. Was she remembering that no one came to be with Jessy when Aaron died? "You know her from the bank?"

"No. Never met her before today."

"So you picked a stranger up off the floor, dusted her off, and brought her home. That's a tough thing to do, Jessy."

With someone else, Jessy could have been flippant. *Tougher than you know.* Or *Not tough at all; I am Super-woman.* But LoLo did know. She'd done way more than her share of picking people up off the floor. Instead of saying anything, Jessy focused on sectioning the orange.

"I was at the bank yesterday."

Heat flooded Jessy's face, and her gut clenched. "I thought you banked onpost."

"I do. I went there with one of my wives." Always supportive, doing anything she could to help the women whose tragedies brought her into their lives. "Someone else's nameplate was on your desk. So were his things."

"Yeah." She mumbled around a piece of orange, sweet and juicy.

"You making a career change?"

Reaching deep inside, Jessy summoned the strength to meet her gaze, to smile brashly. "Yeah. I always hated that job."

"You have any plans?"

Besides falling apart? "I'm thinking about it." She thought about a lot of things. She just never found the energy to actually do anything. Going to get groceries today had been a big deal—and look how that had bitten her on the ass. Two hours now she'd been tied up with Patricia Sanderson, and she didn't know how to extricate herself. She'd hoped the son would head this way as soon as he got the news, but she might as well have told him there were clouds in the sky for all the concern he'd shown.

As long as LoLo and the chaplain were there, she could leave. Even knowing that eventually they would both have to leave, too. Knowing that eventually Patricia would have to be alone in her house, surrounded by memories of her husband, drowning in her grief. Eventually everyone had to be alone.

But not yet. Jessy could cope a while longer. It wasn't like anyone else in the entire world needed her.

"Maybe this time you'll find a job you like." LoLo drained the last of her coffee and squared her shoulders. "I should get back in there."

Jessy watched her go, figuring that in a few minutes the chaplain would come in for coffee and a break. Kind of a tag-team comforting. With her stomach still too empty, she opened the refrigerator, located a couple packages of deli meat, mayo and mustard, some pickles and cheese. Sooner or later, Patricia's friends would start showing up with casseroles, fried and rotisserie chicken, sweets from CaraCakes, pop and doughnuts and disposable dishes, but in the meantime, a sandwich or two would stave off hunger for her, LoLo, and Lieutenant Graham. If Patricia was like Jessy, she wouldn't eat for days. If she was like Therese, she would be sensible and eat even though she had no appetite, and if she was like Lucy, bless her heart, she would stuff herself with food to numb the pain.

Sure enough, about the time she finished putting together the fourth ham and turkey sandwich, Lieutenant Graham came into the kitchen. He wasn't as experienced as LoLo; his lean solemn face showed the bleakness of his burden.

Chaplains made Jessy uncomfortable. She hadn't been raised in church and had never found a reason to start attending as an adult. Aaron's service had been held at the chapel on Fort Murphy, and the memory didn't make her eager to return. Besides, chaplains were good people. Earnest. They didn't make the mistakes Jessy couldn't seem to escape.

"We didn't get lunch. This looks good," the lieutenant said as he accepted a plate. "We called one of her neighbors who's coming over as soon as she can get away from the office. I think she's asked about as many questions as she's capable of processing at the moment."

"She'll think of more." Jessy's first questions had been simple: how had Aaron died, and why. The how had been understandable: he'd been shot by a sniper. She still struggled with the why.

There had been more questions, of course. When would he get home? What did she have to do? How did one arrange a funeral? Where could she bury him?

And more: had he died instantly? Had they tried to save him? Did he suffer? How did they know he didn't suffer?

Would she be able to see him, touch him, kiss once more when he got home?

Could she tell him how very, very sorry she was?

The chaplain took a seat at the breakfast table, ate a bite or two, then gazed at Jessy. "LoLo says you've been through this."

Her hands tightened around the coffee mug. She forced herself to loosen her fingers, pick up a plate, join him at the table, and to take a bite to settle her stomach. "Two and a half years ago," she said at last.

"I'm sorry."

Why did the words sound so much more sincere coming from him than they did from her? Because he'd probably never let anyone down. Never failed to live up to others' expectations. He was a man of God.

She was just a woman.

With way too many flaws and way too many regrets.

About the Authors

New York Times bestselling author **Jill Shalvis** lives in a small town in the Sierras full of quirky characters. Any resemblance to the quirky characters in her books is, um, mostly coincidental. Look for Jill's bestselling, award-winning books wherever romances are sold and visit her website for a complete book list and daily blog detailing her city-girl-living-in-the-mountains adventures.

You can learn more at:
JillShalvis.com
Twitter @jillshalvis
Facebook.com/jillshalvis

Kristen Ashley grew up in Brownsburg, Indiana, and has lived in Denver, Colorado, and the West Country of England. Thus she has been blessed to have friends and family around the globe. Her posse is loopy (to say the least) but loopy is good when you want to write.

Kristen was raised in a house with a large and multi-generational family. They lived on a very small farm in a small town in the heartland, and Kristen grew up listening to the strains of Glenn Miller, The Everly Brothers, REO Speedwagon, and Whitesnake.

Needless to say, growing up in a house full of music and love was a good way to grow up.

And as she keeps growing up, it keeps getting better.

You can learn more at:

KristenAshley.net

Twitter @KristenAshley68

Facebook.com/kristenashleybooks

Hope Ramsay grew up on the North Shore of Long Island, but every summer Momma would pack her off under the care of Aunt Annie to go visiting with relatives in the midlands of South Carolina. Her extended family includes its share of colorful aunts and uncles, as well as cousins by the dozens, who provide the fodder for the characters you'll find in Last Chance, South Carolina. She's a two-time finalist in the Golden Heart and is married to a good ol' Georgia boy who resembles every single one of her heroes. She lives in Fairfax, Virginia, where you can often find her on the back deck, picking on her thirty-five-year-old Martin guitar.

You can learn more at:
HopeRamsay.com
Twitter, @HopeRamsay
Facebook.com/Hope.Ramsay

Molly Cannon lives a charmed life in Texas with her nearly perfect husband and extremely large cat Nelson. When she's not writing, she spends her days reading, taking dance classes with the hubby, and watching all kinds of sports.

You can learn more at:

MollyCannon.com

Twitter, @cannonmolly

Facebook.com/pages/Molly-Cannon

Known for her intensely emotional stories, **Marilyn Pappano** is the *USA Today* bestselling author of nearly eighty books. She has made regular appearances on bestseller lists and has received recognition for her work in the form of numerous awards. Although her husband's Navy career took them across the United States, he and Ms. Pappano now live in Oklahoma high on a hill that overlooks her hometown. They have one son and daughter-in-law, an adorable grandson, and a pack of mischievous dogs.

You can learn more at:

MarilynPappano.net

Twitter, @MarilynPappano

Facebook.com/marilynpappanofanpage

Fall in Love with Forever Romance

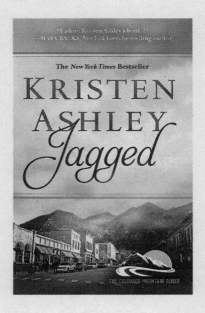

JAGGED

Zara is struggling to make ends meet when her old friend Ham comes back into her life. He wants to help, but a job and a place to live aren't the only things he's offering this time around...Fans of Julie Ann Walker, Lauren Dane, and Julie James will love the fifth book in Kristen Ashley's *New York Times* bestselling Colorado Mountain series, now in print for the first time!

Fall in Love with Forever Romance

ALL FIRED UP

It's a recipe for temptation: Mix a cool-as-a-cucumber event planner with a devastatingly handsome Irish pastry chef. Add sexual chemistry hot enough to start a fire. Let the sparks fly. Fans of Jill Shalvis will flip for the second book in Kate Meader's Hot in the Kitchen series.

Fall in Love with Forever Romance

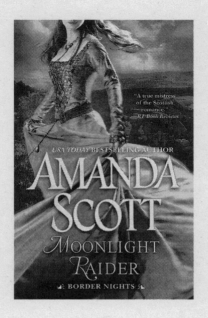

MOONLIGHT RAIDER

USA Today bestselling author Amanda Scott brings to life the history, turmoil, and passion of the Scottish Border as only she can in the first book in her new Border Nights series. Fans of Diana Gabaldon's *Outlander* will be swept away by Scott's tale!

Fall in Love with Forever Romance

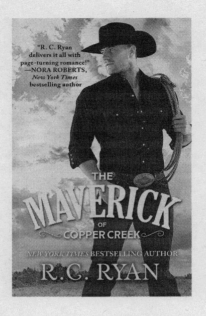

THE MAVERICK OF COPPER CREEK

Fans of Linda Lael Miller, Diana Palmer, and Joan Johnston will love *New York Times* bestselling author R. C. Ryan's THE MAVERICK OF COPPER CREEK, the charming, poignant, and unforgettable first book in her Copper Creek Cowboys series.

Fall in Love with Forever Romance

IT HAPPENED AT CHRISTMAS

Ethan and Skye may want a lot of things this holiday season, but what they get is something they didn't expect. Fans of feel-good romances by *New York Times* bestselling authors Brenda Novak, Robyn Carr, and Jill Shalvis will love the third book in Debbie Mason's series set in Christmas, Colorado—where love is the greatest gift of all.

Fall in Love with Forever Romance

MISTLETOE ON MAIN STREET

Fans of Jill Shalvis, Robyn Carr, and Susan Mallery will love this charming debut from best-selling author Olivia Miles about love, healing, and family at Christmastime.

Fall in Love with Forever Romance

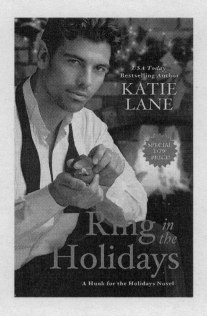

USA Today
Bestselling Author
KATIE
LANE

SPECIAL
LOW
PRICE!

Ring in the
Holidays

A Hunk for the Holidays Novel

RING IN THE HOLIDAYS

For Matthew McPherson, what happens in Vegas definitely doesn't stay there, and that may be a very good thing! Fans of Lori Wilde and Rachel Gibson will fall in love with this sexy series from bestselling author Katie Lane.